HOLD STILL

HOLD STILL

Everybody has a secret

Tim Adler

urbanepublications.com

First published in Great Britain in 2016 by Urbane Publications Ltd

Suite 3, Brown Europe House, 33/34 Gleamingwood Drive, Chatham, Kent ME5 8RZ

Copyright © Tim Adler, 2016

A CIP catalogue record for this book is available from the British Library.

ISBN 978-1-910692-69-1

Design and Typeset by Julie Martin

Cover by Susanna Hickling

Cover image courtesy of www.TinaApple.com

urbanepublications.com

FOR THE REAL KATE

CONTENTS

Tuesday

Wednesday

Thursday

One week later

'A photograph is a secret about a secret. The more it tells you the less you know.'

DIANE ARBUS

Friday

CHAPTER ONE

KATE JULIA PHOTOGRAPHED the moment of her husband's death.

Sliding backwards through the photographs she took that day, she saw everything that led up to his death in reverse. Here were the fireworks exploding over the square in Tirana. White Night, they called it. And here were the tourists sitting in the café below, and Paul standing next to his cousins, and his mother seated in an armchair, and a shot of the hotel entrance. Expanding the iPhone photographs with her fingers, she kept searching for a clue, anything that might have anticipated the terrible thing that happened later. She remembered the painting of Paul's grandfather and Paul telling her he looked as if he didn't have long for this world. Her husband standing in the middle of their room asking if they would always be together. And Paul slumping in the back of the taxi and saying, "Christ, I feel like a ghost."

Then there was the brooding weather, how the sky glowered behind the mountains, anticipating the storm to come. The first fat drops of rain hitting their taxi roof before the heavens opened – rivulets of water chasing each other down the windscreen like tears. But all this was after the fact. You keep looking for clues or signs, she thought, when really there aren't any.

Wait. She stopped at one photograph. There was one clue.

Paul looking wan, after staying up all night.

He had spent the last twelve hours sitting beside his uncle's coffin at his mother's flat. It's the way they do things in a Muslim country, he said. She remembered adjusting his tie and noticing how his longish hair needed cutting. It was already turning grey, and soon he would have to wear it short. Paul turned and looked at himself in the hotel mirror, making final adjustments to his outfit.

They had flown into Tirana from London the previous night. Kate hadn't known what to expect; all she knew about Albania was that it had been cut off from the world by a Communist dictator and that it had a reputation for lawlessness. The Irishman sitting next to her on the plane had warned Kate not to use ATMs. "They copy your card details," he confided. "Me, I always carry my money in my sock. And the officials are the worst. They always want this…" He rubbed his thumb and forefinger together.

It had been dark when they got in, and Paul had headed straight off to the wake. The first morning Kate wanted to see something of Tirana, even if they were on their way to a funeral. All she had glimpsed from the taxi last night was a city much like any other. Yet the way Paul described his country, everything was upside down and back to front. This was his first visit home for a long time; his mother had always come to stay with them in London. But Paul had been close to his uncle, who, he said, had become his dad after his real father died when he was young. So his uncle had paid for his education, enabling his nephew to study computing in London.

Her husband lay down on the bed, and it was Kate's turn to look at herself in the mirror. Smoothing her black dress down, what did she see? A woman in her thirties with long, black hair that she had been dyeing since she was eighteen. A long face that some thought beautiful but she reckoned made her look like a horse. Black horn-rimmed glasses and a gap between her teeth. Good figure. Her thighs, though, were on the heavy side, and she wished that her legs were longer.

"Why do they say no when they mean yes?" she said, shifting in the mirror. The receptionist downstairs had shaken her head last night when Kate had asked if somebody could help them with their luggage.

"It's not really saying no, it's more of a circular motion," said Paul, propping himself up on his elbows. "It's a local custom. I told you, everything's the wrong way round here. Part of its charm, I guess. Did you know the Albanian alphabet has thirty-six letters? That's a lot more than other alphabets."

"Remind me of your cousin's name."

"Which one? I've got so many."

"The one you were closest to. When you were growing up,
I mean."

"Hashim. There were about seven or eight of us who used
to knock around together. We would get into scrapes,
silly stuff. People had big families back then, when the
state took care of everything. Hashim was my best friend,
though; we were like brothers when we were kids." He
paused. "It's funny being back here again. Everything
seems so much smaller. I want to show you around once
we get the funeral out of the way. Not that there's much
to see. There's a national art gallery you might like, full of
hideous paintings. Communist heroes fighting western
imperialism." Paul rose from the bed while Kate fixed her
other diamond earring.

"I'll order some coffee from downstairs. You must be
exhausted."

Kate picked up the telephone and dialled reception,
admiring the bedspread and curtains while she listened
to it ringing. She had designed the textiles for the room,
which is why they'd got such a good deal on the penthouse
suite. She had been freelancing as a textile designer for
the past ten years, after quitting her full-time job at the
Designers Guild. Paul was the one who had encouraged her
to go freelance. A job she'd had designing wall hangings

for a Thai restaurant led to doing interiors for a luxury bed-and-breakfast, which turned into doing a refurb for a flagship hotel. At art school she had wanted to be a photographer, but her teachers had steered her towards textiles. She knew she didn't really have what it took to be a professional snapper, but photography was still a hobby. She glanced at the iPhone on the bedside table. Tomorrow would be a good day for taking photographs. Coffee would be up in a minute, the receptionist told her.

"We could always go to the seaside, if you want. It's only an hour away," said Paul behind her.

"What, in November? It'll be bloody cold."

"There's a fish restaurant on the seafront that does this pasta with clams. Datteri, I think they're called. The Italians rave about them. There's a ban on fishing them in the EU. Not here, of course."

Kate opened the French windows and stepped onto the balcony. On the far side of the square there was a café and, weirdly, a sculpture of an upside-down church with its spire piercing the ground.

"This was an atheist country. Down with religion," said Paul, reading her thoughts. He put his arms around her waist and smelled her hair. "You smell wonderful, like honey."

"Careful," she said as the telephone rang, startling them. Paul went to answer it. It wasn't room service: their taxi was waiting downstairs.

Their boutique hotel was one of many opening in Tirana. Its Italian owners had liked Kate's work for a London branch of the chain and wanted to use the same designs. Her first thought when Paul got the bad news had been to book a room here. She was glad they were getting away, and being offered a deal on the room was a bonus given the size of their overdraft. Lately Paul had been preoccupied and troubled; there was something on his mind, something he was not telling her, and she guessed it was about his business.

Paul owned a website design and hosting company near Liverpool Street station, where she used one of the desks for her freelancing. Business had not been good. Paul had been forced to make some staff redundant, which he hated. But every time she broached the subject, he withdrew into himself. Getting away for a few days would do them both good, she hoped. Most evenings they barely had enough energy to heat up a ready meal, unscrew a bottle of plonk and slump in front of the telly.

Their taxi was waiting on the other side of the revolving door. Crossing the Italianate lobby, Kate noticed a couple of groups of businessmen huddled together.

Their hotel was right in the city centre, the heart of the government area, Paul said, getting into the taxi after her. The driver started the engine, and they circled the square before pulling out into the main avenue. All this was built by Italians before the war, Paul continued, warming to being a tour guide. They passed by an apartment building painted in crazy psychedelic camouflage, and another in bold Mondrian squares. She would photograph this neighbourhood tomorrow, Kate thought. It would make the most wonderful album on Facebook. She reached for Paul's hand. "I told you you would like it," he said.

The taxi had gone down a shopping street, and Kate was amused to see that all the big-name brands they had in London also had stores in Tirana – or rather the shops had misspelled their names to stay one step ahead of the lawyers: "Bloomydales", "Disneey" "Abercromby & Fitch". Wedding dresses were on show in the upper windows. "Why bother buying something if you're only going to wear it once," Paul remarked, but Kate could tell his mind was elsewhere. He kept compulsively checking his mobile.

"Was your mother close to your uncle?" she asked.

"Dad was the older brother, but he hated farming. He wanted to be in the city. So he handed the farm over to my uncle, which was fine with him. My uncle already had five sons and they had a sheep farm."

"You've never told me what your dad did for a living."

"A bit of this and a bit of that. He was a wheeler dealer. You've no idea how hard it was to get things during the Hoxha era."

"So he was a spiv?"

Paul laughed for what seemed the first time in ages. I love to see you like this, Kate thought.

"I hope you're not going to be too shocked by my family. I'm very different from the rest of them."

"How do you mean?"

"It's a tough life in the Highlands. It's where the partisans came from, the ones who fought the Nazis in the war. Tough mountain people."

"What sort of things did your uncle farm?"

"Oh, mainly olive trees, and sheep, of course. I think dad couldn't wait to get out. He loved the city. Mum stayed in her flat in Tirana after dad died and brought me up as a single parent."

"But your uncle paid for your education, right?"

Paul nodded, and Kate thought about the last time she had seen Paul's mother, Marina, during a visit to London. She was a large, heavyset woman dressed in Balkan black who had cleaned their flat immaculately when they got home that first night. The message from her mother-in-law appeared to be that her daughter-in-law didn't look after her son well enough, which left Kate feeling angry and resentful. By now they were in the countryside. They passed a shopping centre that Paul said hadn't been there the last time he had visited. This was where city dwellers fled in the summer when Tirana got too stinking hot, he said. The countryside reminded Kate of Wales, and she noticed castles dotting the hills. Paul said Albanians love castles. The moment they had any money, they wanted to build themselves one.

Looking back, she supposed there was one premonition. "Christ, I feel like a ghost," Paul said, closing his eyes. He slumped in the back seat, and Kate told him to try and get some sleep. How could she have known that her husband would be dead in less than eight hours?

Their taxi wended its way uphill and came to a stop in a queue of cars, all trying to get to the same place. They were in a traffic jam. Paul and the taxi driver began talking in Albanian. "We had better get out and walk," Paul said. Cars were backed up along the single lane that went to the cemetery. Glimpsing the hillside graveyard, Kate noticed how many mourners there were, at least a hundred. There was even a photographer. What was interesting was that the men and women were walking into the graveyard separately.

"Your uncle must have been a popular man," she said.

"It wasn't just me. He did a lot for others. He helped a lot of people."

There was a crack of thunder overhead, and the inevitable rain started. People put up umbrellas. When they reached the cemetery, Paul greeted a group of men who Kate could only describe as a gang of toughs almost comically squeezed into tight suits. Presumably these were Paul's cousins. They all had what she came to know as the Balkan haircut: a crew cut shaved almost bald at the back and sides. Paul was chatting with two of them when he suddenly turned back to look at her. She would always remember that haunted expression on his face.

Kate spotted Paul's mother talking to a group of women and she raised her hand. At that moment, people turned to watch the hearse arrive. The coffin was smothered with flowers, and some mourners held more wreaths in their hands. There was something showy-offy about it, as if they were competing with each other as to who could make the most extravagant gesture. Vulgar, really. Mourners parted to let Paul's aunt through, and Kate could see she was very different from her mother-in-law. There was a steely self-possession about Paul's aunt as she nodded to friends, as if she was used to being listened to and her words acted on.

The mourners stood by the graveside as rain pattered on their umbrellas and the imam began ululating. Paul's aunt threw the first handful of soil on the coffin and some of the women started wailing. Paul's mother pulled at her hair and, again, there was something theatrical about the gesture, as if the women were trying to outdo each other in their grief. Not Paul's aunt, though. She just stared dryly at her husband's coffin. Eventually everybody drifted away, leaving her alone to say goodbye.

"Who will run the farm now that your uncle has gone?" Kate said.

"My cousin Hashim will take over the farm."

"Which one is he?"

"He's not here. Apparently he's out of the country."

"Not to come to your own father's funeral, it's not very respectful."

"He and Uncle Dritan had a falling out. They had a really bad argument. My other cousins think it's what brought on his heart attack. Anyway, cousin Hashim was banished. He was cut out."

"It all sounds very biblical."

"Yes. The old man came to see sense before he died. The return of the prodigal son and all that. I just hope he remembers what happened to Joseph."

"What do you mean?"

"His brothers ganged up on him and threw him down a well."

There was a disturbance as they came out of the cemetery. Kate could see two of Paul's cousins pushing the photographer aside, shoving him in the chest. They were shouting, telling him to go away. One of them grabbed the man's camera and yanked it over his head. For a moment Kate thought he was going to smash it on the ground. Paul raised his eyes and said he would go and sort it out.

Kate watched her husband intervene, separating the arguing men. His cousin refused to give the camera over. She watched Paul reach for his wallet and coolly hand over a wad of notes. He caught Kate's eye and shrugged as if to say, "What else could I do?" Kate wondered what all the commotion had been about. What was so important about a small family funeral that it shouldn't be photographed?

CHAPTER TWO

XHENGO KNEW THE MOMENT he opened his eyes that morning that they meant to kill him. That was why he had to get off this wretched coast. Surely there was one boat that could take him across the sea to Bari. But all the dinghies were wrapped up for winter, and the only sound was the gentle wind chimes from their rigging. Xhengo picked up speed, looking for any sign of life in this closed-up, out-of-season place, but there wasn't any. Even the brown-tipped palm trees sagging in the wind were dying. Everything here was dead.

You don't just kill people in broad daylight, he reasoned. If only he could find somebody to be with, they would protect him. He thought about the bosomy softness of the blonde with dyed hair last night, and how he had fallen cringing into her arms. But she was the one who had betrayed him. If only he hadn't got drunk and shot his mouth off. The girl had sat there listening, nodding while he told her that Zogaj and his gang didn't scare him anymore – Xhengo was the big shot now, with friends in high places. They needed him more than he needed them, he said. Some big shot you are now, he thought. You sonofabitch, you drank all the money. The blonde had told him she needed the toilet, and he drained another brandy and coke while she was away. In one of Zogaj's own places. What a joke. A clean towel and a bar of soap and half an hour with the piggish blonde upstairs. She must have called them while he sat there bragging on the bar stool.

They came for him early that morning.

Xhengo was lying in bed gazing at the weird Tyrolean-forest photographic mural that took up one wall, feeling as if somebody had shat in his head. More knocking on the door. "Two men wanting to see you," the landlady said. If I just stay in this room they can't hurt me, he thought. His eyes felt wet with tears, and he did not want to face today. "Just a minute," he said, swinging his legs off the bed. The floorboard creaked as the landlady moved off downstairs.

So they were here already.

He caught sight of himself in the mirror, a frightened-looking man with watery blue eyes. A tortoise in a wig was what his ex-wife had called him. Carefully he opened the bedroom door, taking care to sidestep the giveaway floorboard, and peered over the banisters. He recognised the top of Sammy's head. The other man was a big stocky fella with a monobrow, who looked as if he never quite understood the question. For a moment Xhengo thought about going downstairs with his arms spread, pretending it had all been a big joke. Right then, Sammy's head whipped round and he gazed up at Xhengo, hate radiating from him, and Xhengo felt like a mongoose being hypnotised by a snake. "Come on upstairs, boys," Xhengo found himself saying.

The heavy stood blocking the doorway like a solid piece of furniture. Sammy, the runt in the leather jacket who looked as if he would enjoy pulling legs off insects, stood in front of his large comrade.

"Hello, Fation," he said. "We hear you've got some new friends."

"What's this all about?"

"Last night, in the bar. You said you'd been talking to the police."

"You know me. I was just talking shit."

"That's not what I heard."

"I was just fucking with you. Look, boys, I've got no beef with you. I want to be your friend."

Sammy sniggered as if he'd just got the punchline of a dirty joke. He turned to the other guy. "He says he wants to be our friend."

Looking round, the wardrobe remarked, "This place is like living in a cuckoo clock."

"You want us to be your friends, the police are your friends, I can't keep up," Sammy said flatly.

"Look, boys, you don't want me. I want to get out, start a new life. I don't know anything."

"Nobody ever leaves, you know that."

Xhengo smiled queasily. "Is that a threat?"

"I don't make threats. I make promises."

Xhengo found it difficult to swallow, and the wallpaper seemed to be sagging in bilious hangover green. They all knew the real reason they were here, so why not get on with it? "What is it you want from me?"

"We want you to come for a little ride. Zogaj wants to see you."

"I heard Zogaj was dead."

"You heard wrong."

They drove through the suburbs of Tirana in their 4x4 Land Cruiser. Deeply hungover, Xhengo sat in the back seat, sweating and remorseful, convinced they would shoot him in the back of the head and dump him in an oil drum, or crucify him in an abattoir and use a cattle prod. They had done worse. Hell, he had even seen what they could do.

The room they led him into was in complete darkness except for a desk lamp. The curtains were drawn. Sammy pushed Xhengo down into a hard chair facing a desk, where he sensed somebody was waiting. The lamp was turned towards him so he couldn't see the person's face. The room smelt musty, as if the windows hadn't been opened for a long time.

"Hello, Fation," a voice said. A woman's voice.

He put his hand up to his face, trying to see who was there. "I came to see Zogaj."

"Is there anything you need? Are you thirsty? Hungry?"

He ran his tongue over his lips. They felt cracked. "I could use a glass of water."

"We hear you've been talking to people." Her voice was soothing and reasonable.

"I told Sammy. The police called me in for questioning. They offered me a deal, said they'd pay me for information."

"Become an informant, you mean."

"I suppose so. Yes."

"And why would you want to do that?"

"You don't pay me enough. For what I do for you, I mean. If they caught me I could go to jail. It's not enough money."

"There's never enough money."

Xhengo squirmed in his seat. If only he didn't have this pounding headache. "The joke was on them. I took their money."

"What did you tell them?"

"Nothing much. A few names. They said they knew them already."

"You crossed a line."

Sammy nudged Xhengo's shoulder and handed him a tumbler. The water tasted funny, a little brackish, but he drained it anyway.

"Thank you," he gasped, wiping his mouth.

"We don't like people we can't count on."

"I'm not well. I want to get out. You don't need me anymore."

"Oh, but we do."

"Why me? You'll find someone else."

To his amazement and surprise, Sammy and the other man dropped him back home. All Xhengo could think about was getting out; he didn't want to have anything more to do with Zogaj and his whole stinking crew. Where was that detective when he needed protection? The stinking head's phone went through to voicemail every time Xhengo called. "Sure we'll protect you, give you a new identity," the detective had said as Xhengo drew a map of the organisation on the police station whiteboard. A new life. Dabbling his feet in the shore of the Ionian, some olive trees, a few goats. Yes, that was it. He was just a white-goods salesman, for goodness' sake.

"Be seeing you," was the last thing Sammy had said as he turned on the steps. That was when Xhengo knew they were going to kill him.

Two hours later and here he was, looking for a boat to get him away from the coast. Zogaj had eyes everywhere in the airport and docks. Xhengo was a dead man, he knew that now.

The quay stretched out before him in the desolate seaside resort, the boats shrouded for winter. A deserted fairground was on his right, with a tarpaulined waltzer and a closed switchback ride with badly airbrushed portraits of the stars (Was that really Michael Jackson, he wondered). Ever since that interview, Xhengo had felt that something bad was happening out of the corner of his eye, just where he couldn't see it. He didn't feel well. You're just being paranoid, he thought, you've got to get a grip. A building was open ahead, thank God, an amusement arcade with a string of light bulbs swagged along the guttering.

That was when he heard them.

"Frey-end," Sammy called mockingly. "Frey-end." The wind swallowed up their words.

"Leave me alone," Xhengo shouted back. "I've done nothing to you. Why can't you just leave me alone?"

Sammy said something, and he and the other man started to laugh.

A lumpy, bored-looking girl was sitting behind the booth in the arcade. Fruit machines whistled with cascading bloops and tinny explosions around them.

"Please. You must help me. I'm being followed."

The girl shrugged and turned back to her magazine.

"You must help me. Call the police," Xhengo persisted.

"I can give you change for the phone if you want."

He placed his hand on the Perspex window separating them. To his surprise, the plastic seemed to bend as he pressed his fingers into it. What was happening to him? "I don't want to play any games," Xhengo pleaded.

"So you can use the phone."

"Where is the nearest phone?"

"Dunno."

Sammy and his muscle were threading their way through the arcade games and slot machines. Getting nearer. "Please," Xhengo begged.

"Fation, there you are," Sammy said, slapping him on the back. His accomplice slipped his arm through Xhengo's, ready to lead him away. Sammy grinned and waggled his fingers, making the had-too-much-to-drink sign to the cashier. Something weird was definitely happening to him, Xhengo thought. The colours and noise had become intense, as if somebody had turned up the volume, and the greasy fried-food smell was unbearable. He had to get away before he was sick. Xhengo wrested his arm free and lurched outside, clattering down the metal steps.

Both men followed, the big one and the short one, like a

nightmare comedy act. They were relentless. His calves felt like they were bleeding as he staggered along the promenade. He had to get away. Why wasn't anybody helping? Couldn't they see what was happening? The fairground organ music swirled around him, up into the sky. It was becoming harder to run. Xhengo tittered. The whole ridiculousness of the situation struck him for the first time; I mean what did any of it matter when he could simply fly away to safety? I really can fly, he thought.

The pedestrian walkway ended here, and the track narrowed to a rocky causeway. Up ahead, a castle seemed to be rippling in a heat haze. The rocky track was becoming gluey and unstable, and he had an irresistible urge to laugh his head off. Sammy and the other man were gaining and Xhengo looked down at his feet, where the stones seemed to be breathing. Somewhere far off in a corner of his mind, he knew the men had spiked his drink. Fascinated, despite himself, he dropped to his knees to study the rocks more deeply. The pebbles had whorls in them that seemed terribly important, that contained a tantalising secret just out of reach, a message that would unlock everything. Xhengo looked up. There, straight ahead, was the blessed sight of a waiting police car. Thank God he was safe. Except that now he couldn't walk. He sat on his haunches rocking with laughter as the gangsters caught up with him. Everything was so killingly funny. He was laughing so hard he thought he was going to vomit.

Fairground organ music swirled around him. All he wanted to do was dabble his feet in the water. You don't just kill people in broad daylight, he told himself. Boots crunched right up beside him and Sammy looked down, blocking the tepid winter sun. "Funny guy, it's time to go home," the little man said.

CHAPTER THREE

NOW THAT THE FUNERAL WAS OVER, Kate hoped her husband could relax. She reminded him that he'd promised to show her around the city again. Paul said he would try and make time, work permitting, barely looking up from his mobile phone. Kate felt resentful at always having to compete with the wretched thing.

Their taxi was following the line of cars back to Tirana, and she reached for his hand again.

"Paul," she said. "You know you can talk to me about anything, don't you?"

"Yes, I know that."

"I mean, if anything was wrong you would tell me, wouldn't you?"

"Oh, for God's sake," said Paul, snatching his hand back. "I keep telling you, there's nothing wrong."

Stung, Kate persisted. "Look, I know you're worried about the business, but you've got to keep the faith. We're in a recession. Everybody's in the same boat. I could go back to work full-time if you want me to. John Lewis is looking for people."

"Please. Just drop it. It's not just the business, it's everything to do with my uncle. It's all on my shoulders. There's going to be a lot of sorting out to do over the next few days."

The rest of the journey was spent in resentful silence. Rain drummed on the taxi roof and Kate listened to the thock of the windscreen wipers, feeling hurt and confused. Why was this all on Paul's shoulders? What about his large family? Couldn't they take some of the responsibility?

Eventually they pulled up outside the block of flats Paul had grown up in. It was a ratty, bombed-out Communist-era block that looked either half-built or abandoned. Washing draped over balconies. A tangle of sagging wires. Paul ran round and opened the car door for Kate. The rain had become torrential, turning the gulch that ran through the middle of the potholed street into a stream. Kate's tights got soaked as she ran towards the entrance.

Inside was even worse. The staircase had a raw, unfinished look, as if hand-to-hand fighting had only just ended. Broken tiles. Rough, slapped-together concrete. So this was where her husband had spent his childhood; clearly Paul's father had not left the family much money. She felt truly sorry for him, only now understanding how poverty-stricken he had been.

The couple trudged up five flights of stairs to where Paul's aunt and his mother were receiving guests. The two women sat in overstuffed leather armchairs while people leaned down and whispered. Not speaking Albanian, Kate felt left out. Her attention wandered to a painting on the wall above the sofa; it showed a young man dressed in partisan uniform with mountains behind him. Half-turned away, he had a wistful quality, as if he was already saying goodbye. But what really struck her was his haunted expression. He and Paul had the same eyes.

"He doesn't look long for this world, does he?" said Paul, handing her a drink.

"Who was he?"

"My grandfather, who died fighting the Nazis. He was shot in the mountains trying to stop the Germans invading Tirana. He never liked Hoxha, apparently. Said he was a tyrant. Turned out he was right."

Enver Hoxha was the dictator who had made Albania one of the most paranoid countries on Earth. The countryside was pustulated with thousands of cement bunkers, waiting for an invasion that never came. You saw them on the hillsides outside the city.

Paul got back on his mobile phone the moment they returned to their hotel. It was already dark outside. Kate left him downstairs, pacing and gesticulating. Honestly, he was never off the thing; it was like the third person in their marriage. Kate went upstairs and took off her hat, placing it on the bed. She hated arguing. A marriage going well is the closest any of us know of ecstasy, she thought. A relationship that had soured was a living hell, a burning bed.

She took her iPhone from the dressing table, opened the French windows and stepped outside. It was evening now and blustery, although the rain had stopped. She snapped away at the buildings and at the people in the café across the square. Some hardy folk were sitting outside. A waiter threaded about, rearranging chairs and wiping a table. Suddenly there was a boom overhead and Kate looked up to see phosphorescent firework trails crackling and fizzing into nothingness. This was the White Night Paul had told her about, when Albanians celebrated victory over the Nazis. There was another explosion, this time a pulsing red-and-blue jellyfish.

She heard Paul come into the room and braced herself for another argument. Kate tried to remember the last time they had been happy. She turned to face him.

"Fireworks. Look," he said.

He stood by the bed with remorse on his face. "Kate, I'm sorry. I'm sorry about arguing in the car. You were right. Everybody wants a part of me. I feel like one of those rubber dolls with stretchy arms, and my arms are being stretched tighter and tighter."

Those were the soft words she needed to hear. She took his hands. "It's okay. You don't need to fight me. I'm in your corner."

"I don't know what I'd do without you. You know that."

They kissed tentatively and then again, this time deeper. Paul's tongue opened her mouth and his hands dropped to her breasts. He pulled her close, and she could tell how hungry he was. Part of her resisted, still angry with him, while another part wanted the healing to begin. They hadn't had sex for weeks. Paul had been impotent the last time they'd tried, blaming work stress. His hands cupped her buttocks and she felt his erection through his trousers. She was getting wet. He roughly hitched up her dress and slid his finger into her knickers, touching her clitoris. She wanted him badly now. "Come over here," he said thickly, leading her by the hand to the bed.

Afterward, Kate felt sated and happy, as if the world had clicked back into place. A peaceful kind of sleepiness came over her. Paul lay flat on top of her, and she could feel his sticky erection shrink up. Her stomach was damp with sweat and she felt his cum leaking out of her, but she didn't want to move just yet. Instead, she gazed at her husband, whose eyes were closed. He had a lean face and his expression was often amused and a little wry. When they first met at her degree show, she had wondered if he was gay. "Fey" was the word the Scots used. He had worn his hair in a pony-tail then. His face was rounder now, and he had put on a little weight each year of their marriage. She still thought he was beautiful, though. In her mind's eye he would always be twenty-three, like one of those Bonnard paintings where the artist depicted his wife as a young woman, even when she was elderly. Her mind wandered to what their first child would be like. Her girlfriends had started having babies, and she felt jealous every time somebody updated her Facebook status with a new arrival. Her doctor had told her she could postpone having a baby until she was in her forties, but she was starting to wonder if it was true. She had stopped using the pill without telling Paul, afraid that her fertility was ebbing. Would this be the moment it happened?

Lying there, she held on to the moment. Then Paul's wretched mobile pinged with an incoming message and he opened his eyes, rolling onto his side to answer it. The text must have been important, because he got up to read it properly. He stood in the middle of the room gazing concernedly down at his mobile. Kate was in a playful mood and she reached for her iPhone on the bedside table. She framed him with her smartphone, admiring his naked torso.

"Hold still," she said. The iPhone shutter snapped.

"We're always going to be together, aren't we," said Paul. It was more of a statement than a question.

"Of course we are. I love you."

Paul gave her a brave little smile and she turned away, tagging the photo #holdstill and pinging it to him on Snapchat. It would make him laugh.

She heard the French doors open, and moments later a car horn blared. Sounds of panic and commotion came up from the street. She rose from the bed, already knowing something bad had happened. "Paul…" she said. He wasn't in the room. Kate pushed her way through the net curtains and reached the balustrade.

Looking down, she saw her naked husband lying half under a truck. His arms and legs were at funny angles, as if a child had thrown down a doll. A woman was screaming uncontrollably, and the driver had got out of his truck clutching his head. People were gathering around Paul's body and somebody looked up at her. Kate's kneecaps dissolved and she fell to the patio, unable to comprehend what had just happened. One part of her was observing the other, watching herself as she sat there shaking. Only then did she realise that the woman screaming was herself.

CHAPTER FOUR

BOOM-SSHH. The waves broke on the bitterly cold beach and spume rolled over the sand, edging up over his feet. The wind flapped around his jacket and trousers. Hashim hated Zogaj for sending him here. How typical of the boss to get others to do the dirty work while Zogaj was probably asleep in a comfortable bed two-and-a-half-thousand kilometres away. He compared the godforsaken spot with home, thinking of the avenue lined with palm trees that led up to the mosque, the hot pinks and acid greens of the seafront. He thought about its shrieking electric amusements and how he'd occasionally catch the eye of a Macedonian factory worker who'd come to Durres for a cheap holiday.

The biting wind brought Hashim back to the here and now. According to the numerals on his army watch, they were late. Goddamn them for making him do this. Did they think he was no better than some whore-beater?

A light flashed in the darkness, and he was so caught up in his bitterness that he almost forgot to signal. Hashim gave the boat three long flashes. The whores would be climbing into the inflatable now. Any resistance would have been beaten out of them back home. They realised by now that there were no jobs waiting for them here as beauticians and au pairs. They were not going to save their families from their miserable lives.

His hatred of Zogaj was graven right down to his bone. Hashim hadn't been there when his father had been murdered. Later they told him that his mother had just stood watching while a pillow was placed over his head. His father had struggled half-heartedly under the blankets and then given up. Of course, Papa had been ill for a long time, and the sweetish smell of death had always been in the room, crouched like a gargoyle in a corner. But now his cousin would inherit everything. Why had his mother never wanted him? He remembered her summoning him once to her bedroom and asking what he would do if he found her dead. He had still been only a child. Call a doctor, he had replied. "No, extract my gold teeth and sell them. You always were a weakling," she said dismissively.

His feeling of not being wanted was partly the reason he spent so much time away from the farm. He had devoted his youth to looking after sheep, on endless rocky tracks strewn with droppings. Hard scrabble up mountains where the weather could change from sun to rain to snow within an hour. When Hashim was a boy, the family kept what it really did for a living from him. But somehow he always knew. Conversations would stop when he entered a room; there were guilty looks and large amounts of cash lying around.

In those early days, the family knew the war was there but they didn't go to it. Hashim saw smoke rising from the villages across the border, but his family kept to their side of the mountains. The Serbians were looting houses, setting villages alight and digging mass graves, they said. We must do something. Really, the Kosovans and the Albanians are the same people. One day, a grey NATO jet flew overhead and its sound hit him only a second later, as if somebody had torn the sky in two. That was the night Papa told them that the war was getting nearer and that their brothers in Kosovo would need arms. So they started trading their marijuana with the Italians for weapons: Kalashnikovs, grenades, even an anti-aircraft gun.

One afternoon they found a Serbian soldier wandering dazed in the mountains. He'd become separated from his unit. One eye was puffy and black and closed-up, and he was acting confused; later his father said he had shellshock. He kept mumbling and slapping his forehead as if he'd forgotten something. So that evening they led him down to the village, which looked so warm and inviting, in the valley below. Hashim thought the farmers would look after him. The whole village posed for a photograph with the soldier, looking stiffly formal like in one of those Victorian portraits. His father told him that he and his cousin were to turn the soldier over to the KLA.

He would always remember what happened next.

Hashim dug his hands into his pockets, cursing the wind

while his lungs ached for a cigarette. But he'd left them in the van. The dinghy's outboard engine was getting nearer, the inflatable smacking down like an open hand on the water. Once they were inside the van, their orders were to drive back up the motorway to a service station where cars were waiting to send the girls all over England: Bristol, Manchester, Birmingham and Leeds. They may be my brothers, he thought, but the Bangladeshis were the worst. They paid a high price, the younger the better. He tried imagining what it would be like to be with a woman, to touch her down there, but that was the problem. He had no imagination.

Sammy cut the engine and let the waves carry the dinghy the rest of the way. Hashim helped haul the inflatable up onto the sand to stop it sliding back into the water. Sammy shouted at the whores to get out. He was a sick fucker, that one. He once told Hashim that when he was a kid, the dogcatcher who lived upstairs taught him how to masturbate the strays they caught. Hashim would have to keep a close eye on him.

The handover went smoothly, and eventually there were just three of them sitting in the driver's cab. Sammy sat on the far left wearing his stupid wraparound sunglasses, thinking they made him look like Bono. The girl sat between them. Hashim wanted to tell her that everything was going to be all right, that nothing would happen as long as she did what she was told, but he didn't speak Vietnamese and, he guessed, she didn't speak Albanian.

Papa had treated his cousin like a son after he came to live with them. His cousin must have been eight years old. At first, they used to tumble over each other like puppies, but the older his cousin got, the more different they became. It was as if he could see further than Hashim, think about things longer and deeper, and had grown embarrassed by his cloddish cousin. Sitting there at the family dining table, Hashim felt dull resentment whenever he looked at him. Why should his cousin usurp what was rightfully his?

The business had changed, too. The Albanians have always been pirates, his cousin said, but there was a new kind of piracy. Today there were billions of leks to be made from cybercrime. Say, somebody wanted to download music. You sent them back a file – and then he used all these words Hashim didn't understand, like malware and Trojans. What he did understand was that it was like old-fashioned protection. The family held their computers to ransom: either the person paid up or they destroyed what was on it. Plus, they'd stolen everything that was on it anyway. Our friends in Italy would pay good money for credit card details, his cousin said. The old man just sat there nodding; in truth he was only a peasant goatherd. Hashim's uncle had always been the one with the brains.

The three of them drove mostly in silence into south London. It always surprised Hashim how many people were awake even at five in the morning as he watched a bus pull out in front of him.

Other gangs caught on to what they were doing. It was like picking low-hanging fruit. Hashim's job was to be the muscle, to make sure that other families didn't get in on the action. A couple of brothers gave them a lot of trouble, though. They shut up after a grenade was tossed through their front window.

The nail bar was in a side street. Looking for the turn, Hashim noticed with distaste the number of hairdressing salons and nail bars catering to the blacks. The nail bar was sandwiched between a pawnbroker and a vet. A dumpy Vietnamese woman, grey with tiredness, opened the door in her dressing gown. Her son stood behind her, and a flash of recognition passed between them. "People like us always recognise each other," he thought. The walls of the place were painted a hideous magenta, and it reminded him of the pink house. "Upstairs," the woman grunted in a thick, rubbery accent. They followed the tough-looking youth through a beaded curtain and up the steps to a bedroom. The madam switched on the overhead light. A single mattress, stained brown with what could have been blood, lay in one corner. The Vietnamese girl sat down on the mattress, drawing her knees up against her chest. Watching, afraid of what was going to happen next.

The pink house. His father told them to drive the Serbian soldier to a pink house near Tirana airport. During Hoxha's time, the only flights that came in to Tirana were from Communist China. So the teenager didn't understand why they were taking the Serb to the airport – were they flying him to China? His cousin said he didn't know, best not ask. The soldier lay across both footwells with his hands tied and a sack over his head. Hashim's boots rested on top of him. The pink house, when they got there, was a nothing sort of place with a scrubby garden and a few chickens pecking about. The walls were a wedding-cake pink that changed to grey halfway up, as if they'd run out of paint and had just decided to carry on painting. It was dusk by now. You could hear planes in the distance coming in to land at the nearby airport. Hashim hauled the soldier out of the car and pulled him towards the house, but the closer they got, the worse he felt about it. A strong chemical smell clogged his nostrils. His cousin was to take the Serbian inside while Hashim waited in the car. To his surprise, a man in blue hospital scrubs opened the door, all dressed up like a surgeon.

Hashim sat in the driver's seat smoking cigarettes and waiting for his cousin to come out. All the while an ominous feeling kept building, like something bad was about to happen. Ten minutes. Twenty minutes. After three quarters of an hour, Hashim was about to get out and see what was going on when his cousin appeared holding a plastic picnic cooler. When he got back in the car, Hashim could tell something was wrong.

"You were a fucking long time. What took you so long?"

"Just shut up and drive. I don't want to talk about it."

"Hey, I was just asking–"

"You don't want to talk about it either."

They'd been told to go to a gate away from the main building. All the way there, Hashim knew there was something bad in the picnic box on the back seat. A guard waved them through. A private jet was parked beside the hanger, and there were men waiting to do the handover. "You do it," his cousin said. "I need to get some air." Hauling the picnic box out, Hashim set off towards the aircraft steps, noticing the Turkish flag on the plane tail. His cousin walked around the car breathing in deeply. He looked as if he was going to be sick.

The present knifed into the past. Dumping his rucksack on the bedroom floor, Hashim rummaged through a front pocket for his carefully wrapped needles. Then he set his ink bottle down. He had always enjoyed drawing: flowers, birds, hands clasped in prayer. In prison they'd called him Picasso. Which was why that stupid kuff had asked him to draw a tattoo of a cross on his neck. Instead, he'd drawn a great black ugly penis with hair sticking out of its balls like an old-fashioned sea mine. The brothers all had a good laugh over that. Except that he'd found a chunky turd in his bed that night when he threw back the cover. Hashim remembered looking in the shower-room mirror

and calmly knowing that he would kill the fucker down the
hall that night. That was the first time he had murdered. He
remembered the slight resistance as the shiv went in, and
the pop-eyed "Wait, this can't be happening" look on the
infidel's face. Later, Hashim felt bad. The kuff came to him
as a ghost, sitting on the end of his bed and not saying a
word, just looking at him reproachfully. That's why Hashim
decided to tattoo a black teardrop above his left eye – as a
way of showing his remorse. It also told the others to keep
away. He was a murderer now.

"Give me your hand," Hashim said in English. When the
whore looked confused, he grabbed her hand and held on.
He kept the wrist tight as he dipped the needle into the ink,
jabbing it into her forearm. He could feel her panicking,
like a bird battering its wings against the side of a cage.

Slowly he tattooed the letter Z into her skin. Papa
compared it to marking sheep up the hillside. After
Hashim had finished and rewrapped his bloody needle, the
whore just stared at her reddened forearm. Even if she tried
running away, anybody who picked her up would know
who she belonged to. Zogaj.

CHAPTER FIVE

KATE DIDN'T REMEMBER how long she had sat there.
Eventually she got up to answer the hesitant knock on the
door, taking in the flashing blue lights below. The police
must already be here. She knotted her dressing gown,
feeling strangely detached, as if this was all happening
to somebody else. A dapper man with a Van Dyck beard
stood outside in the corridor. The hotel manager, she
supposed. Was she all right? A dreadful accident. Her
husband must have lost his balance and fallen over the
edge. The police were on their way upstairs now and
wanted to speak to her.

She didn't remember getting dressed or how she got into a
police car to drive to the hospital. What she did remember
was the ambulance's blue light splintering and reflecting
back in shop windows. She kept seeing Paul's body, his
arms and legs at funny angles, and the way the man in
the crowd had looked up when he heard her screams. The
occasional yip of the ambulance siren cut through her
thoughts. The ambulance men weren't in a hurry to get
anywhere; to them this was just another dead body in the
back, not the person they were going to spend the rest of
their life with.

A memory. It must have been the first time they went on a date. Paul had taken her to see a revival of an old Marx Brothers film at the National Film Theatre; it was one of the few American films they were allowed to see growing up in Albania, he had said. At first she hadn't liked the film. It seemed stagey and old-fashioned, yet there was a scene where the Marx Brothers were all clambering over each other in a ship's cabin that made her cry with laughter.

Afterward, they had walked over the bridge to Embankment, and Paul had stopped to admire the city at night: St Paul's and the science-fiction skyscrapers behind it.

"It's so different from where I grew up," he said.

"What do you mean?"

"You have no idea. There was no colour, everything was grey. I remember the first time I saw an orange, I couldn't believe how colourful it was, the orangey-ness of it. My Dad brought one home. A lorry had appeared in the street selling them off the back. I think they were from Cuba. We were so cut off from the rest of the world."

There was a sadness about him as he looked out over the bridge, and she wanted to tell him it was going to be okay. He turned to look at her. Kiss me now, she thought.

"I could fall into you," he said. At the time she hadn't understood what he meant, but now she knew.

One moment he was there. The next he was gone.

A policeman escorted her along the hospital corridor to a waiting area. Nurses chatted behind the reception desk. A man was shouting behind a curtained-off bed. Kate tried to take it all in, feeling far away from herself. This was the kind of thing that happened to other people, not to you. The policeman showed her to a line of bucket seats in the corridor and jerked his chin for her to sit down. Kate sat there in a daze, unable to comprehend what had just happened. What was the message Paul had received on his phone just before he jumped? What had been so terrible that he'd taken his own life? His mobile was still lying on the dressing table next to her make-up purse. Thinking about Paul's mobile, she rummaged in her bag for her iPhone. She needed to see that final photograph. She swiped through images she'd taken that day in Tirana, gazing at the last photo of her husband, the one of him standing naked with a hopeless look on his face. She put her finger on the screen, wanting to touch him one more time. My darling, come back to me. I love you so much. Wait, there was something else. Through her tears, she spread her fingers over the screen, enlarging the picture.

Somebody was standing behind him.

A bearded man loomed though the curtains behind her husband. The wind had blown the net curtains out, imprinting them on the man's face. Had he been waiting to push Paul off? Who was he? A burglar caught in the act? She rose from her seat, wanting to show the policeman standing guard, but he shook his head and put his hand on her shoulder. The way he pressed down made Kate realise for the first time that the police thought she had something to do with Paul's death. How ridiculous. Surely they didn't think she had pushed her husband off the balcony? A kaleidoscope of thoughts went through her head, each one turning into another.

A young doctor in hospital scrubs came towards them. "Mrs Julia?" he asked in English. She nodded. "Please would you come with me? The police need you to identify your husband's body. I'm sorry."

Patients shuffled past them as they turned this way and that down hospital corridors. A porter pushed a stunned-looking old woman in a wheelchair with a drip up her nose. Somewhere a mournful alarm sounded. Finally they came to what Kate guessed was the morgue viewing area. Her body walked through the door, but her mind didn't. Not my husband, she thought, not my husband. The walls were painted coral pink. A box of tissues lay on the table, and through the louvered windows she could see two men in blue scrubs standing over a gurney.

Paul was stretched out on the gurney. Her husband was just sleeping, that was all.

A paper doily covered his face, and the reality of his death hit her for the first time. Until now she hadn't really believed he was dead. Somehow she had imagined that

Paul would walk in, leading the clapping, and she would feign astonishment as the reality TV hoax was revealed. Except that this was no hoax: this was her life.

Another man was waiting for her in the anteroom. He was small and nearly bald, with glasses that comically magnified his eyes. His spectacles were old-fashioned Seventies frames and his eyes, large and strange, seemed to float behind the lenses. "Mrs Julia? My name is Inspector Poda from the Albania State Police. I am the officer assigned to you. I am sorry about what has happened." His English was good, tinged with an Italian accent. "Before we go any further, I need you to identify the body. Are you okay with that?" Kate swallowed and nodded. She was determined to get through this, no matter how painful it would be. "Your husband was run over by a car," Poda continued. "There was a lot of damage to his face after he hit the pavement." That explained the oddly dainty touch with the doily. He rapped on the glass and nodded.

Neither of the two mortuary attendants moved. One was big with a round, grave face and a greasy ponytail – he reminded Kate of the butler in those Addams Family movies she had watched as a kid – while the other was barely more than a child. He had that sullen, pasty-faced look of somebody brought up on a tough estate, and he made her think of a white rat with red eyes. Neither man seemed willing to make the first move. They both kept gesturing, as if urging the other to take the first step.

Finally, the kid who looked like a white rat came forward and lifted Paul's wrist. "Do you recognise this tattoo?" the detective inspector asked. On the back of Paul's hand was the faded grey tattoo he had got as a teenager, a crude Z. A certain disintegration was occurring in Kate's chest, an increasing shakiness. She nodded. The inspector nodded back and the attendant stepped forward to close the blinds.

Her husband was lying dead in front of her, and the only question now was how to make funeral arrangements. She felt defeated. "What happens now?" she asked, lifting her face. She was a child needing to be looked after, this was so overwhelming. The detective looked at Kate sympathetically.

"I need to ask you some questions," he said.

"Why? Am I under arrest?"

Poda shrugged. "No. Do you think you should be?"

"Of course not."

"I need you to tell me what happened. So we can eliminate you from our enquiry." He gestured for her to sit down. "Do you have any idea why your husband killed himself?"

Even the words he was using made her want to giggle, the idea of Paul killing himself was so ridiculous.

"None whatsoever. We flew into Tirana yesterday for his uncle's funeral. It was this afternoon. Paul seemed fine when we got back to the hotel. We watched the fireworks and then..."

"This uncle. Who was he?"

"A farmer who lived in what Paul called the Highlands. He took over Paul's family farm when he was a boy, after his father died. I don't know his name."

"But you have family in Tirana, yes?"

"Yes, Paul's mother lives in the city. We went to her flat after the funeral."

"I need the name and address of your mother-in-law. I also want to speak to other witnesses, people at the hotel."

The policeman nodded as he wrote in his notebook. "You get back to the hotel and your husband does this thing." The inspector stopped writing and looked up. "So this was completely unexpected? You had no argument, there was no fighting?"

"We did argue. Paul had been having money problems at work. He runs an internet business in London. Business hasn't been so good. I knew he was worried."

"So money worries were the reason he killed himself?"

Kate sighed. Suddenly she felt absolutely drained. The detective inspector was going too fast, trying to make her say things she didn't mean. He was attempting to get things wrapped up quickly, pushing for a simple explanation instead of the truth.

"There's something else you should know. Just before Paul jumped, he got a text message. He read it, and the next thing I knew he was dead."

The inspector looked surprised. "Where is this text message? Do you have his mobile phone? I need to look at it."

"It's back at the hotel. I left it there. In the confusion."

The inspector stood up. "We'd better get going. The National, yes?"

The first thing Kate noticed when she got back to their room was the silence. The French windows were still open and the net curtains were moving about. She closed the windows and only then did she pick up Paul's mobile. The detective inspector stood there awkwardly, probably wondering whether to interrupt this private moment. She turned her back to him. For some reason, what the Irishman said came back to her – about all Albanians being thieves – and she forwarded the text to herself. Just for safekeeping. "Here," she said. "Look for yourself." Both of them stood over the mobile. There was no message, just a photo attachment: it looked like a CCTV screen-shot of Paul standing next to a young Asian woman. Paul had his arms raised as if he was shouting. The black-and-white image was grainy, but it looked as if they were indoors.

"Have you ever seen this photo before?"

Kate shook her head. "No, never."

"You don't know who this woman is? Or who sent the photograph?" She shook her head again. "Try phoning the number."

Kate tapped the call button and listened to the single dial tone. Whoever had sent the message was obviously abroad. The automated voicemail cut in and she ended the call. Voicemail, she said. The inspector dug his hand into his pocket and pulled out a plastic bag. Carefully, he took the mobile from her hand, reversing the bag over it. Evidence, he replied. Kate went through Paul's jacket and handed over his wallet and notebook, and then went to the safe for his passport. The inspector said she could have them back in a couple of days, once his investigation was complete. "So what happens now?" she asked. Poda blinked behind his funny magnified spectacles. "You make funeral arrangements," he said flatly.

Silence reasserted itself once she was left alone in the room. Kate felt like a small child again. Who would look after her now? She wanted her husband to hold her, to tell her everything was going to be okay. But, of course, nothing was going to be okay. The one person she needed was gone. A tsunami of things she needed to do was bearing down on her. Being practical, yes, that was the only way she would get through this. "That's one of the things I love about you most," Paul had told her. "You're so down to earth." But what would happen once she ran out of things to do, what then? Her chest felt tight, so tight.

Don't leave me, my darling, I love you so much. Finally the tears came. Sitting there on the bed, she was wracked with great heaving sobs. Kate had never felt more abandoned or alone.

Saturday

CHAPTER SIX

A HEAVY WEIGHT was pressing down on her, making even the thought of getting up impossible. What was the point of leaving the bed? Everything seemed hopeless. She felt for Paul's side of the mattress, but of course it was cold and empty. Grief was building like a wave about to break, and she knew she had to fight it, otherwise Paul might as well have grabbed her, too, and they would both have toppled over together, their brains dashed on the pavement.

Paul wouldn't have wanted her to feel this way. "If anything ever happens to me, I want you to remarry," he had told her only a few weeks ago. She remembered looking up from her Macintosh, wondering what had brought that on. Perhaps he had already made up his mind. Guilt weighed down on her. Kate gazed up at the hotel ceiling, trying to remember if Paul had given her any other clues about what he'd planned to do. Was there anything she could have done to stop him? Some indication of his state of mind?

What a way to go. She tried to imagine what it must have been like, standing on the edge of the balcony and then tipping over, seeing the square rush up to meet you. She screwed her eyes shut, trying to block out the image.

And who was the woman in the text message? Why was Paul arguing with her? What had that to do with Paul's decision to jump?

Thoughts about how her husband had killed himself, and who the woman in the photograph was, twisted round each other. The fact was, however, that Kate had unknowingly failed her husband in some way, and now he was lying dead on a hospital gurney.

What she needed to do was tell people, let them know her pain and shock. This was the first time she had felt compelled to play to the gallery. She must testify to the calamity that had befallen her, and this urge would grow stronger over the coming days. She would tell taxi drivers, shopkeepers and anybody else she came across what her husband had done. Like a character in a Greek tragedy, she wanted to tear her clothes, wail and beat her breasts.

The telephone cut through her thoughts.

"Hello?"

"Kate, this is Marina. I heard on the news this morning. Somebody at the hotel threw themselves off roof. Are you both all right?"

It was painful to swallow. How do you tell a mother that her son is dead? "Marina – I'm very sorry. There's been some bad news. Paul–"

"Oh, God. Don't tell me that. Please don't tell me it was Paul."

"There was an accident. He fell off the balcony."

Silence. Paul's mother began crying on the other end of the line. It was a horrible, keening moan, and Kate could imagine the black O of her mother-in-law's mouth. She couldn't think of anything worse than a mother outliving her son. It was so unnatural.

A memory. Her classics teacher budged up next to her at a school desk, translating the Greek together: What greater grief can there be for mortals than to see their children dead?

"He must have lost his balance and toppled over the edge," Kate told her, parroting what the policeman had said. In her heart, though, she knew this wasn't true. She thought about the man on the balcony, the face looming through the net curtains. "Please. I want to come and see you."

"My son, my son. I loved him so much. You can't–"

Half an hour later, she was in a taxi heading towards her mother-in-law's. The taxi driver was the same man who'd driven her and Paul back to the hotel. Her husband had been alive less than twelve hours ago. It felt like a different life. They passed by a dingy clothes shop calling itself Harrrods, and she made a mental note to remember to tell Paul because he would find it funny – only to realise that she would never tell him anything again. That was hard.

She screwed up her eyes to stop herself from tearing up as they lurched over another pothole. Soon they were back in the rundown side street with black wire spewing out of the apartment-block wall. She handed over two thousand lek and told the driver he would get the other half on her return. No problem, he said. Kids stopped playing football as she got out of the car, as if they had never seen a taxi before.

Her mother-in-law seemed to have aged even since yesterday. She took the chain off the door and shuffled back down the hall to her sitting room. A hideous Communist-era shelving unit dominated one wall and Kate noticed the apartment's smell for the first time, a curious mixture of mustiness and linseed oil she would come to associate with Albania. Marina sat down heavily in her overstuffed leather armchair and lit a cigarette. "Tell me what happened," she said dully. Kate went through the whole story from beginning to end. How she knew Paul was under pressure at work, their row in the taxi and Paul jumping from their seventh-floor balcony. She left out the part about the text message.

"Whatever had been on his mind about work, we could have talked it through. We would have found a solution," Kate said.

"Paul was not happy. He tell me."

"I know he wasn't happy. It had been building for weeks. If

only he had seen a doctor–"

"He tell me he has big debts. He feel trapped. He say everything on his shoulders, how he can't see any way out. I am sorry, Kate, I should have told you."

"When did he tell you?"

"The night you arrive. At his uncle's wake. I can see he is unhappy. A mother knows."

"You should have said something. Depression is an illness. It can be treated."

"Kate, you are good woman. I do not want to hurt you. What Paul tell me–" Marina shrugged.

"Hurt me? What did Paul tell you?"

"At the wake. He talk about everything, his life–"

"Yes? And what did he say?"

"He say he feel trapped. He want new life."

"Yes, he told me he felt responsible for everything."

Marina twisted the tissue in her lap harder. "With you, I mean. He was unhappy with you."

"I don't understand."

"He tell me he do not love you anymore."

Kate's brain pulsed with shock the moment she said it. Her lips felt thick, and it took a moment before she could think of what to say. "The thing is, Marina," she said, recovering,

"I don't believe Paul's death was an accident. I think he was murdered."

Marina shifted in her seat. "What make you say that?"

She reached into her handbag and pulled out her iPhone, swiping through photographs with her finger. Handing the mobile across, she showed Marina the photo of Paul in their bedroom, naked and vulnerable.

Now it was Marina's turn not to understand.

"Look closer. Behind Paul on the balcony. There's a man standing outside. Waiting for him. You can see his face where the net curtains have blown onto him."

Marina studied the phone before handing it back. "I don't see anything."

"Don't tell me you can't see it."

"It was just wind. You see things that are no there. Kate, listen. I am sorry for you, I am sorry for my son. I don't know how long I can go on knowing that he's dead. It is the one thing I feared most in the world. But you have to accept truth–"

Anger heated through her, and there was fire in Kate's belly. She could not believe Paul's own mother was so quick to dismiss her. Goddammit, she would prove that her husband was murdered. Somebody had pushed Paul off that balcony, and she was determined to find out who. She slipped her mobile back in her bag. "Fine," she said acidly.

"If you don't believe me, I'll find somebody who does."

"Kate, wait–"

"Don't bother getting up. I'll see myself out."

Tears stung her eyes as she weaved down the corridor. She didn't really know where she was going. How could this woman say such a vile thing? Of course Paul loved her. What had happened was an aberration, a thin streak of the irrational that runs through everything.

Back outside, Kate felt as if she couldn't get enough air into her lungs. Her thoughts turned to the man lurking on the balcony, the one who had pushed her husband to his death. The problem was that she knew only one other person in Tirana who might believe her.

The taxi driver was standing beside his car waiting. He dropped his cigarette when he saw Kate and looked faintly alarmed when she told him where they were going. She was a woman possessed. Like a Fury, she would pursue whoever had done this to her husband to the ends of the Earth.

CHAPTER SEVEN

ANOTHER CORRIDOR. Canary-yellow walls and a powder-blue, mica-flecked floor. Notices in Albanian. Police headquarters was located on the outskirts of the city centre. Policemen walking past looked down at Kate curiously as she sat in the corridor gathering her thoughts. A man had been lurking outside ready to push her husband off their balcony, she was convinced of it. A burglar surprised in the act when they arrived back so unexpectedly. But what if Marina was right and it was all just a trick of the light? Vast edifices of conspiracy had been erected around the Moon landings because of the way light had fallen in a photograph. Maybe this *was* all in her mind: she'd invented it because she couldn't cope with the truth. These two voices vied in her head until Inspector Poda came downstairs to greet her. The funny-looking detective looked worried.

"Mrs Julia? We're not ready to release your husband's body yet. Our investigation is ongoing. We need to do a post-mortem first and then issue a death certificate."

"Have you found anything?" she said, standing up.

"It is still early in the investigation. We will get witness statements, talk to people. You can take your husband home once the post-mortem is finished."

"I haven't come about that. I need to show you something. Another photograph," she said, realising how lame this sounded.

"Another photograph? We're still trying to find the person who sent your husband the text."

"Please. Can we talk somewhere in private?"

The inspector signed her in and escorted her through the turnstile before they went upstairs. In the bad old days, there had been a secret police as well, its headquarters up the road from her hotel. Poda gestured for the two detectives in the room to leave. Looking round at the grubby beige computers, desks and whiteboards, Kate thought they could have been in any sales office.

"So, how can I help you?" the inspector said, leaning forward. Kate showed him her iPhone and they went through the same routine again, with Poda looking quizzically at the photo. Except this time he nodded.

"What am I looking at?"

"This was the last photograph I took of my husband. You can see somebody else on the balcony behind him."

"Yes, I can see his face in the curtain."

"You believe me?"

"There's definitely somebody there."

"I thought I was going mad." Kate tried to keep the excitement out of her voice. "I thought it must be a burglar."

Poda turned serious. "We need to show this to the hotel. Perhaps they know who it is. Often these people have friends on the inside, people who work as cleaners."

"Thank God. I can't tell you what a relief this is."

"You are not going mad, Mrs Julia. Whoever that man is, we will catch him."

So grief had not driven her insane. The Albanian police did believe her, and if the police believed her, then her husband's killer could soon be behind bars.

Inspector Poda escorted Kate to the car park. He had a peculiar rolling, bandy-legged walk, as if he'd once been a sailor. Bypassing a line of police cars, he ushered her into a beat-up Fiat. "Best not let them know we're coming," he explained. "Otherwise, we'll set the cat among the pigeons, yes?"

They exited the police headquarters and turned right up the dual carriageway. A gulch ran through the middle of four lanes of traffic. The inspector was driving her back to her hotel, and the nearer they got to the city centre, the worse the traffic became. Poda drummed agitatedly on the steering wheel with his thumb. "There was never any traffic before there were women drivers," he muttered.

Ten minutes later, they pulled up outside the National. The police tape keeping onlookers back had gone, and it could have been any normal Saturday morning. Normal for everybody else, that is. Through the window, Kate glanced up at the hateful balcony that her husband had fallen from. When she got out of the car, she noticed that the pavement looked clean. The management clearly didn't want anybody reminded of last night. For them it was business as usual. Except that whoever had cleaned the pavement had not done a very good job. There was still a dark patch where her husband's brains had been dashed. She shuddered as she stepped over it.

As they walked through the double doors, the receptionist looked embarrassed to see them. She wouldn't meet Kate's eye. "Good morning, Mrs Julia. We are sorry for your loss."

The inspector interrupted. "We need to speak to the manager," he said.

"Of course. I'll just see if he's free. Who shall I say needs to see him?"

"Inspector Poda of the Albania State Police."

Kate took in the chandeliers and marble floor while they waited. The hotel had a classical feel. She remembered Paul telling her that an Italian architect had designed it as the economics ministry before the war. It had been government offices right up until the Nineties.

The manager with the Van Dyck beard appeared. He

reminded Kate of those drawings of Willy Wonka in a Roald Dahl paperback she had as a child.

"Who ordered the crime scene outside to be taken down?" Poda asked in English.

"I don't know. One of your colleagues, I suppose. They said they had everything they needed." The manager looked nervous, as if he wanted them out of there. Bad for business. "How can I help you?"

"We need to show you a photograph." Poda gave Kate a look indicating that she should get out her iPhone. "Do you recognise this man?"

"Yes, it's the man who killed himself." Then, remembering who Kate was: "Sorry, madam, I meant no offence."

"No, not him, the man behind, the one coming through the curtains."

It was a moment of vaudeville comedy, and Kate wished she had never embarked on such a wild goose chase. The manager looked dubious and then slowly nodded. "I suppose there could be somebody there. It might just the way the curtain's moving." He stroked his beard. "Yes, I'm pretty certain I know who that is."

"You know this man on the balcony?" repeated the detective inspector. Kate's heart thickened with surprise. This was all going much faster than she had expected. Maybe the police could even have Paul's murderer under arrest within the hour, she thought optimistically.

"Yes. He works as a dishwasher. We've had a lot of stuff going missing: jewellery, passports. We've never been able to prove anything, though."

"What makes you think it's him?"

"He's just trouble. He's always late or too hungover for work."

"Is this dishwasher on duty now?"

The manager looked at his watch. The wall clock behind him said nearly noon. "He should be here. Do you want me to find him?"

They filed downstairs through the basement restaurant and turned to the right. The manager ushered them into a typical industrial stainless-steel kitchen. Two cooks in chef's whites were getting lunch ready, and the one chopping vegetables looked up as the manager held the door open. The dishwasher stood with his back to them rinsing plates, his long hair in a ratty ponytail. The manager said something sharply in Albanian, and the dishwasher turned around. With his unkempt grey beard and tied-back hair, he looked like a California mountain man. There was no doubt in Kate's mind: this was the man who had been lurking on their balcony.

The man who had murdered her husband. The stranger who had pushed him to his death.

The four of them sat in the restaurant, the only people there. It was that empty hour before lunchtime service began. The dishwasher sprawled in his chair. For somebody being interviewed by the police, he looked almost relaxed, even bored. The inspector began speaking in Albanian and showed Kate's iPhone to the dishwasher, who shook his head. The conversation became heated. Kate didn't have a clue what was going on, and eventually the dishwasher folded his arms. Poda turned to Kate and said, "He says he wasn't in the hotel last night. He was watching the fireworks with his girlfriend. She was with him all night, apparently. Of course, we will check." The inspector spoke to the dishwasher again, who shrugged. Their suspect had agreed that they could speak to the woman who'd been with him last night. Suddenly, Kate didn't feel so confident.

They left the dishwasher with the manager watching over him. Poda said he needed to call headquarters for backup.

The detective inspector turned to Kate while they waited. "The hotel must have paid off my colleagues to take down the crime scene. Not good for business. This whole country's on the take. What do the Italians call it? *La mordida*. The bite. One hand washes the other." He mimed washing his hands.

"Will it hurt your investigation?"

"Probably not. Forensics got everything they needed. I'm more interested in what happened on your balcony. We'll need to dust for prints again. Check CCTV."

A dark blue Volkswagen marked Policia pulled up outside the hotel, and a couple of tough-looking policemen got out. They, too, had Balkan meathead haircuts, short on top and shaved sides. You wouldn't want to get on the wrong side of them, Kate thought. A minute later they were marching the dishwasher across the lobby and through the revolving door. She and Poda would follow in the inspector's beat-up Fiat.

The outskirts of Tirana were even more chaotic than where Paul's mother lived. There was a confusion of shops with wedding dresses stuck in the upper windows. Everything looked as if it was being built or had been abandoned. Cranes were everywhere. If anything, the potholes were even worse on this side of town.

Flanked by two policemen, the dishwasher walked up the worn stone steps of his apartment block. There was no lift. He lived on the top floor, and Kate peered over the handrail down the central stairwell as they made their ascent. Paul's body sprawled at the bottom flashed into her mind, and she yanked her head back. She felt nauseous. Perhaps Paul's death had given her vertigo as well.

The top-floor landing was a long corridor with doors on either side. All the woodwork was painted chocolate brown, and there was a strong smell of cabbage. The policemen stood outside one door and knocked. A young woman tying a dressing gown opened the door, looking at them suspiciously. They exchanged words in Albanian and the dishwasher went in.

The room the couple shared was really just a bedsit, with a double bed taking up most of the space. There was a wardrobe and a table covered with ratty-looking velvet on which a couple of electric rings stood. A corner vanity basin doubled as the sink, and all the woodwork was painted the same shit brown.

The four of them stood jammed in a corner until the inspector shook himself free, shooting a look at his officers as if to say, you idiots. The chambermaid answered his questions quietly, and after a brief exchange Poda turned to Kate. "She says they were together all last night. They watched the parade and then the fireworks. They have friends who saw them together." Kate was starting to have qualms. Who was she to ruin a man's life, and on the basis of what, a Snapchat photo? And in any case, what did it matter? Her husband was dead. The man she had loved with every atom of her being had gone, and everything else seemed pointless. "Tell him I'm sorry. There's been a mistake. I'm not going to press charges," Kate said. The dishwasher nodded at her gravely; clearly he understood some English.

"That's not for you to decide," said Poda.

He began looking round the room, opening wardrobe

doors. The young woman stared down at the floor. Poda picked up a book from the bedside table, flicked through the pages and then shook it, as if he expected something to fall out. The tension became palpable. It was like an awful game of hot and cold as Poda rattled open a table drawer, jangling the cutlery. He reached in with his arm and pulled out a watch: a Cartier Tank. Kate recognised the design. Holding it up with an I-told-you-so expression on his face, Poda searched again, and this time he pulled out a passport. At this, the chambermaid began shouting at her dishwasher boyfriend. One of the policemen cut in and shoved her down on the bed. The inspector said something sharply, and the cops hustled the protesting dishwasher out. "I'm arresting him on suspicion of stealing from hotel guests," said Poda before he turned to the woman, speaking softly to her. She looked dejected.

Kate didn't want to be in this squalid room anymore. In fact, she wanted to be anywhere but here. So Paul had been killed because they'd panicked a burglar – and for what? Apart from her iPhone and Paul's MacBook, there hadn't been much else in the room. She imagined the life they could have had together: Paul's baby growing inside her, jolly family days on the beach, helping their son – it was always a son – get ready for his first day at school. Well, none of that would happen now. This man had erased whatever future with Paul she might have had. She waited outside until the inspector joined her in the corridor.

The two of them leaned over the balcony and watched the policemen taking the dishwasher downstairs. He was struggling and complaining. The chambermaid had just admitted he had bullied her into giving him her pass key, Poda said. Her boyfriend stole from hotel guests and sold the goods on to a fence. Suddenly the dishwasher looked up and stared directly at Kate. It was as if he was looking right into her. "The man who die," he called up. "I know nothing. I know nothing."

Pushing the dishwasher's head down into the police car, neither officer paid much attention to the homeless man trundling a supermarket trolley along the street. His filthy clothes were stiff with dirt and his hair was matted with dreadlocks. It was the smell that was worst: people got out of the way because of the stink of booze and urine. The trolley's wonky front wheel made it veer off course. The tramp stopped to pick some litter off the pavement, all the while watching the police car. He dug a Samsung phone out of his rags and spoke softly into it. "Tell Zogaj they've made an arrest."

CHAPTER EIGHT

THE ROOM WAS PACKED with men standing shoulder to shoulder, bearded men, mostly shopkeepers, and a few local students. Hashim was one of the last to be let in. The imam, who was sitting on a carved wooden chair, was in the middle of his talk as the Albanian squeezed his way through. The digital clock behind the imam told the local time. In fact, there were clocks everywhere, giving the time both here and in Mecca. The imam's voice was comforting and reminded Hashim of home, of golden minarets rippling in the midday heat, a call to prayer ululating over the city, a mystery as old and timeless as the Qube itself. He jostled in-between his fellow believers as the imam stood up, revealing a crescent and star carved into the seat. The bearded cleric broke off and looked round the room for support, as if he wasn't quite sure as to the truth of what he was saying.

His talk over – homosexuality, the most corrupting and hideous of sins, was a vile perversion that went against human nature, *fitrah* – the imam sat back as a Pakistani in a djellaba stood chanting with his back to the room. As one, the worshippers dropped their gaze to the elaborate

Persian carpet and Hashim noticed that his right sock had a hole in it. He wiggled his big toe where it poked through. The worshippers dropped down again on their haunches, prostrating themselves, and Hashim heard the man next to him whispering urgently.

Quickly it was all over and Hashim emerged into the street, ignoring the man in a hi-vis jacket collecting donations in an empty curry-sauce bucket. The mosque was a shop front in a busy Soho street. All around them were kuff sex shops: women in chains being throttled, beaten and grabbed by the hair while men finished off in their insensible faces. Turning his leather collar up, Hashim pushed his way past the other men chatting and joshing each other, smoking cigarettes as they made plans. This place was on its knees as well. The smell of corruption stank in his nostrils. Soho was gearing up for Saturday night: the tourists and staggering-drunk women, the lonely men who slipped into the hostess bars. Zogaj owned most of them. Hashim nodded to a bored peroxide blonde sitting on a bar stool touting for custom.

One of his early jobs had been to persuade the owners to sell up to Zogaj. "We supply the girls. Now we want to own the bars as well," Zogaj had told him. He'd had to get rough with some of them, but that was the thing: prison didn't frighten Hashim; it was better than where he'd come from. The English guys, it was like there was a cut-off point as to stuff they wouldn't do. Hashim never felt like that. For him, there were no limits.

His bedsit was down the road from the shop-front mosque. He trudged upstairs past the grubby anaglypta wallpaper and the sign saying "Model First Floor". Hashim glanced up at the red naked light bulb. The whole place stank of cat piss. Letting himself in, he looked round the shabby room and lay down on the single bed, not bothering to take his boots off. He tapped one of the strong Greek cigarettes he'd brought over on the crushed packet and sparked up, exhaling through his nostrils. Only one left.

His father featured in one of his earliest memories. He couldn't have been more than three or four. There had been one hot, airless night in particular, the heavens swagged with pendulous stars. Papa had carried him up the mountain on his shoulders, and they had lain on the hillside gazing up at the stars as he explained the constellations. Could he see the shape of a plough? And there was the Archer, shaped like a bow and arrow. Thoughts of Papa turned into other thoughts: how Zogaj had clamped a pillow over the old man's head. "Zogaj always wins, Zogaj never loses," was what they said. Well, not this time, thought Hashim. Zogaj, Zogaj – the name was like an abscess leaking its poison into his nerves. They said that revenge was a dish best served cold. Well, he would just bide his time.

There was a knock on the door. Hashim wondered who it was; hardly anybody knew he was back in London. A couple of teenagers stood on the landing, probably up on a school trip. The one in front was a red-headed Yid, brashly confident, while his friend looked away down the stairs. "Can I see the model, please?" the Yid asked. "Not here," Hashim said. The shy one tugged his friend's elbow, signalling for them to go. He was attractive in an adolescent way and Hashim felt the familiar stirrings, hating himself at the same time. The Koran was clear: Whenever you catch somebody committing the act of the people of Lut, then kill both parties to the act. He wondered what it would be like to unbutton the boy's school shirt and kiss his nipples, put his hand down his trousers and feel his cock and his silky balls. Why did Allah torment him like this, what did he want with him? Hashim thought for the thousandth time that day as he watched the boys go downstairs and out into the street. They would kill him if they knew his thoughts. The punishment was death by stoning. He could see them standing in front of him, hatred on their faces, his surprise as the first stone struck a glancing blow. The stones would come thick and fast after that, an incoming sleet of rock. Seeing his own death gave Hashim pleasure. Lying there under a pitiless Albanian sky with the crowd standing over him, his torment would finally be over.

As he lay back down on the nubbly magenta bedspread, Hashim gazed at the neon sign rippling outside, a glass of drink pouring electric bubbles into a glass. The bedspread reminded him of the pink house. His thoughts turned back to that day with the Serbian soldier. His cousin had later told him what he'd seen. The pink house near the airport must have been a school before they used it for this. Three school desks had been jammed together; on the floor beneath them was what looked like dried blood. Medical rubbish was heaped in one corner: busted-open packaging, empty drip bags and plastic tubing. It had dawned on his cousin that this was a makeshift operating theatre. When they took the plastic bag off the soldier's head, he had also realised what was going on, and that's when he really started to struggle. For a moment his cousin had stood rooted to the spot, not quite believing what was happening. "Are you going to fucking help?" a doctor had said. It had taken all four of them to lift the private onto the tables and get him sedated. The soldier was still shouting and struggling, and his final words as he went under, his cousin said later, were "Bože pomozi mi. Nemojte to da mi radite." God help me. Please don't do this to me.

There were voices on the stairs and Hashim realised that he had better get going. Besides, he was hungry. Just one more message to deliver for Zogaj. They treated him like a messenger boy and not a family member, he thought resentfully.

The Vietnamese restaurant was busy, and there was a small queue by the door. Waiters bustled about with plates of food. Hashim sat down, studied the photos on the menu and ordered a bowl of noodles. He wondered if the waitress who took his order was one of theirs. But no, there was a defiance about her, plus the nose ring and the sleeve of tattoos. Probably a student. The girls who worked for them were too afraid to meet your eye. Any resistance had been beaten out of them long ago. He remembered reassuring one of them that he was her best friend, and she had believed him – even when the police raided the nail bar where she worked and transferred her to hospital, she escaped and came back.

The last of his broth pooled in his spoon and, satisfied, Hashim pushed the bowl away. He fished in his leather jacket for the crumpled box of cigarettes and lit his last one, tasting a crumb of sweet tobacco on his tongue. Almost immediately, the waitress noticed what he was doing and came over. "You can't do that. No smoking," she said, affronted. Let the bitch stew. He drew on the cigarette and exhaled slowly in her face. She looked askance and then belligerent. "You get manager," Hashim challenged her. Sure enough, the owner came out wearing dirty chef's whites and wiping his hands on a filthy tea towel. Flames shot up behind him as another cook furiously beat a wok. "What you problem?" the restaurant owner said, flinging the cloth over his left shoulder. "No smoking here." He was a big man in his mid-sixties who'd let himself run to fat. Zogaj said he'd been something during the war, that he'd made money selling heroin to American GIs. The proprietor stood over Hashim.

"I said, what's your problem?" he repeated. The owner placed both hands on the table and brought his face close to Hashim's. He noticed grease spots on the chef's whites.

"Zogaj say you owe money. You pay Zogaj what you owe."

The Vietnamese man looked surprised. "You know Zogaj? Zogaj send you here?"

"He want his money by tomorrow. I come and collect. He say that unless you pay him what you owe him, there'll be trouble."

"No fucky Muslamic tell me what to do. You tell Zogaj I pay when I'm good and ready."

"Listen, I wanna tell you a story. Back home, these guys make bad talk about Zogaj. 'We take business from Zogaj, Zogaj old man.' So he say, I hear you don't like what I'm doing, you come and we talk. Plenty food, plenty girls. Everybody happy, right? Zogaj meet these guys and the next minute, they all dead for disrespecting him." He gripped the cook's wrist and held it to the table. "If he do that to people who show him no respect, what do you think he do to people who owe him money?"

Sensing a disturbance, some of the diners turned around. The restaurant owner gave a queasy we're-all-friends-together smile.

"Okay, boss, you tell Zogaj I get money. I just need time."

Hashim extinguished the tip of his cigarette on the back of the manager's hand, who yelped like a little girl. Hashim hissed, "You get money you owe tomorrow. I come back same time."

"Please. I don't want no trouble." Fear showed in his eyes.

The Vietnamese cook's hand was still pinned to the table, and his little finger was just too tempting. Hashim started pulling it back despite the owner's whimpering until there was an unforgiving click.

When he stood up, he sensed the fear in the room; none of the other diners would meet his eye. Looking back, he saw the restaurant owner hopping about with his left hand under his armpit. Fuck it, he should be grateful. At least Hashim had broken the finger he used the least. Zogaj always wins, he repeated, Zogaj never loses.

Stepping out into the street, Hashim felt his phone vibrate with an incoming text message. He could see it was from Zogaj, who had sent him a photograph: so this was what she looked like. It was funny, but he had expected somebody different. She had a long horse face and glasses, and her hair was centre-parted like that Greek singer they used to watch on TV when he was a kid. Nana somebody. She wasn't like his usual girls. The message in Albanian read, "Gjej të saj dhe për të sjellë atë për mua." Find her and bring her to me.

Sunday

CHAPTER NINE

NOBODY TELLS YOU how much paperwork is involved when somebody dies. Kate hugged a manila envelope to her chest as she trudged from one department to another. There were empty waiting rooms with railway station clocks, cramped offices with brown linoleum floors, and always the sound of typing. She was questioned, cross-questioned, photographed; she dictated statements, gave her signature and initialled documents. Men gathered in doorways and would glance at her sympathetically, yet they didn't want to get too close in case her bad luck was contagious. She felt far away from herself, as if all this was happening to somebody else. She wanted to tell the officials that it had been a dreadful mistake, and that her husband would be coming to collect her at any moment. The words they used – "victim", "tragic accident" and "assailant" – meant nothing to her. They could have been talking about somebody else. Mostly, though, she just felt numb. Her emotions were simply unavailable to her as she sat there waiting, always waiting, in a corridor, her ankles tucked beneath her, hugging that manila envelope.

The British Embassy staff could not have been more

sympathetic to her, a young widow whose husband had
fallen to his death from a hotel balcony. You have our every
sympathy, said the ambassador. "You look as if you're
coping very well," he continued, handing Kate a cup of tea.
"I don't think it's really sunk in yet," she admitted.

The police said they needed to keep Paul's body until
the results of the post-mortem were known. After that it
would be up to her whether she wanted Paul's coffin flown
back to England or whether, because he was an Albanian
national, he would be buried in Tirana. That would be up
for discussion with his family. Christ, he would probably
be buried in the same cemetery where we buried his uncle,
she thought, what, the day before yesterday?

One moment he was there. The next he was gone.

Kate called Paul's mother, saying she needed to see her.
She swallowed her pride before making the call. Grief does
strange things to your mind, she thought. It's like going
to a foreign country. That's why Marina had said such
unforgivable things: she was unhinged by the enormity of
what had happened. They both were. Kate told her mother-
in-law that they needed to discuss funeral arrangements,
and that she didn't want them to part on bad terms. Marina
suggested meeting in the park that afternoon before
sunset. Kate could hear the flatness in her mother-in-law's
voice. That was why suicides were so selfish, she reflected,
because it was the rest of us who had to carry on living.

The park was only a ten-minute walk away, and it would be good for Kate to leave her hotel room. The four walls were closing in on her; she needed to get out and clear her head. On their way to the funeral, she remembered Paul pointing out the national art gallery. It was only five minutes from the hotel and, as this was Sunday in a Muslim country, it would be open that afternoon. Yes, that's what she would do: she would go to the art gallery.

The gallery was next to a building that looked like a crash-landed Millennium Falcon. Teenagers sat like starlings on the roof, while others slid down one of its sides. "The dictator's museum," Paul had told her. He had warned her that most of the paintings inside were ghastly super-heroic Social Realism works from the Communist era ("Friends of the Mechanics Factory"). Kate wandered round the mostly empty gallery gazing at the vaguely Tom of Finland-like paintings of aviators standing around in leather chaps. For a moment it was a relief not to think about Paul's death. Then she heard his voice in her head, clear as a bell, as if he was standing right next to her. She was looking at a naive painting of children playing with wooden guns. It must have been one of their earliest conversations when they were going out, after that moment on the Embankment; she even remembered what she'd had to eat.

"We used to have those guns. I remember playing with them at nursery school. It was what we had instead of toys. The whole country was primed for invasion at any time.

That was when the country was atheist, of course."

"What happened after Hoxha died?"

"Christian missionaries came into the country in droves. Albania had always been Muslim before, so a lot of people went back to that. My mother got religion in a big way. You'll see when you meet her."

"So you're not a believer?"

Paul had finished eating and pushed his plate away. "Nah. Hoxha was right. It's all superstition, all that fasting and prayer. There's nobody out there. When I die I don't even want to be buried, just cremated. I don't believe. I'm not a real Muslim."

Kate's mum was disappointed when Paul insisted on a register-office wedding. What mother hasn't wanted to see her little girl married in church? And Kate, too, was quietly upset not to have a full church wedding, but Paul had been resolute, insistent: "Listen, you have to be a believer to be married in church, and I don't believe. Besides, you wouldn't want me to go down there." He pointed downward with his index finger and laughed.

The other thing Paul had insisted on was that his family shouldn't be present. Just his mother. It was the first time they had really had an argument, but Paul had been immovable, cruelly deriding his family back in Albania as peasants who had only recently stopped hanging from the trees by their tails. Kate hadn't heard that tone in his voice before. Perhaps he thought his family would embarrass him, or that they didn't fit in with his new life and her boringly middle-class family. "Goddammit, which part of that didn't you understand?" he had said, bringing his hand down on the table. The sudden violence had been unnerving.

Kate thought of what Paul had said about wanting to be cremated, and that made up her mind. When and where had he been happiest? That would be the spot where she'd pour his ashes. She thought about the party they'd had after their civil ceremony in Bishop's Palace, posing for photographs and laughing at Colin's best-man speech. Emerging through a blizzard of confetti. They had posed against one tree in particular. Yes, that was where she would scatter them. According to her watch, she had a quarter of an hour before she was due to meet Paul's mother. She took one last look at the painting of children playing, then turned on her heel and left.

Chunky Albanians in tracksuits huffed and puffed their way around the jogging track. The sun was setting over Tirana Park, the pleasure garden in the city centre with its vast lake. Marina had told Kate to meet her in the open-air cinema.

Paul's mother was sitting alone in the crumbling amphitheatre. The cement stone circles of the outdoor cinema were graffitied and decaying. A teenage skateboarder was doing tricks in the semicircle where the screen would have been. There was a heaviness about Marina, as if she, too, had had the life sucked out of her. For the first time, Kate glimpsed what her mother-in-law would look like as an old woman.

"We used to bring Paul here every Sunday to watch movie. You bring cushions and picnic to watch film," Marina said.

"Was this before you had television?"

"We had television. One channel. No, this was government-approved movies. Every week we used to come when Paul was little boy."

"What sort of movies? Soviet war films?" Kate pictured the jut-jawed hero staring resolutely ahead while his wife/girlfriend clung to his side, begging him to stay.

"Norman Wisdom."

"What, the British comedian?" Kate dimly remembered a clown in a flat cap swaggering and taking a pratfall.

"The Party said he was example of little man not being crushed by counter-revolutionary capitalist system. Chaplin, too." Marina turned to her daughter-in-law. "I am sorry about what I said yesterday. I was angry. Disappointed. I wanted to hurt you. Now I am sad for you both."

"You were wrong about the photo."

"What do you mean?"

"The photograph I took of Paul. There was a man on the

balcony. The police believe me. It was a dishwasher who works in the hotel. They think he was burgling our room when we got back unexpectedly. The police found stolen property where he lives. He's under arrest."

"My God. Do you think he killed Paul?"

"He denies it. He says he was watching the fireworks along with everybody else on Friday night."

"What do you think?"

"I really don't know. I don't know about anything anymore."

Marina shook her head. "Murder–"

"Marina – what you were saying yesterday about Paul being so unhappy. Did he ever mention to you that he was seeing somebody else?"

"You think Paul had mistress?"

"I didn't want to tell you this, but before he jumped, somebody sent him a photo."

"What photo?"

"A photograph of him and another woman. I know you were close. I thought he might have told you something."

"Oh, Kate, I am so sorry."

"So he never said anything to you?"

Her great shoulders slumped. "What son tell his mother such a thing?"

"I thought I could find this woman."

"What would be point? What's done is done. Nothing will bring my son back."

"I suppose you're right." Even as she said this, Kate knew she had to find the woman in the photograph, she needed to confront her.

"Have you thought about what happens next? With Paul's body, I mean. He could be buried in family graveyard next to his father and uncle–"

"Marina, I wanted to talk to you about that. Paul didn't believe. In fact, he was an atheist. He told me that when he died he wanted to be cremated. I want to take his ashes back with me to London. I want to scatter them where he was happiest."

Marina's eyes widened at Kate's words. She gripped her daughter-in-law's wrist almost painfully. "You cannot do that. Cremation does not exist here, this is Muslim country." She shook her head. "In any case, Paul is Albanian. He must be buried next to his father and uncle. All his family are buried there, going back generations. Please, I am begging you."

"I'm sorry, Marina, but my mind's made up. As Paul's wife and next of kin, it's up to me to decide."

Marina was about to say something when, mercifully, Kate's iPhone started ringing. Fishing her mobile out of her bag, she could see it was a foreign number. Her heart contracted with foreboding.

"Hello?"

"Hello, Mrs Julia? Inspector Poda from Albania State Police. The man from the hotel we arrested, he was not on your balcony."

"How do you know that?" She apologised to Marina with her eyes and got up from the concrete seats.

"He was with two friends watching the parade. And a barman remembers seeing him. He even remembers the time. The dishwasher was drunk and got into an argument in the bar. There was no way he could have been in your hotel."

"Is he still under arrest?"

"Sure. For stealing from hotel guests. But not for the other thing, no."

"Wait a minute, so you're telling me the dishwasher is not the man we're looking for?"

"I'm sorry. The man from the hotel, he didn't kill your husband."

CHAPTER TEN

KATE LOOKED DOWN at the orderly collectivised fields from the window as the aircraft gained altitude, but she wasn't really taking anything in. The detective inspector had rung her in her hotel room that morning while she was rescheduling her flight back home. The coroner had completed his post-mortem, he said. Poda had asked for it to be summarised in English so that Kate could read it. "That was quick," she said. Because Albania is a Muslim country, everybody works on Sundays, he replied.

Moments later Kate's iPhone pinged with a message. An email with two attachments had landed in her in-box. She double-clicked on the English version and started speed reading: "Because of the fall, the ribs punctured the lung. Most of the injuries were on the right side of the body. The pattern of injuries was indicative of falling from the seventh floor. The ribs were fractured both on the chest and side. Thoracic and lumbar spine fractured with thoracolumbar junction badly damaged. Os calcis and ankle joint fractured. Distal radius shattered." Then, further on – "Rigor mortis was present of a 3 to 4+ throughout his entire body. No other trauma found, and fatal injuries are consistent with suicide jump. Foul play is not suspected at this time."

So that was it, then.

The autopsy stated that Paul had died from blunt head trauma when his skull struck the pavement. Kate remembered the sound, like an axe splitting a wet log, and shuddered.

"Are you still there?"

"Yes, I'm still here. It's just a lot to take in, that's all."

"Our investigation is over. We have no other suspects, Mrs Julia. Your husband did kill himself." She heard Poda breathe on the other end. "Do you want the name of an undertaker? I know one in Tirana. This is not the first time a foreigner has died here."

"My husband wanted to be cremated. I want to bring his ashes home with me."

"Cremation?" the detective said doubtfully. "This is a Muslim country. We don't have cremation–" The line went muffled, and she heard him speak in Albanian. After a moment he said, "Yes, the hospital can create your husband."

"What do you want me to do?"

"You must come to the hospital to sign some papers." More Albanian to the person he was talking to. "The hospital will do the cremation. After that, you can take your husband home."

She knew that she was acting partly out of spite, as a way of punishing her mother-in-law.

"How long will it take? I was planning to go back to England tonight."

"I don't know. We've never done this before."

"What will happen to the man you arrested? The dishwasher?"

"He lost his job. The hotel fired him. He will be fined, maybe go to prison. Mrs Julia, I am sorry for your loss. I wish we had met under different circumstances."

"No, Inspector, thank you. For everything you have done."

What was she doing sounding like Lady Bountiful? As if she were opening a garden fete or something. Poda rang off, leaving Kate listening to the dial tone. It really was all over.

The detective inspector instructed her to collect Paul's ashes that afternoon, and she picked them up on her way to the airport. As she walked towards the reception desk, everything felt so unreal. Slow motion. The ground beneath her feet felt gluey and unstable, as if there was nothing to hang on to anymore.

What was left of her husband had been boxed up, like a package ready for delivery.

The woman at the airport check-in had looked at Kate strangely when she presented her husband's ashes to take on board as carry-on luggage. Kate wasn't in her right mind, she could feel it. The desk clerk was flustered as she smoothed a hold baggage sticker on the cardboard box. The check-in assistant read the paperwork, including Paul's death certificate, and handed it back with a fixed, synthetic smile.

Paul's suitcase was in the hold along with her own. Packing up his things that afternoon had been the moment his death really hit home. Opening their hotel room wardrobe, she took hold of his jacket sleeve and breathed in, wanting the smell of him. Perhaps if she kept his clothes just as they were, he might come back. "Hello, kitty-kat," he would say as he walked in. Another wave of grief was building and she stared at the plane safety procedure card, determined not to cry. Grief kept coming, though: her throat felt tight, and she couldn't get enough air into her lungs. She told herself to just keep breathing, but she still felt as if she were being punished for a crime she had not committed.

Three hours later, Kate was collecting their suitcases from the baggage hall at Gatwick.

The taxi dropped her outside their block of flats. Struggling in through the front door with Paul's ashes and both suitcases, she caught her upstairs neighbour on his way out. She didn't think she'd ever said more than two words to the elderly gentleman, who was always so immaculately dressed. He lived on the ground floor with his dog and was, she had always assumed, a widower. He held the door open and, as she struggled past, she had the most peculiar feeling, as if somebody had walked over her grave.

The entrance door slammed shut and Kate paused in the entrance hall, wondering what had just spooked her. She had seen the man before somewhere. Of course you have, she told herself, he's your downstairs neighbour. No, somewhere he shouldn't have been, someplace else.

Closing the front door behind her, the first thing that struck her was the silence. So far she had managed to keep herself busy, signing forms and speaking to hospital staff. It gave her the illusion of movement – at least she was doing something. Now, though, alone in the stillness, everything reminded her of him. Paul making breakfast as they chatted about what they were doing that day, watching television together curled up on the sofa, and making love in the shower, his hands on her hips as she placed her palms on the tiles. She would never have him inside her again.

Kate dumped their carry-on luggage in the bedroom, unable to face unpacking it. His ashes she slid on top of the bookshelf in the sitting room. Their wedding photo was on the cupboard beside the fireplace, in a tortoiseshell frame. Her head was resting on Paul's shoulder and he was smiling. Colin, Paul's best man, had done the reading: "For now we see, through a glass darkly." Well, now she saw things as they bloody well were all right, oh yes.

Kate made herself a stiff gin and tonic and swallowed
one of the Temazepam the hospital had prescribed for
her. The first thing she needed to do was tell everybody
what had happened. She sat down on the sofa, telephoned
her mother and told her the dreadful news. "Oh my God,
darling. And you had no idea something was on his mind?"
Kate felt the solid wall of the painkiller take hold. By the
time she hung up, Kate had promised to spend this coming
weekend with her mum. No, she didn't want her to come
and stay, she needed to be alone.

Kate felt restless, still wanting to make telephone calls.

Colin, Paul's second-in-command at work, was the next
person she spoke to. It was Colin who had introduced them
at her degree show, and she'd had the distinct impression
he was showing her off as a prize to be won. He was
quadriplegic and had been wheelchair-bound for the past
twenty years – he'd had an accident on a university skiing
trip, mistiming a jump that had left him almost paralysed
from the neck down. When he woke up, he couldn't move
his arms or legs. What he was, though, was a brilliant
programmer, and he was the one who oversaw coding
while Paul went out and hustled for business. Ha, what
business? That was one of the reasons Paul had committed
suicide, she told herself. Orders had pretty much dried up.

"Colin, I've got some bad news. Paul had an accident in
Albania. I don't know how to put this. He's dead." She
found herself laughing as she said this.

"What do you mean, he's dead?"

"I mean he fell from our top-floor balcony. He's dead, Colin. Dead." Her chin wobbled, and she could feel herself losing it again.

"Jesus Christ, Kate. Are you okay? Tell me what happened."

"You know we went to Tirana on Thursday night for his uncle's funeral. He'd been in a strange mood all day. Withdrawn. There was something on his mind, something he wasn't telling me. He got back from his uncle's wake, we were talking, and the next thing I knew, he'd fallen or jumped, I don't know which. Our room was on the seventh floor. There was no way he could have survived."

Colin waited before speaking again, his mathematical brain calculating all the possibilities.

"He jumped off the balcony?"

"It all happened so quickly. Why would he do something like that? Why would he leave us?"

"Did you have an argument? Did he leave a suicide note?"

"No, nothing like that."

"I know he was worried about the business, but this–"

"There's something else you should know. I was convinced there was somebody on our balcony, that Paul had surprised a burglar. It sounds stupid now, I know. The police arrested a man who worked in the hotel, but he didn't do it. He had an alibi to say he was watching a street parade. It was all in my mind. I thought I'd seen something in a photo I took on my iPhone, a trick of the light, the way the wind blew on the curtains."

She was gabbling, vomiting up everything that had happened.

"Good Lord. Do you want me to come over? You shouldn't be alone."

"I'm fine, Colin, really. I need to be on my own tonight, I don't know why."

"What about funeral arrangements? When will they fly Paul's body home?"

"He's already here. In fact, I'm looking at him." She laughed unnaturally and took a swig of her gin and tonic. "Albania's a Muslim country. His mother wanted him buried in the family plot where his uncle is, but I said no. I wanted him here. Paul always said that coming to England felt like coming home."

"Christ, Kate, I am so sorry." Colin paused. "What does this mean for the business?"

"Paul would have wanted you to carry on. You know the business made a big loss last year. The bank had called in its loan. I saw the letters. Paul couldn't think of a way out apart from selling up. There's some value left in the lease. But he didn't want to let everybody down."

Colin waited again for her to continue, and she noticed she

had already finished her drink. It hadn't even touched the sides.

"What do you want me to tell everybody?"

"Just tell them the truth. I'll come into the office, explain everything."

"Paul dead. Jesus. You mean you saw it happen?"

There was nothing she could say to that. Yes, she thought, and I even caught it on camera.

They rang off, with Kate promising to speak to everybody first thing Tuesday. By now she felt utterly drained. It was all she could do to get up off the sofa and crawl into bed. There was still one more thing, though. Opening up her MacBook, she connected her iPhone and dragged her Albania photos onto the desktop. Double clicked on the folder. There was Paul, looking haunted with the curtains blowing behind him. Here were the photographs of the fireworks exploding over the hotel. More photographs of architectural features that had caught her eye. Looking closer, she noticed a man standing in shadow in a room across the square. His balcony faced theirs. He was in darkness, but he was clearly there, probably watching the fireworks along with everybody else. She kept going backwards. Kate wasn't quite sure what she was searching for, but whatever it was, she could feel it wriggling away, and she had to trap its tail between her fingers. Something was nagging at her. There. The photo of the café lit up at night, the waiter darting between tables and customers wrapped up against the cold. She zoomed in on the photo until it became almost abstract, a meaningless collage of pixels, zoomed out until the image returned.

There, seated at a café table, was her downstairs neighbour.

CHAPTER ELEVEN

HASHIM ALWAYS KNEW he was capable of murder. There was a side of himself he didn't like. He could become devoid of feeling for others. Unemotional. He knew what he was doing was wrong, but he went ahead and did it anyway, as if he couldn't control himself. It was like watching somebody else in a movie.

The Peckham gymnasium was at the top of a steep flight of steps off the street. Hashim wondered what the girl on reception saw as he came up the stairs. Did she see a murderer? Or did she just see a hollowed-out, mournful-looking man with a teardrop tattooed beneath one eye? The girl looked up from her gossip magazine. "I'm looking for Sammy," he said. "Is he in?" She told him to try the changing room.

A few Muscle Marys were straining with weights while Seventies disco thumped from the speakers. The place looked like a cross between a nightclub and a prison exercise yard. Hashim remembered that clang of dropped weights so well. So many hours spent in the prison exercise yard when it was too stifling in the cells. Even the guards took pity on them sweltering in that oven with three other men. So they sat in the shade watching other prisoners lift weights in the searing heat.

An older man was standing over a younger man while he struggled with the bench press, spotting him in case he collapsed. "I wouldn't eat that muck she gives me. I'd rather eat here," the older man was saying as the young one agonised the weight up. Hashim's eyes flicked to the older man.

Men were padding about in towels in the changing room. No sign of Sammy. There was a sharp smell of bleach and chlorine, and Sammy's bucket and mop stood propped beside a door with a strip of electric white-blue light beneath it. So the vain little fucker was getting himself a suntan. Hashim tiptoed in. Ghostly bluish light seeped out from around the sunbed, and there was the whoosh of cooling fans above the powerful hum. Hashim pulled the coffin lid up without warning. Lying there in an absurdly tight pair of briefs, Sammy would've looked almost normal if his legs had been longer. Hashim suspected that one of his grandparents had been a dwarf. It took Sammy a moment to figure out what was going on, and he almost hit his head on the fluorescent tubes as he sat up.

"Çfarë qij?" he said. "Oh, it's you. You nearly gave me a fucking heart attack."

"Zogaj has another job for us."

"What, another delivery? That's two in one week."

"No, just one woman. Zogaj wants to meet her. We're to bring her to Tirana."

Sammy still had little brass cones stuck to his eyes. "What does Zogaj want her for?"

"Zogaj wants something from her. You know, they never tell us anything."

"If she doesn't want to come with us, can I force her?" There was a touch of wheeziness in his voice, as if the idea excited him.

"Only if we have to. Zogaj wants to interrogate her personally."

"How much?" Sammy asked, peeling the cones off.

"Five thousand euros upfront and another five thousand on delivery. That's ten thousand each."

"Zogaj must want her pretty bad. When do we start?"

"Tomorrow. Zogaj has told me where she lives. We're just to keep an eye on her and, when the time is right, snatch her. The thing is, there can't be any witnesses. We'll smuggle her out through the usual route."

"What if somebody does see us?"

Hashim shrugged, and Sammy grinned like a badly carved Halloween pumpkin.

"I'll need to get things," Hashim said, thinking of duct tape and a strong knife.

"What's the hurry? Now you're here, you might as well relax a bit. Get some sun."

"Sunbeds give you cancer."

"Have a swim, then. Use the steam room or the sauna."

"I don't have any trunks."

"Come with me."

Sammy climbed into his cleaning-staff outfit and Hashim followed him down the corridor. His office was really the laundry room, with folded towels piled high on the shelves. He rummaged in a plastic box and handed over a pair of Speedos.

"There, those should fit you."

"Have you got any heat with you?"

Sammy waddled over to a pile of towels and lifted one corner. Not for the first time, Hashim thought about how powerful his squat legs were and wondered if his insane rages came from all the steroids he skin-popped. There, bedded in-between the towels, was a Glock handgun.

"Stupid place to keep it," Hashim said. "Put it under the spare wheel in the van."

Hashim unlaced his workman's boots and hung his leather jacket and grey hoodie in the locker.

The swimming pool stank of chlorine, and the water was too warm as he dived in. Warm like blood. The soft life was getting to him, he thought, as the cloud of bubbles cleared and he came up to breathe. His head plunged down as he began a powerful crawl up to the far end. The water felt like a cleansing, an absolution for everything he had done. If indeed a believer sins, a black spot will appear on his heart. If he stops from his sin, and seeks forgiveness from it, his heart becomes clean again. But if he persists, it increases until it covers his heart. Was his heart rotten-black with cancer? He could picture it, shrivelled and fibrous with stumps for ventricles. The water was absolving him of his sins, washing them away, like that time–

Zogaj had told him to go and clean up the mess. His cousin had arranged a sit-down with the Petrela brothers, saying it was better to stop all the violence and grow the pie rather than all these fire-bombings and shootings. The government was putting pressure on the mayor to do something. Everybody knew he was on the take and that his officials were corrupt. It won't do any good, Zogaj said, the brothers are ignorant people.

Something must have gone wrong. Hashim was only one block away when Zogaj called him on his mobile: your cousin lost his temper and now there's a big mess you've got to clean up before the cops get there.

People were leaning out of their windows as he approached the garage. A fucking dog was howling inside.

Brick dust was still hanging in the air along with the smell of cordite. A bit of weak winter sun filtered through the grimy back window. You could see motes of it dancing, and that damn dog had been tied by a leash to the axle of a lorry and it just kept on howling – Hashim wished somebody would just shut it the fuck up. The two brothers were lying on the floor of the cold, dark garage. Or rather one of them was lying on his back with blood pooled round his head and a surprised look on his face. Blood dark as motor oil oozed across the concrete floor and slid thickly down the drain. The other brother had crawled up against a table as if trying to get away. Somebody shut up that damn dog. My God, he thought, if this is what he's capable of, God help us all when he really gets angry. It was the savagery of the attack that shocked him, like a dog that turns on you without warning. One day Hashim would have to put that dog down, he now knew that.

It was hard work getting rid of the bodies. You'd be surprised how much blood there is inside a human being. Eventually he had to use a hacksaw, and fed the body parts into an incinerator. As he watched the head through the observation window, the heat lifted up the corpse's hair and opened the older Petrela brother's eyes so he was staring right at him. That freaked Hashim out.

Hauling himself out of the water, Hashim walked back to the changing room, dripping. Oh yes, he was a bad man, he wasn't a nice person. Every moment was a fresh beginning, though, wasn't it? The man he'd spotted earlier with the moustache was watching from the Jacuzzi with his arms draped over the sides. The water foamed away. At the last moment, Hashim turned and slid in beside him. The water was so hot, dizzying in fact. Neither of them said anything, and Hashim luxuriated in the water jet massaging his back. Sure enough, he felt the other's man's hand brush his thigh. Blood roared in his head, and all he felt was this overwhelming lust. Why can't you control yourself, you mustn't give in, you mustn't.

The other man got out of the Jacuzzi and headed for the sauna. The message was unmistakable. Hashim waited for a moment to see if anybody was watching.

The older man was sitting in a corner wearing a towel. The wooden bench was almost unbearably hot, and Hashim kept on looking straight ahead. His throat had gone quite dry. The stones hissed sharply as he poured water over them, and a wave of heat fell across their backs. Sweat popped on his skin. He ran his hand along his tattooed forearm, wiping the sweat and tasting the salt on his forefinger. He was conscious of this other man's body so close to his, and wondered what it would be like to lick his chest and drop his hand to his balls. His lust was so overwhelming, he thought he was going to faint. The older man had dropped his towel and was now touching himself in a muzzy cloud of pubic hair. "Feels good," he said. "Want some?"

Monday

CHAPTER TWELVE

IN HER DREAM, she saw a death's head looming through the net curtains, two black holes for eyes and a maw where the mouth should have been. "You'll never find who killed me," Paul's voice spoke clearly, his voice in her head.

Then she woke up, with a sob, as if she had spent too long underwater. The dream faded and Kate was left alone where she had always been, back in their empty marital bed.

They said you couldn't die of grief, but this pain was unbearable. She kept her eyes closed, not wanting to face today.

What she did need to do, though, was pee. Wrapping a dressing gown around herself, she padded down the hall to the loo. When she'd finished, she went into the kitchen, switched on the radio and made herself a cup of instant coffee. They were out of the real stuff. As she spooned the coffee into a mug, a line by TS Eliot from her schoolgirl English lessons came back to her, the one about counting our lives out in coffee spoons. How many cups of coffee before she could join her husband?

Stop being so bloody morbid, she thought. Either she could fight this or give up. You told Colin that Paul would have wanted him to keep the business going, she said to herself. He wanted you to remarry as well, if anything happened to him. She wondered why Paul had even said that. Was it because he had a premonition of what he was going to do, that things were going to end badly?

Her iPhone calendar reminded her that she had an appointment that morning with an American woman who handled soft furnishings for one of the big US hotel chains. She had seen Kate's bedspreads and curtains for luxury hotels and wanted to know if she could make cheaper versions for the budget market. Big bucks if she could get into that. Ker-ching, Paul had said when she told him: America was the holy grail for any business. Kate cursed herself for not remembering to cancel the eleven o'clock appointment. Right now even the idea of dressing herself seemed impossible.

Kate forced herself to shower and put some clothes on. Her mind felt thick with sleeplessness and drained of feeling. Burying herself in work would be the only answer. Work harder. Don't feel sorry for yourself. Get used to being on your own. That was the mantra for widowhood. She stared numbly at the computer screen. What did any of this matter now that the very worst had happened? She knew she needed to speak to somebody, a therapist perhaps, because she could not function like this. Even putting one foot in front of another seemed impossible. She picked up the phone and called her doctor's surgery.

Yes, the receptionist said, there had been a last-minute cancellation. Her regular doctor was away but she could see his temporary replacement. Kate told the woman she could be there shortly.

Half an hour later, she was sitting on a plastic bench between a heavily pregnant woman and a teenager holding a cardboard bowl to vomit into. He kept dry heaving and Kate wanted to move away, but no other seats were available. The waiting room was full even this early in the morning. A dot-matrix screen announced which patients were to be seen next. With nothing else to do, she studied the notice boards and pamphlets offering advice on contraception, how to spot a stroke and sexually transmitted diseases.

Dr Giri was standing in for Kate's regular doctor. She reckoned the Indian woman was in her mid-twenties. She had a round, moon face and warm, intelligent eyes. Kate liked her immediately. Dr Giri looked up from her computer screen and gestured for her patient to sit down.

"Good morning, Mrs–"

"Julia. Kate Julia. I usually see Dr Muir."

"Please. Sit down. How can I help you?" she asked, running an eye over Kate's notes.

The widow cleared her throat. "My husband died this weekend. I'm not sure that I can cope. I need to speak to somebody. A therapist–"

Dr Giri's voice softened. "Oh, I am so sorry. Have you been sleeping, eating?"

"Not really, no. I thought if I could talk to somebody–"

"Of course. You need to see a grief counsellor. How did your husband die?"

"He killed himself."

"Suicide?" Dr Giri's eyes widened, and you could see her wondering about her patient. "How terrible. When did you find out?"

"I saw him jump, when we were at a family funeral in Albania. I don't think I've actually accepted it yet. Nothing seems quite real. I think I'm still in shock. It's as if there's nothing to hold on to."

The locum doctor moved her PC mouse around and peered at her screen. "The problem is that you can't see anyone immediately. There's a waiting list."

"I was hoping to see somebody today."

"That's impossible. The earliest somebody could see you is in three months."

"Three months?"

"Of course, you could see somebody privately. I could

prescribe something in the meantime."

"I don't want pills."

"Anti-depressants can help in the short-term." Dr Giri wrote out a prescription on a pad. "The pills might make you feel funny for the first couple of days, but keep taking them. They will help."

"I told you, I just need to speak to somebody."

Dr Giri looked at Kate sympathetically. "There are also counselling groups. People who've been through similar experiences to yours." She returned to her computer and typed something into a search engine. Google, really? "Yes, here we are ... family support for those dealing with murder or manslaughter overseas. You're in luck. I mean, they've got a meeting tonight."

She wrote down an address on a Post-It note and slid it across her desk. Support After Death Overseas was meeting that evening in a church hall in north London. Kate, crumpling the note into her bag, wondered what kind of people would be there.

"Thank you for seeing me," she said, standing up. "I don't want to take up any more of your time."

Dr Giri smiled encouragingly. Most people stepped back from suicide, treating it as if it was a contagious disease. "Please. Call me if you need a repeat prescription. And go to the group tonight. Talking to other people can help. You can always speak to a private therapist. I can find you the name of somebody if you like."

"That would be very kind. Yes, I'd like that."

The chemist handed Kate the cardboard box. Walking back home, she read the tiny wording on the packet: side-effects could include nausea and sleeplessness. "Do not take if suffering from acute depression or having thoughts of suicide." What a joke. That's exactly why she wanted the pills.

She pondered what she'd told the doctor about not wanting to take anything, but she needed to numb this grief. Kate busted open the foil package and swallowed two anti-depressants right there in the street.

CHAPTER THIRTEEN

THERE WAS A RICH STINK of fox shit from the hedge
as Kate walked back home. The sun tried to shine through
the witchy-fingered branches. The days were getting short.
A black van was parked along with the usual cars and Kate
noticed something odd about it: its windows were mirrored.
And, as she got closer, she saw a plastic novelty dildo
on the dashboard, the kind of thing you wound up and it
clattered around on plastic feet. You could see it where the
silver mirroring had worn away. It gave her the creeps.

Yet when she got home, she couldn't face being alone.
Spending the rest of the afternoon within those four walls
would truly drive her mad. Please, somebody just call me,
she thought – her mother, anybody – willing the telephone
to ring. She longed for some human contact, anything to
stop this pain. Kate's thoughts turned to the old man who
lived downstairs, and she wondered what he had been
doing in Tirana on Friday night.

She decided to find out. Kate went and knocked on his door.

A dog barked inside. The distinguished-looking man
opened up but kept the chain on. He held a pipe in one
hand.

"Yes? How can I help you?" he said.

"Hi, you don't know me, but I live upstairs." Kate glanced around. She didn't want to get into this standing in the hall. "Please may I come in? I need to speak to you."

"Can you tell me what this is about?"

"Not standing on your doorstep, no. It's personal."

The old man must have decided that the young woman looked presentable enough. He put his pipe in his mouth and slid the chain off.

"My name's Kate, by the way. Kate Julia." The dog reached up to be petted and she stroked its fur.

"Charles. Charles Lazenby," he said, gesturing down the hall.

Lazenby's sitting room looked as if the contents of a much larger house had been crammed into it. There were big chintz armchairs and a sofa facing the fireplace. Photographs were everywhere: on the occasional tables and the mantelpiece. Kate had been right in thinking he was a widower who'd moved somewhere smaller when his wife had died.

"Would you like some tea? I was just making some."

Kate said no, studying one photograph. It showed a much younger Lazenby standing in a khaki uniform beside a pretty woman in a sundress shielding her eyes. Wherever they were, it looked hot.

Lazenby sat back on the sofa while his dog jumped up

beside him, yawned and stretched out its front legs.

"So how can I help you?"

"It's none of my business, but were you in Tirana on Friday night?"

The old man frowned. "Why yes, I was. How do you know that?"

"What were you doing there?"

"I don't see what business it is of yours."

"Please. It's important."

"Visiting some war graves, if you must know. My brother was a special agent during the war. SOE. He died in Tirana helping the partisans, as did many of his friends. There's a memorial to them in the park. A sentimental journey, I suppose. Why do you ask?"

"I was in Tirana as well. Don't you think that's a coincidence? Us both being in Tirana on Friday night, seeing as I only live upstairs?"

Lazenby started to light his pipe, sucking in two or three times before he got it going. He waved his spindly blackened match before placing it in the ashtray. "I suppose so, yes. These things do happen."

The kettle began to whistle in the kitchen. Lazenby stood up and the dog, wondering what was going on, jumped down. He asked her again if she wanted some tea, and this time Kate said yes.

While he was out of the room, she studied some of the other photographs on the walls: mostly they were in black and white, and Kate suspected he had taken them himself. Clearly her neighbour was something of an amateur photographer. One showed a cool, mini-skirted blonde surrounded by City gents in bowler hats holding umbrellas – she guessed he had taken it in the Sixties.

Kate was studying the photograph more closely when Lazenby returned carrying mugs of tea.

"Did you take all of these?"

"Yes, I did. It's always been a hobby. My wife used to get cross at the amount of money I'd spend. That's why it's the perfect man's pastime. There's always another bit of equipment to buy." He laughed with a crackly smoker's cough.

"I saw you down in the square opposite my hotel. What were you doing there?"

"Watching the fireworks. I speak some Albanian. I must tell you something. There was a little boy at the next table also watching the fireworks, who said to his father, 'Dad, I must be dreaming.' Very sweet, really." He coughed again. "You must have been there when that dreadful business happened, the man who fell from the balcony."

"Yes." She paused, not sure how much to divulge. "The man who died was my husband."

"Oh, my dear, I am so sorry," Lazenby said, sitting up. The dog, disturbed, opened its eyes but didn't move.

"The police first thought my husband had discovered a burglar. Now they think it was suicide." They sat there in silence for a moment, listening to the gas fire bubble. "Did you take any photographs that night? It might help the police."

"Yes, why yes, as a matter of fact I did. I was too busy photographing the fireworks, though, to see what was going on. I glimpsed what was happening, but by then it was too late."

"But you were using your camera." Her heart thumped. Combined with her iPhone photos, she could start making a collage of who was exactly where right at the moment of Paul's death. Her mind was gabbling ahead. Using social media, she could make a huge Cubist collage on her wall, an almost 3D mosaic showing where everybody was in the square that night. The police did the same thing. Except they called it a murder wall.

"Do you have them here?"

"They're on my computer."

A laptop and what looked like a digital projector were standing on a folded-down oak table. Kate shifted some candlesticks and opened up the table while Lazenby unhooked a painting from the wall.

They sat back down as the old man pointed to the wall with a clicker. The slide show began: a bleak out-of-season seafront ("That's Durres, a jolly cross between Miami and Blackpool. Macedonians go there for cheap holidays."); the crash-landed spaceship of the Enver Hoxha museum; the war memorial that Lazenby had gone to Tirana to visit. More photos showed dusk over the city. Here was the White Night parade, excited children walking past, a man on stilts, men holding flaming torches. "Here we are in the square," said Lazenby. It was exactly how she'd remembered: whistling rockets and then a pause before the boom, blossoming jellyfish of pinks and purples, swags of gold evaporating into nothingness. Oh, Paul, why did you leave me? She could just see the top of the National roof in one photograph. Then another shot, further back this time, showing the hotel frontage.

"Stop. Can you hold it here?" Kate stood up and put her finger on their balcony, creating a long, deep shadow. "Here's where our room was. On the top floor."

"I think you're mistaken. The man I saw fell from the sixth floor. The floor below."

"But we had a penthouse suite."

"Then the man I saw didn't fall from your balcony. He fell from the floor below."

"I don't understand."

Lazenby shook his head emphatically. "I'm sorry. I'm quite

certain about this. The man I saw fell to his death from the balcony beneath yours."

CHAPTER FOURTEEN

GOOGLE MAPS WAS WRONG. It took an hour and a half to reach the address on the Post-It note the doctor had given her, a church hall in north London. Cross with herself for being so late, Kate hurried towards the ugly Thirties building, fretting because the meeting had already started. She pictured the church hall full of people sharing the pain she was going through.

Instead, there were just three people sitting in a circle of nearly empty seats. So this was the London branch of the overseas bereavement group. A young man who seemed to be in charge acknowledged her as the door swung shut. "–a few housekeeping notes. Jean has offered to become treasurer," he was saying. Jean was a warm-looking woman in her seventies wearing a coral cardigan. Another woman looked up gravely, with sorrowful eyes hidden behind her fringe. Kate sat down and apologised for being late, wondering what was going to happen next.

The young man was about to speak when the swing door banged shut again and a second latecomer hurried in. He lifted off his hood as he sat down, also apologising. "I can see we have some new faces tonight. Welcome," the group leader said. Her fellow laggard was black and had a hunted expression on his face. He, too, was out of breath. "As I have the heart card tonight, I thought I would start things off," the leader continued. He began telling a story about how he'd had a perfectly all-right day, and then felt guilty about not thinking about his sister, who'd drowned over a decade ago on a beach holiday. Kate became impatient. She could not see what any of this had to do with actual bereavement. What she needed was practical help as to how she was going to get through the next hour – and the next day and the day after that. How she was going to keep putting one foot in front of the other.

The room lapsed into silence and the atmosphere became so reverential she had to fight rising hysteria not to take her clothes off and run screaming round the church hall. It was like being at a funeral. Finally, the other latecomer spoke.

"My name is John, and I lost my wife a year ago," he said in a strong Birmingham accent. The others muttered "Welcome".

"It were all my fault. We went on holiday in Sicily and it were cheaper to fly back from Naples than from the island. So we got the ferry to Naples, and I thought we could spend the day wandering around. I dunno why we did it. After breakfast we started walking, and that's when I first noticed him. My wife looked so pretty that day. She was wearing a white dress she'd bought special, like."

He stopped and sniffed, rubbing his eye with his finger. "I knew we were being followed, but I didn't want to say anything. Didn't want to frighten her, I s'pose. We took a wrong turn down a side street, and I remember looking up at these lines of washing, thinking there must be another way out, when it happened. This bloke grabbed my wife's bag. I were too frightened to move. He ran off, and I remember turning to her and asking, 'How much money was in it?', when I saw the stain. She looked down, and we both saw this dark circle spreading. She looked at me and then she fell on her knees before toppling over. I'll always remember that. She never said a word." He stopped, shook his head and blew out his cheeks, as if the memory was still too raw for him to cope with. "Anyway, the Italian police couldn't wait to have her cremated. No body, no investigation. They weren't interested in solving the murder of a British tourist. I didn't know any better. And the authorities couldn't care less either. As far as they were concerned, this had all happened in a foreign country."

The others muttered agreement, and a yawning chasm of dread opened up beneath Kate. "What did you mean when you said there couldn't be any police investigation?" she asked. "Once you'd cremated your wife's body, I mean."

The group leader interrupted. "We don't allow cross sharing," he said.

Sitting there, Kate realised they were all trapped in their own grief, each of them banging on the glass, trying desperately to get somebody's attention. What had happened to her was entirely without precedent. People's husbands just don't throw themselves off hotel balconies. There were no comforting truths to be found, and suffering was not going to ennoble her. Kate was alone. That was why they were all here, straining to hold hands with blind-worm hunger. She needed to speak to this stranger whose experience so closely matched her own. Jean, the woman in the coral-pink cardigan, told an interminable story about her legal battle with the New York police after they threw her husband in the drunk tank when he had had a stroke in a hotel lobby. They had assumed he was drunk and that's where he died.

The meeting ended with them all holding hands and affirming that together they were stronger. Kate felt acutely embarrassed and self-conscious linking hands with these strangers. It all seemed so childish.

She got her chance to talk to the other newcomer once the meeting was over and he was stacking chairs. "Excuse me, my name's Kate," she said. "I was wondering if I could have a word."

The man turned around and she registered how handsome he was: he had a strong, masculine jawline and warm, sensitive eyes. The tight curls of his hair were cut short. He also looked very fit.

"My name's Priest. John Priest. Pleased to meet you."

"What you were saying just now, about the police wanting your wife to be cremated, what did you mean?"

"Foreign police always want you to cremate. It saves them having to investigate. I didn't know it at the time."

"I think I've done something really stupid. My husband died, and I was the one who pushed for cremation. We were in a Muslim country, and my husband's family wanted his body in the ground quickly. It was a way of punishing them, I suppose. I was angry. The coroner's report had come back, so I thought, 'Well, that's it then.' None of what you said even occurred to me."

"They know that you're vulnerable." He looked at her warmly and smiled. "Listen, do you want to go and get a drink or summat? There's a pub over the road."

Her immediate instinct was to say no, and then she thought, why the hell not? "Yes. I'd like that very much."

Priest ordered a dry white wine for Kate while she took in the hideous swirly carpet, Sky Sports and tinny cascading bleeps from the fruit machine. The place smelled of stale beer.

"There you go. Cheers. I'm still not used to these London prices."

Kate clinked his pint glass and they both took a sip. She needed that. "So how long have you been going to meetings?"

"Not as often as I should. There's a group up in Brum, where I come from. It's been a year since Kelly died. They were really helpful at first, and then I let things slip. It was the anniversary of her death last week, so I felt I ought to go. I don't really know anybody in London."

"How long have you been here?"

"I only moved down a couple of weeks ago. I work for a car dealership. We're buying a chain of garages in south London, expanding, like. I don't know London at all. Me head office just gave me the address of a flat and told me to collect keys."

"Which area do you live in?"

"Fulham. On Fulham Palace Road."

"We must be near each other. I only live around the corner. In a mansion block called The Cloisters. Do you know it?"

He shook his head. "So what do you do for a living?"

"I'm a textile designer. Seats on trains. Hotel furnishings. Car interiors. Perhaps you sell some of mine."

"Which manufacturer did you work for?"

She gave him the name of a Korean car firm.

"We only do Vauxhall," he said, taking another sip. "So you work from home then?"

"I have a desk at my husband's office. The thing is," she said, setting her glass down, "my husband only died three days ago." Priest said nothing, just looked at her.

She told him about how they'd gone to Albania for his uncle's funeral, and how her husband had thrown himself off the hotel balcony. She was gabbling, but she had this compulsion to keep telling people her story.

"I'm still in shock. You read about these things happening to other people, and you never imagine they're going to happen to you. I mean, there was nothing wrong with our marriage. One minute you're looking at a clear blue sky, and the next, it's like an aircraft has slammed into the side of the Twin Towers. There's nothing left. Everything's vaporised."

Priest contemplated her for a moment and then shook his head, as if to say, that's quite a story. "I'm amazed you're even out of the house. I didn't want to see anybody."

"My first thought was that Paul had been murdered. There was a dishwasher in the hotel who'd been stealing from guests, and I thought he was on the balcony. But he had a solid alibi and he swears he had nothing to do with Paul's death."

"Do the police believe him?"

"He has an alibi for the evening it happened. He was in a bar with his girlfriend watching a parade."

"So, if your husband jumped, why are you worried about the police not being able to investigate? If it's an open-and-shut case, like?"

"There are things that don't make sense. I was taking photographs from our hotel balcony the night Paul died. There was something niggling at me, but I couldn't put my finger on it until I got home. My downstairs neighbour was also in the square that night. How strange is that?"

"Have you spoken to him?"

"Yes. He says he was in Tirana visiting war graves. His brother died there. He had fought with the Partisans during the Second World War."

Priest shrugged. "Sounds like a coincidence," he said.

"There's no such thing as a coincidence. Here's another thing." Kate paused, wondering how much to tell him, but once she had started, she couldn't stop. "The moment before Paul died he got a text message. He looked at his phone, put it down on the table, walked outside and jumped."

"What did the text say?"

"It wasn't a text, it was a photograph. Of him and another woman."

Priest looked doubtful. "When Kelly died, I tortured myself looking for answers."

"Wait, there's something else. There was another man watching from a balcony across the square." She needed to tell somebody what she'd found – how all these coincidences added up. There had to be a meaning to everything, only she just couldn't see it yet. "What I'm getting at is ... there's got to be a connection. The man on the balcony. The woman in the text message. My downstairs neighbour. I know somehow it all means something."

"It's all a bit over my head," Priest said dubiously.

"I believe everybody in the photographs had something to do with his murder," Kate said, coming to the realisation for the first time.

Priest looked at her for a moment. "Sometimes bad things happen and we don't know why. We look for reasons when there aren't any. Computers do it all the time. It's called pattern recognition. Except the patterns aren't really there. The computers are just seeing patterns where they don't exist, not really. Sorry, I can be a bit of a computer nerd sometimes."

"So you're saying I'm making this all up?"

"I mean, it's human nature, isn't it? Creating order out of chaos."

"I suppose it's a question of whether life has any meaning, or whether it's all random." Kate picked up her drink. "What you're really asking is, is there a God?"

"Sorry, that's a bit deep for me."

In her heart, she knew that what Priest was saying made sense, but she still wasn't convinced. Her companion asked if she wanted anything to eat and she shook her head. She hadn't eaten anything since the plane, but she found the idea of food nauseating, especially meat, since she had seen Paul dead in the street. Priest got up to order from the bar and left Kate brooding. He was wrong about there not being a pattern to anything. Now she understood something about Paul's death.

There was no way she could prove it, but deep down she knew it was true.

Everybody in the photograph was waiting for Paul to jump.

Tuesday

CHAPTER FIFTEEN

"Do you believe in ghosts?"

"No, I don't. Why do you ask?"

"Paul was standing in our kitchen last night when I got home. I only glimpsed him for a second, and then he was gone. It's not the first time I've seen him either. I catch glimpses of him here and there: at the top of the stairs or in the hallway. It's like he's just walked out of the room. Do you think I'm going mad?"

"People see what they want to see," the therapist replied. "In your case, you've suffered a terrible loss. It's only natural that you project what you want to be real. Your husband has died quite suddenly, not giving you any time to grieve, but that's all it is, only a projection. You do understand that, don't you?"

"He looked so real, as if I could touch him."

"That's very common at this stage of grief. We all do it. When my mother died, I was convinced I saw her one night on the lawn. Perhaps it's where the idea of ghosts comes from, our longing for somebody to come back."

Kate had taken Dr Giri's advice and had contacted a

grief counsellor. This woman therapist specialised in counselling the bereaved. Better yet, Liz Gilchriest lived nearby, in one of the bigger houses off Fulham Palace Road, and in one of the streets known locally as the Alphabet Streets. Even better, she could see Kate first thing.

The woman who answered the door had a purple flattop haircut and overlarge clear white Ray-Bans that made her look like an early Eighties pop singer. She radiated a warmth, though, that made Kate want to unburden herself.

Kate continued. "They talk about the stages of the grieving process – disbelief, anger, then acceptance – happening one after the other, but for me it's like they're all happening at the same time. I feel different emotions each second, then this blankness, this nothingness, as if I'm dead as well."

The therapist shifted on the sofa, doing that irritating thing of sitting cross-legged on a normal seat. Kate looked round the room, which was furnished in high-end hippie chic: Indian carvings and esoteric images on the walls, good furniture and shelves crammed floor-to-ceiling with books.

"What would you do if your husband was sitting right here in that chair?" Gilchriest said.

"Tell him that he was a coward. That he took the easy way out."

"What makes you say that?"

"He's left me to pick up the pieces. As his executor, I have to wind up his company. He has a business that is teetering on the brink of bankruptcy. How do you think it makes me feel, having to make all those people redundant? Paul couldn't face it – I believe that's partly the reason he jumped."

"Do you know what another reason might be?"

"Yes. I suspect he was having an affair."

"That must be really hurtful."

"You could say that," she said acidly. "If I'd suspected, I would have asked him why he had to go outside our marriage. Whatever was missing, we could have found a way forward. I believe that."

"A leg that's been broken is often stronger after the fracture heals," the therapist said, nodding.

"I'd also tell him that I forgive him," Kate said. "Many people have affairs; they don't end ... like this." Her chin wobbled and she felt herself going again. An ominous-looking box of tissues was ready on the carved wooden table.

"What about forgiving his mistress? Could you do that?"

"I don't understand. What do you mean?"

"It might help you understand. Why he did what he did. If you talked to her, I mean."

"Are you suggesting that I speak to her?"

"That's up to you. I'm just trying to give you tools to cope."

"I don't even know who she is. She's just a woman in a photograph." Kate felt that she was in a highly suggestible state, that the wrong course of action might set her down a path she would later regret. "I'll think about it," she said.

The next thing she had to do was the one she had been dreading.

When and where had she been happiest? On her wedding day. It was a spring afternoon, and the sun had come out just as they were posing for photographs. Relatives chatting as the wedding photographer motioned for them to stand closer together. She remembered how cold Paul's hand had been as they stood in front of the tree in Bishop's Palace, lilies draped over her arm, squinting in the breezy sunshine. And now here she was, spreading her husband's remains around the stump of the tree. She poured the line of grey-black ashes around the knotty base. Completing the circle felt like a full stop.

Most people haven't got a clue about grief, she thought. Not real grief. Kate used to think that grief was something inside that you could fight and overcome. Like cancer. Your grief would shrink and shrink until one day it wasn't there anymore: you had conquered it by zapping it with chemo and radiation or dropping it into a jar labelled "shrinking liquid". That wasn't true. And it wasn't going to go away either. You just had to accept that it would always be there, sitting on your shoulder, a monkey on your back.

Suffering was slowly destroying her; Paul's suicide was never going to go away. Looking in the bathroom mirror that morning, she had barely recognised herself, she looked so dreadful.

Walking back home, relieved to have got the ordeal over, she thought, this must be my fixed point – my grief will get smaller the further I move away from this moment. It has to. She kept on seeing him lying there. Oh, Paul, tell me what to do. My life was stolen that night. The best part of me was killed, too. What did you mean when you asked if we would always be together? Was it a clue? A message? What if he hadn't died at all, and the body she saw in the hospital was somebody else's?

Stop being so ridiculous, she thought, you've watched too many TV thrillers. Yet her downstairs neighbour was adamant that he'd seen Paul fall from the balcony below. But why? And even if it was true, and Paul had somehow found somebody else to take his place in the morgue, why on earth would he do that? Questions drummed like rain on a roof. What he did must have something to do with that photograph, the one of him and that woman, the text message sent moments before his death. Wait, that didn't make sense either. Doing something like faking your own death would take days or even weeks of planning. She dismissed these thoughts as grasping at straws, but something still niggled at her.

Kate carried her cup of coffee through to the sitting room and switched on her MacBook. Quickly she trawled through social media looking for any other photographs from people who had been in the square. She found several photos on Instagram showing the square from different angles, then some snaps posted on Facebook taken in the café. She printed them off, along with her own photographs and Charles Lazenby's, Blu-Tacking them to the wall to create a rippling, distorted Hockney-esque collage of who was exactly where that night.

There was also the photo that had been texted. There was no doubt in her mind that this really was Paul. He was wearing the cashmere hoodie she'd given him for Christmas under his leather bomber jacket. His arms were raised as if he was arguing with the woman. Who was she? Even though her back was to the camera, you could tell that she was slight. Not very tall. Why was he so angry? The thought crossed her mind that he was breaking up with her, telling her that they had no future together. Yeah, right.

Marina's words came back to her, how Paul had been so unhappy being married and that he had wanted a way out. Part of Kate still hated him for this humiliation, yet she nonetheless felt a keening loss. Her seesawing emotions kept getting worse – waves of grief and then anger, back and forth. Everything they had talked about, all their dreams, had been based on a lie. Had he been fucking this woman all the time? Things he'd said, things she hadn't understood at the time, suddenly made sense. Had they been making love in their bed while Kate was out drumming up work? The thought made her want to claw her face and tear herself into a thousand pieces.

Still, what the therapist said about contacting this woman, trying to find out why Paul had been so unhappy, came back to her.

The key was the photograph.

She uploaded the CCTV image into Photoshop and started playing around with it, increasing the DPI until the pattern of the carpet they were standing on became crystal sharp. Her guess was that they were in a hotel: you could see the carpet had an unusual deco-style tulip print. Somewhere at the back of her mind, she knew she had seen this design before. Kate's Pinterest board was where she clipped photos for inspiration, other people's interiors and fabric designs. She trawled through hundreds of images but came up empty-handed. Tapping her pen against her teeth, she then went through iPhone photos she had taken of places she had visited and Facebook updates showing travel destinations, as well as her Instagram timeline. Nothing. She couldn't find anything in her older scrapbook ring binders where she kept clippings, stapled fabric swatches and Sellotaped magazine pictures. But she was still convinced she'd seen the carpet somewhere. It was just maddeningly out of reach.

Her friend Rachel worked for a carpet manufacturer down in Wiltshire. The firm specialised in hotel carpets, and Kate had placed a big order with Rachel for the Albania hotel and others in the past. The carpet in the bar of the National came from that company. Surely they would have access to thousands of designs. Kate zoomed in on the carpet, cut-and-pasted the close-up and emailed it to her friend. Had Rachel ever seen it before?

The computer clock said it was half past twelve in Tirana. She had better phone Inspector Poda, telling him what her downstairs neighbour had said. Somehow she doubted the Albanian police were going to take a man in his eighties with failing eyesight seriously. And what that man last night, John Priest, had said about them shutting down the investigation came back to her. She berated herself for having been so naive.

"Hello? Inspector Poda? It's Kate Julia in London."

Was there the faintest sigh in his voice? "Hello, Mrs Julia. How can I help you this time?"

"I found somebody who was in the square on Friday night. He was taking photographs. It's my downstairs neighbour. Isn't that amazing?"

"Your downstairs neighbour was taking photographs?"

"Yes, he was visiting Tirana as well."

"What a coincidence." The police chief went silent. There's

no such thing as coincidence, Kate reminded herself. "So, how can I help you?"

"Well, he's convinced that Paul fell from the balcony below ours, not the top floor."

She let her words hang, realising how mad they sounded. "This neighbour. Did he see the accident?"

"Not exactly, he says it all happened too quickly. But he's convinced that Paul fell from the sixth floor, not the seventh."

"It's not possible that your husband didn't kill himself. The dental records match. The man who died was your husband."

"I'm not saying that my husband didn't kill himself, but I think there are too many coincidences for you not to reopen the investigation."

"Such as?"

"Well, there was another man in the square on Friday night. Watching us from another balcony. He was staring right into our room."

"It was White Night. There were fireworks. Everybody was looking up at the sky."

"So you're not going to investigate, despite what I've told you."

"All you've told me is that a witness got confused as to which balcony your husband fell from."

"Put like that, I suppose you're right."

"I told you. Our investigation is finished. We have no other lines of enquiry."

That's what you think, she thought. If Poda was not going to investigate her husband's death, then she would do it herself. Kate would be the one who brought her husband's killer to justice, so help her God.

Even as she was thinking this, an email dropped into her inbox. It was from Rachel:

Hi Kate,

Nice to hear from you. Yes, the hotel carpet is one of ours. It's the Savile Hotel on Park Lane. They had a big refit about a year ago. It was a major order for us. Let me know if you want me to send you a sample for your next job. The hotel was very pleased with it, and we can do a deal on the price.

Hope the Albanian hotel launch was successful, and that everything's going well for you.

Best regards,

Rachel

CHAPTER SIXTEEN

KATE DUG HER HANDS deeper into her pockets for warmth as cyclists and a few hardy joggers overtook her. The bare branches lining the avenue receded in infinite perspective above her head. She had decided to walk though Hyde Park to the Savile Hotel, which was above the Dorchester on Park Lane. It was one of those big international hotels that, living in London, you never really notice. Its Chinese owners had opened hotels in Shanghai and Dubai before taking over this venerable institution.

The man on reception asked if he could help. Kate told him she needed to see the manager. The receptionist leaned forward: "Might I ask what this is about?" She fingered the iPhone in her pocket. "Just tell him it's personal," she said. He nodded and told her to wait.

Whoever had styled the interior had done a good job. Painfully modern furniture had replaced the sagging chintz and horse prints of the previous hotel. Watching guests check in, Kate wondered why Paul had chosen this place. It wasn't like him at all. An image of him sprawled on the pavement, his arms and legs at right angles, was seared in her memory, and it was going to stay with her forever.

She looked up at the approaching sound of heels. It was the desk receptionist. Would she come this way? The manager was ready to see her now.

They went upstairs in a lift that didn't seem to be moving.

A menu signed by the Duke of Windsor was framed on the hotel manager's wall. Kate was thinking about how bland the prewar menu sounded when the manager himself came in. "Christian De Schutter," he said, offering her a chair. She sat down opposite him.

"How may I help you?"

"I know this sounds strange, but somebody texted my husband this photo. I believe it was taken in your hotel."

She handed her phone across and De Schutter studied it. He became serious. "How did you get hold of this?"

"I told you. Somebody texted it to my husband. I don't know who."

"You don't know who sent you this photograph?"

Kate shook her head.

"How do you know the photo was taken in this hotel? Do you know the people in the photograph?"

"I design hotel interiors for a living. I recognised the carpet." Kate leaned forward. "Look, I don't want to cause you any trouble, but I need to find this woman. Do you have any idea who she is?"

De Schutter smiled unhappily. "Would you excuse me for a moment?" He picked up his telephone and pressed a number on speed dial. "Hello? Myra, there's somebody I need you to meet. Could you come to my office, please?"

They sat in silence, waiting for whoever this Myra was to arrive. Eventually, for the sake of saying something, Kate remarked: "The man in the photograph is my husband."

De Schutter did a double-take, something she'd only seen people do on television. "Did the police send you here?"

"The police? Why, what have the police got to do with it?"

"Your husband is the man in the photograph?"

A large, tough-looking woman came into the room holding a walkie-talkie. She was wearing a black trouser suit and her blonde hair was swept back behind her ears, where Kate noticed a fine, almost transparent loop. The hotel's head of security, she supposed.

The hotel manager seemed flustered. "Myra, this woman–"

"Mrs Julia. Kate Julia."

"–has identified the man on the CCTV footage. She says it's her husband." The police were looking for Paul? The manager passed Kate's phone to his security chief. The woman studied her phone and looked up at Kate with no emotion whatsoever. Her lack of expression was unnerving.

"Please, could you tell me what's going on?"

"Mrs Julia, you really have no idea who sent you this?"

Kate shook her head.

"Where is your husband now?"

The widow looked down at her hands in her lap. "My husband killed himself four days ago. He received this text message and then he committed suicide."

The hotel manager and his head of security exchanged a look. "Mrs Julia, I am sorry for your loss."

That bloody expression again. "You haven't answered my question."

He cleared his throat. "Like any big hotel, we have a lot of international visitors. We can't control what they do. Sometimes they use, um, services–"

Her husband was seeing a prostitute?

"To be honest, it's very unusual. You go to Russia or some of these places and it's everywhere," the security chief interrupted.

De Schutter looked as if beads of perspiration were about to pop out on his forehead. "There's nothing we can do to stop them. I don't quite know how to tell you this, but your husband visited this hotel with one of these women. This time last week."

The security chief looked at Kate shrewdly. "What was unusual was that this escort booked the room in her own name. Tran An Na. Usually her customers were guests here."

Kate gripped the floor with her toes, determined to hang on. First his betrayal, and now this. Inside, she was reeling. "How do you know my husband was with this–" She couldn't bring herself to say the word. "–woman?"

"We have CCTV throughout the hotel."

Kate blinked hard to stop herself from crying. She felt as if she had been punched in the face. "You're telling me that my husband visited this hotel with a prostitute? You must have video footage. The video this frame was taken from. Please. I need to see it."

The security chief said, "I'm sorry. We have data-protection rules–"

"I'm sure we can make an exception in this case," the manager interrupted. The security chief nodded. "In that case, would you come this way, please?"

The hotel manager tried to do his best to look gracious, extending his arm to indicate the way out.

The security centre was a couple of doors down from the manager's office, at the back of the hotel. Fifteen or so colour monitors showed the hotel from different angles, switching between empty stairwells and reception to bedroom corridors. They grouped around a security guard's chair as they watched the recordings.

"We've got around two hundred cameras in the hotel," the Myra woman said. "What's unusual is that this man keeps his hood up and his head down. He knows he's being watched." Her voice softened. "If this man is your husband, of course–"

Kate turned to her. "There's no doubt about it. It is my husband." They watched Paul and the Asian woman walking towards and then away from the camera. "I don't understand why he was so careful about being spotted in a hotel corridor yet allowed himself to be seen in the lobby."

You're a cool customer, you could see the security chief thinking. "He probably didn't realise he was being filmed. Security cameras are hidden inside wall sconces in the lobby. One of the waitresses remembers them arguing. Then they went upstairs."

"You need to tell all this to the police," the manager said. "Tell them everything you know."

"You said this kind of thing, people using the hotel, happens all the time."

"To be honest, I've rarely encountered it," said the security chief. "It only becomes an issue when it becomes an issue, if you know what I mean. A guest complains that a woman accosted him in the bar. Or a man refuses to pay when he's done."

"Who had access to this footage?" Kate asked.

"Just my security department. Nobody else is allowed in here usually. The police, of course. They have a copy of what we've just shown you."

The manager placed his hand gently on Kate's shoulder. "Mrs Julia. There's something else you should know. This prostitute was found dead. She had overdosed on pills. Your husband had left the room an hour earlier."

Kate felt herself going into shock.

First, her husband was having an affair, and then it turned out he was seeing prostitutes. And now he was wanted for questioning over somebody else's suicide.

"I need to sit down," Kate said.

"Would you like a glass of water?" the manager asked.

"We did an audit of the lock," the security chief continued. "Nobody else entered the room between the two of them going in and your husband coming out."

Kate could picture the scene. First, the hesitant knocking becoming more insistent. Then the chambermaid getting her pass card out and opening the door. Dust motes hanging in the air in-between a gap in the curtains. A body still in bed with an arm dangling towards the floor. The chambermaid approaching, asking if everything was all right, noticing a cairn of pills beside a tipped-over bottle on the bedside table.

"Do the police have any idea why she killed herself?" Kate asked numbly.

"The problem is timing," the security chief began, before

the manager cut her off with a little shake of his head.

The hotel manager telephoned the police from his office, handing the phone over to Kate.

"DI Sumner. How can I help you?"

"My name is Kate Julia. You don't know me. I need to come and see you. I have information about the man you're looking for – the man in the Savile Hotel."

"Which man are you referring to?"

"I'm standing in the manager's office. He told me to ring you. The man's name is Paul Julia. He's my husband," she said, before correcting herself. "I mean, he was."

"You mean, he's your ex-husband?" The man's voice was warmly northern.

"No. He's dead. He died four days ago."

There was rustling as the detective covered the phone and said something. "Can you come to Belgravia police station? We need to speak to you. I can send a car."

"Yes. I'll be here."

The manager made a gesture asking if they could send a car to the back of the hotel. Kate put the phone down. A police car would be there in ten minutes, she told them.

Another police station. The same plastic bucket seats. So her husband had not just betrayed her, he'd committed adultery with a prostitute as well. Kate's skin crawled. It was almost as if he was enjoying humiliating her from beyond the grave; all she had ever shown him was love, and this was how he had repaid her.

A perky-looking policewoman showed Kate into the interview room and asked if she wanted a cup of tea. Kate shook her head. Walking around the bare room, she touched the chunky black recorder on the table. The interview room was something she'd seen so often on television, and it felt strange actually being in here. A plastic strip ran along all four walls: an alarm, probably. When she tried moving a chair it wouldn't budge. To stop suspects throwing them around, she supposed.

Detective Inspector Sumner came into the room. He was a thickset man with an owlish face and staring, rather protuberant eyes. She also noticed how tired he looked. The DI pulled out a chair and placed a manila folder on the table. When he spoke, his tone was concerned.

"Thank you for coming to see me, Mrs Julia. I appreciate it. My name is DI Sumner, and I am leading this investigation."

Every time you came into contact with somebody official, you had to start all over again, Kate thought. She went through her story one more time.

"How do you know your husband even visited the Savile Hotel?" Sumner sounded mildly sceptical.

"Somebody texted my husband a photo showing him and

this woman together. Before you ask, I don't know who sent it."

"Why would somebody do that?"

Kate shook her head. "At first, I thought it might be the woman's husband or boyfriend."

"Do you have the phone? May I see it?"

The widow handed the phone across, and the detective inspector studied it. "Who else has seen this photo?"

"Nobody apart from you and the hotel manager. Oh, and the police in Albania."

"Albania? What's Albania got to do with it?" Sumner looked surprised.

"We were in Albania when the message was sent. My husband killed himself within moments of receiving this photo. He jumped off our hotel balcony."

"He did what?"

Even as she said this, she realised how absurd it sounded. "My husband committed suicide last Friday. I think he knew he was about to be found out."

"Your husband killed himself because he was having an affair? People have affairs all the time."

"It's the only explanation I can think of."

"Are you willing to put all this in a statement?"

Kate nodded.

"There's something else you need to know. My downstairs neighbour saw Paul jump. But he says Paul jumped from the balcony below ours, not the top floor."

"Pardon?" Kate could sense she was losing him. Sumner tapped his pen on the table.

"You have to believe me. That's what happened."

"So you're saying that although you saw your husband jump from your hotel balcony, an eyewitness says he fell from the floor below? What do the Albanian police say?"

"The investigation is over as far as they are concerned."

Sumner looked surprised. "So soon? How can they be so certain?"

"I did something stupid and had Paul cremated. I was too hasty. His family wanted him buried in Tirana. It's a Muslim country, so they want you in the ground as quickly as possible."

"...And once that happened they lost interest," Sumner said, finishing her sentence for her.

Kate looked boldly up at the inspector. "There are so many things about his death that don't make sense. Will you help me?"

"Help you how? We can't do a post-mortem. In any case, it would only tell you what you already know. I'm sorry to be so blunt."

Kate folded her arms. "I see. So you won't do anything."

"It's not that I don't want to help you, but how?"

Kate was about to reply when the fire alarm went off. They both sat there, waiting for the noise to stop, and the DI mouthed that it was just a practice. After a moment, they both realised that this was no fire drill. Sumner stood up and said he would find out what was going on.

He had left his closed folder on the table.

Kate sat there with the alarm fibrillating her eardrums until curiosity got the better of her. If she was quick, the detective would never know. She pulled the file towards her with one finger, opened it and started reading. The first part of the report consisted of an officer's notes, describing how he had found the prostitute's body. There was lots of detail about how it was positioned and that sleeping pills were found on the carpet. Her eyes drank in as much as she could. A section at the end of the report gave more background detail. Kate slowed down. The alarm shut off but still she couldn't stop reading. Her heart was racing: the detective could return at any minute.

"...Tran An Na, 18, was a known prostitute working the West End hotels mostly through escort services. Her online profile was widely available through a variety of aliases. During the day she worked as a beautician at E-Z American Nails, 147 Streatham High Road, in south London. E-Z American Nails has been under surveillance as a front for a brothel on its upper floors. Vietnamese sex workers are smuggled–"

She pushed the folder away quickly as the detective inspector re-entered. Kate must have looked guilty as hell.

"False alarm after all," the DI said, glancing down at the table.

"I'm ready to give you my statement."

"Before we get started, there's something I need to know. There's no easy way to ask you this. Did your husband often, um, see other women?"

Kate felt affronted – how dare he ask me that? – and then realised that the man was only doing his job. "You have to understand, this is all new to me. Until last week I thought we had the perfect marriage. Friends told me they used to measure their happiness against ours. Now I find out that I never really knew the man I was married to. Do any of us really know anybody else anyway?" She felt herself disintegrating again. "So the answer is no, to the best of my knowledge my husband didn't regularly visit prostitutes."

Sumner turned down the corners of his mouth. "There's something else you should know. We are treating this woman's death as suspicious."

"But the hotel said she took an overdose."

"That was before we got the results back from her post-mortem. In our experience, pregnant women don't kill themselves."

CHAPTER SEVENTEEN

PEOPLE WERE CRUSHED up against each other in a fug of humanity. There was a nasty scraping sound in the Underground carriage as the lights stuttered. Looking at the people around her going to work, how Kate longed to be one of them – tapping away on her office keyboard and then popping out to Tesco for a sandwich at lunchtime. Instead, her life was unravelling before her. The police had asked for a strand of Paul's hair so they could test for DNA and confirm the baby was his. She felt sick to her stomach. This felt like a nightmare she wanted to wake up from but couldn't.

Their marriage had been so happy, and what had happened was so unexpected. Had their union really been so perfect, though? She replayed arguments they'd had in her head, searching for that tiny crack in the glass that would eventually spread and shatter everything.

Kate got off at Putney Bridge and trudged back to the flat she and Paul had once shared, thinking how everything in her life had changed. There was a Chinese saying that once everything was perfect in the garden, the wind would come and knock it down.

The moment she inserted her door key, she knew something was wrong.

Hello, she called as her front door swung open. There had been a disturbance. Bills were swept from the hall table onto the carpet. Bending down to pick them up, she glimpsed the chaos in the sitting room. Books had been pulled down from bookshelves and family photographs overturned, while the carpet was a sea of downy feathers. Someone had even slashed the curtains and sofa cushions. Fear pooled in her stomach. She had been burgled. Hello, Kate called out for a second time. What if somebody was still inside the flat, waiting for her to come home, about to attack? She froze, unable to move.

Panicking now, she crept into the bedroom and saw her clothes heaped on the floor, all her blouses and dresses screwed up. She felt utterly violated. Had they been watching her when she left this afternoon? Her mind strayed back to that creepy black van with the mirrored windows. She knew she had to leave in case anyone was still in the flat, yet she had to see the rest of the damage.

The kitchen was the worst. Jars and bottles had been pulled from the shelves, slicking the floor with oily glop. Broken glass was everywhere, and the whole place reeked. Tiptoeing around the mess, she could see how they had got in: the back-door window was smashed, enabling them to reach round and open the door from the inside. The kitchen door led onto the back stairs, originally used by servants and tradesmen, and she had been telling Paul for weeks that they needed better security. Only now did it occur to Kate what was missing. Her laptop. Sure enough, when she went back into the sitting room, there were a couple of cables on the desk where her computer had been. Shit. Everything had been on it, all her work and personal stuff, photos, hundreds of pictures of Paul and her together. Her entire digital memory. No, wait, everything had been saved on the external hard drive. Going round the side of the desk, she saw that it had been stolen as well.

Her first instinct was to put everything right, to restore order. She began gathering clothes off the floor but her hands felt like stumps. She sat back and slid down the wall, her legs shaking uncontrollably. It was all too much for her to cope with.

Two police constables eventually arrived after an hour. The three of them stood in her sitting room while the older one questioned her.

Had she noticed anything unusual when she went out this morning? the policeman asked.

No, she hadn't, but she'd had a lot on her mind.

Apart from her laptop, had anything else of value been taken?

She didn't think so. A pair of diamond studs Paul had given Kate for her birthday were still in the box on her dressing table.

The younger PC stood by the sitting room window, looking up at the nearby tower block. There'd been a spate of break-ins recently, addicts from the estate looking for stuff to nick.

"If you wait a few days, your laptop will probably turn up at a pawnshop on the High Street," he said. He jerked his head towards the window. "Either that or online. There's a fence on the estate who flogs stuff that way."

"What are the chances I'll get it back?"

The constable shook his head. "Negligible, I'd say. They'll get about fifty quid for it. Look, here's your crime reference number. You'll need it when you're making a claim on the insurance."

His colleague called out that he'd finished dusting for prints in the kitchen.

They stood on the doorstep and the older policeman said he'd be in touch. Kate stood in the hallway watching the PC write up his notes once the men were back in their car. Suddenly she couldn't bear to be alone. She needed to be with people, but who? Her mum was down in Somerset, and anyway, she would see her this weekend. Her best friend Estelle was away at a trade show – she'd seen her Facebook update this morning. When she'd married Paul, she had let her old friends drop: only now did she realise how completely she had bound her life to his.

Priest, the man from the victim support group, lived only

round the corner. Perhaps he could help her get everything straight. It was after six, so he might be back from work already. Kate rummaged in her bag for Priest's business card. Found it. Priest answered on the fourth ring.

"Hello?" He sounded cautious, as if he was unused to people calling him on his mobile.

"John, it's Kate. Kate Julia."

"Oh, hello, how are you doing?"

"Something bad has happened. I've been burgled." Kate sighed. "It never rains but it pours, right?"

Priest offered to help her clear up once she'd told him what had happened.

Twenty minutes later he buzzed the doorbell. He tutted when he saw the mess. "They really did you over, didn't they?" She felt weak. Less than four days ago, she had been happily cocooned from the harsher side of life in her supposedly perfect marriage; the worst that had happened was the occasional parking ticket. Those comforting veils had been ripped away, and now she saw things as they really were. A line of classroom Shakespeare came back to her: "He that dies this year is quit for the next." Paul had taken the easy way out.

It took a couple of hours to put the flat right. Priest duct-taped the slashed cushions ("Working in the trade, you realise everything can be fixed with either duct tape or

WD40") while Kate rehung her clothes. Picking up an armful of Paul's crumpled suits, she couldn't resist inhaling deeply.

Her new friend came out of the kitchen drying his hands on a tea towel. "Don't go in there. The floor's wet," he said. Her Good Samaritan had cleaned everything up; you wouldn't have known there had been a break-in apart from the cardboard patched on the kitchen door. Kate felt drained, her head thick with exhaustion. All she wanted to do was have a drink and go to bed. As if reading her mind, Priest asked if there was any booze in the house. "I think there's a bottle of wine on the shelf," Kate said, remembering a dusty bottle they'd been saving for a special occasion.

"Why don't you sit down? Is there anything to eat in the fridge?" Priest asked.

"I don't know. I haven't been to the shops since I got back. To be honest, I'm not hungry."

"You must eat something."

"There's some pasta sauce in the cupboard. I think we've got some spaghetti."

"We can do better than that."

There was the comforting pop of a cork, and Priest poured out wine for them both. Kate took a sip. The wine tasted dry and rich, like being licked by a cat's tongue. Priest rattled the salad drawer in the fridge and pulled out some tomatoes and a half-destroyed garlic. It would never have occurred to Kate to use up what was in there rather than pop out and get something ready-made. Squeezing the tomatoes and nodding, Priest banged pans about. Watching him bend over, Kate noticed how strong his back was beneath his grey marl tee-shirt. For God's sake, she thought, you've only just scattered your husband's ashes. She felt guilty and cross with herself for even thinking of Priest that way.

It was a pleasure to watch him cooking, though. Soon a rich tomato sauce was bubbling on the stove while the spaghetti boiled.

"Comfort food," he said, setting her plate down. It certainly smelled delicious.

"Where did you learn to cook like this?"

"I had to learn. Me mum worked in a factory shop during the day and as an office cleaner at night. She would get in late."

"What about your dad? Where was he?"

"I never knew me dad. He fucked off when I was small. Mum says he could have charmed the birds from the trees. He was in the motor trade, like. It must run in the family." Priest grinned and ate a mouthful of pasta.

Kate felt herself being restored with each mouthful. "Christ, what an awful day. By the way–" She giggled nervously. "I found out my husband had been seeing a prostitute."

"Blimey, how did you find that out, then?"

"Remember that photo I told you about? The text that Paul was sent? It was taken at the Savile, the big hotel on Park Lane. The manager told me that Paul met a Vietnamese prostitute there. They were filmed going upstairs."

Priest put down his fork. "Was that something you knew about?"

"Of course not, no, but then again, it turns out I never really knew the man I married."

"How did you find the hotel?"

"Wait, it gets worse: the police are treating the death as suspicious. The prostitute was found dead in the hotel room. She'd taken an overdose."

Priest considered what she had just said. "Bloody hell. You're a regular Miss Marple, aren't you? What do the police say?"

"Wait, I haven't finished yet. It turns out this girl was pregnant." Priest's mouth fell open at this. "This prostitute – really, she was just a girl, a teenager, for God's sake – worked in a nail bar in Streatham." Kate paused. "I thought I'd go and visit, see if I could find out anything."

Priest shook his head. "You don't want to do that. Listen, these are not nice people. Leave it to the police."

"Okay, okay, you're right," Kate lied. "It's just that ... can you imagine what it's like to not know the man you were married to, to realise he had this double life?"

"I'm no expert, but lots of men go outside their marriage. If there's something they're not getting, I mean."

"What are you saying? That Paul wanted to be tied up and spanked? God, I'm no prude. Why didn't he just talk to me?"

Priest placed his hand over hers. The touch of somebody else's skin felt so good. Kate realised it was the first time anybody had touched her since Paul's death. "You're gonna drive yourself mad asking all these questions. There's got to be a point where you start letting go."

Kate giggled again. Her laughter was tinged with a note of hysteria. "No, wait, there's more. There's something else I need to tell you. Remember I said I went to see the old boy who lives downstairs? The one visiting his brother's war grave in Albania?" Priest nodded. "He did see Paul fall from the balcony, except he says Paul didn't fall from the penthouse but from the floor below."

Priest's eyes widened. "I don't understand."

"He's saying that Paul didn't jump from our balcony but from the one below ours."

"That doesn't make any sense. Anyway, how can he be so sure? It must have been over so quick, like."

"He's adamant." Kate drained her glass. "In the end, it doesn't matter, does it? I have the post-mortem. Paul died when he hit the pavement."

The conversation reached a natural pause and Priest got up to clear the plates. Kate offered to help but Priest told her to stay seated. He loaded the dishwasher, dried his hands and swallowed his last mouthful of wine. Kate felt pleasantly boozed and stuffed.

"Right. I'd better get going. I'm driving to a showroom in Clacton tomorrow. Are you sure you're gonna be all right?"

She knew now that she didn't want him to leave. The thought of being left alone in the flat scared her. What if whoever had burgled the flat came back? She imagined her bedroom door being thrust open and a man in black entering the room, his torch light crazily swinging about as he held her down on the bed while the knife bit into her neck, preparing–

"Please, John, don't go. I don't think I can be alone tonight."

Priest stood over Kate and held her by her shoulders. She looked up into his warm brown eyes. "You're going to be fine. Whoever it was isn't coming back."

"John, you can sleep on the sofa. It's not safe for me here."

"I've got to get up really early."

"Please, John. I wouldn't ask–"

"All right," he said reluctantly. "I'll stay. I have to be up early, mind."

There was a spare duvet and a pillow on top of the wardrobe. Kate changed into pyjama bottoms and a pretty tee-shirt. She caught sight of herself in the bathroom mirror as she brushed her teeth. There were dark smudges of exhaustion beneath her eyes.

She called out goodnight and shut the bedroom door. She didn't think she'd ever been so grateful to crawl into bed. Christ, what a day. The faces of the hotel manager and the detective at the police station came back to her, then the CCTV photo of Paul meeting the prostitute. It was like a ghastly merry-go-round she wanted to get off. Still, she couldn't sleep. Her mind was too wound up with what had happened. Remembering the touch of Priest's skin, she felt the need for human contact. Anything to stop the pain of being alone.

Would he still be awake? What she needed was to be held, to be told that everything was going to be okay.

Edging down the hall, Kate began to have second thoughts. Priest would think she was a slut. Her husband was barely in the ground and here she was, creeping into another man's bed. Kate stopped. A floorboard they'd never got around to fixing creaked. "Kate, everything all right?" Priest called out. Too late now. She pushed the sitting room door open. Acid orange light from the street lamp spilled from behind the curtain. He was lying there still awake, with his arms behind his head.

Kate stood in the doorway. Priest sat up in bed and again asked if anything was the matter. Instead of replying, Kate crossed the room and slipped in beside him. The warmth in her heart dropped down to her loins, and she bent down to kiss his shoulder and then his nipple. "Kate, stop. This isn't a good idea," he said. Instead, she pulled the duvet down, wanting to see his naked body. She smoothed her hand over his hard chest. That's when she saw the faded tattoo on his upper arm, a yin-yang that had almost gone grey. Flashback. The mortuary attendant raising Paul's wrist in the hospital in Tirana, showing off his homemade Z. She choked on the memory. Suddenly she couldn't do this anymore. Her throat felt tight and she let out a sob. "Hey, it's all right," Priest said gently, touching her hair. It was as if he'd given her permission to let go, and they lay there in the dark as great convulsive sobs swept over her. She felt as if she was never going to get all of it out. Priest just lay there, touching her hair and reassuring her that everything was going to be okay, nothing bad was going to happen to her. But of course, nothing would ever be all right again.

Wednesday

CHAPTER EIGHTEEN

LIVERPOOL STREET STATION was disorienting when you emerged onto the concourse. Men and women barged past Kate as an announcement about the late arrival of the Stansted Express ping-ponged over the station tannoy. She stood looking for an exit, not sure which way she was facing.

She could see that it was a bright, clear morning, one of those crisp, perfect days you get before winter properly sets in. Paul's office was further north up Bishopsgate, in a cobbled street off Spitalfields. His office block was due for demolition, with another high rise set to take its place. They would have to find somewhere cheaper. If the company stayed in business, that is. A year ago Paul might have sold it as a going concern, the accountant had told her over the phone that morning. Right now, all we're looking at is a muddy hole in the ground, he had said dryly. Nobody was going to buy the company today.

The goods lift gate rattled shut and the lift jerked upwards.

The East London Hosting Company was almost a cliché: about twenty, mostly young staff were tapping away at Macs. The bearded men wore tight, dark blue jeans and neat gingham shirts, while the few women had a hippie-ish look, with peasant skirts and strands of dreadlocks. Designer light-bulbs hung down above the exposed brickwork. The whole thing was making a statement. We're creatives! Working in Shoreditch! Well, not for much longer, Kate thought grimly. Soon this would be an empty dusty space with outlines where the furniture had once been.

Colin swung round when he saw her. Kate noticed that he'd put on some weight, one of the problems when you were pretty much paralysed from the neck down. They'd met when Colin was trying to put his life back together after the skiing accident. Paul was doing a degree in marketing while Colin had studied computing. They'd talked about what would become known as the cloud and how, in the future, everything would be stored on the internet and not on PCs. At the time, Kate hadn't really understood what they were talking about. They set up a company building and hosting high-end websites. At first business boomed: their clients included several government organisations and public campaigns. Then the recession hit in 2008 – the government made what it called a bonfire of the quangos, scrapping their key clients. Then it decided to take everything in-house. The new edict was that Whitehall would build its own websites. Business dried up.

"Hello, Kate."

"It's good to see you, Colin." She felt a rush of comfort at seeing an old friend.

"You look a lot better than I thought you would. How are you feeling?"

"Pretty banged about. It comes in waves. Sometimes there are moments when I almost feel normal."

"You know how devastated we all are. He was my best friend, you know."

Kate touched his hand, which was resting on the wheelchair joystick, curled up like a reptilian balled fist. "I know that. Thank you for the flowers."

"Do you have any better idea of what happened? How he fell, I mean?"

Yes, she thought, he jumped because the police wanted to charge him with murder. He went behind my back with a teenage Vietnamese prostitute and got her pregnant. He killed himself because he couldn't face what he had done. She said: "I honestly think it was an accident. He lost his balance and toppled over."

"You seem to be holding up."

I don't know how. Everything I thought about my husband has turned out to be a lie. "You know what they say, one day at a time."

"I've told everybody to assemble in the meeting room at eleven. Are you sure you want to go through with this?"

They'd spoken on the phone early that morning, rehearsing what Kate was going to say. Unless they found a buyer, everybody would be made redundant. There wasn't enough money in the bank to keep the business going indefinitely.

Somebody touched Kate on the shoulder and she turned to see her friend Jackie, the bookkeeper. Jackie was a warm, older woman who'd been widowed herself after her husband died of cancer, leaving her with two young children to support. She had a wry sense of humour and, best of all, the quality that Kate prized most in another woman: she was intensely practical.

"If you want to talk," Jackie said simply.

"Thanks. Perhaps we could grab a sandwich after this meeting."

"Sure thing, babe. You know where to find me."

"Yes, I'd like that very much."

"Kate, we really should get going," Colin interrupted.

Colin's wheelchair jerked backward before he wheeled around and trundled across the office floor. A couple of employees looked up from their computers. Their grim expressions told her they expected the worst. Somewhere deep below a Tube train rumbled.

A sea of mostly young faces looked expectantly at Kate. Some had moved down to London for this, their first job. Others had just bought their first flat or had celebrated the arrival of a baby. Paul liked to think of them as his family, and he'd pledged to keep going through thick and thin. But there was hardly any petrol left in the tank, and the East London Hosting Company was running on fumes. Now his widow was switching off the engine.

"Thank you all for being here this morning. As you know, Paul died last week when we were in Albania for a family funeral." There were sympathetic murmurs round the table. "He fell from the balcony of the hotel we were staying in. It was a tragic accident. You know how much he loved this company he created with Colin, and how much he loved all of you. When they started, the cloud was something that rain came out of." Laughter. "Colin persuaded Paul that servers and hosting were the future. It was Paul's job to persuade others of this vision. That was a tough sell when you're dealing with governments and organisations that want to hang on to their data. And this was the first company to do it, which gave us first-mover advantage. We won some big accounts – the Department for Work and Pensions, the Welsh tourist board – then the big boys caught on, the Accentures and the PricewaterhouseCoopers of this world. That's the problem with first-mover advantage."

Kate paused, bracing herself for what was coming. The staff seemed to sense a change in her mood, and the atmosphere in the room became more serious.

"We've found it harder to get and maintain clients since the recession hit and the big fish moved in. We're just a tiny minnow that led the way. Now government has taken everything in-house. Those years of outsourcing are over. The company made a loss for the first time the year before last. That loss got deeper this year, which means rethinking." Here it comes, you could see them thinking, these kids who had put their faith in her husband. He loved this company. Goddammit, he should never have thrown in the towel so quickly – he should have fought on, she thought, anything to keep going – "but I want to assure you that your jobs are safe for now. By hook or by crook, the East London Hosting Company will keep trading. We're not going to let them push us out of business, I tell you that."

Kate had no idea what she was saying. It just came out of her mouth. She simply couldn't do it, she couldn't let those kids down. Colin looked as surprised as she felt, while Jackie furrowed her brow. The meeting broke up and people drifted back to their desks. There were no questions. You could sense the relief, though. Colin watched the others leave before he turned to her.

"That was unexpected. What made you change your mind?"

"I looked at their faces. They were so trusting. Paul would have wanted me to fight on."

"So what's Plan B?"

"Go to the bank. Throw myself at their mercy. We've never borrowed a penny before. Nobody would lend to Paul when he started out. He always said that banks only give you an umbrella when it's not raining."

Colin looked doubtful. "But we've made a thumping loss for two years running."

"If you've got any better ideas, let me have them."

"I mean, why would the bank lend to us now? It's not logical."

"For God's sake, Colin, what do you want me to say? I'm trying to keep people's jobs here." She flung her hands wide.

"You're right. I'm sorry."

"I didn't mean to snap. Do you know the name of your bank manager?"

"Our business relationship adviser, you mean. Funnily enough, he came to see us a few months ago. I think I've got his card in my desk."

Only Colin and Paul had private offices, which were next to each other beside the meeting room. The glass was frosted so you couldn't see inside. Colin rolled into his office and pulled open a desk drawer. Kate dawdled for a moment outside Paul's room, summoning up the courage to go in.

It was exactly how he had left it. Kate felt as if he had just popped out and was coming back at any moment. She trailed her fingers along his desk. There was their wedding photograph next to his keyboard. What a joke. Colin called out from next door.

He handed her the business card with his better arm. "Umar Omar?" Kate queried, studying it. "Who calls their child Umar Omar?" Colin shrugged. Kate telephoned the bank from his office, asking to make an appointment. The call centre said that Mr Omar had a slot available that afternoon.

Finally, she couldn't keep Paul's secret any longer. This was something she needed to get off her chest.

"Colin, I need to talk to you about something. Paul's death wasn't as straightforward as I said."

Colin swivelled round to face her. "What do you mean?"

"Just before he jumped, somebody sent Paul a text message. It was a CCTV photo. Taken in the Savile Hotel on Park Lane. He'd met a Vietnamese prostitute there. They went upstairs and argued, and she took an overdose. The police wanted to question Paul over her death. I think that's why he jumped, that and the hole the company was in. He was frightened everything was falling apart."

"Paul was wanted for murder?" Colin repeated.

She nodded.

"Do you believe he was capable of murder?"

"Of course not."

"What do the police say?"

"Now that Paul is dead, there's nothing they can do."

Colin thought for a moment. "Who had access to the CCTV footage?" He had put his finger on the one question she could not answer. Paul always said that Colin had a touch of Asperger's Syndrome, a mild form of autism. He would become fixated on a seemingly unimportant detail: useful when writing software, maddening most of the rest of the time.

"Just the hotel security team. And the police, but they wouldn't have sent it."

"Bizarre." Colin sighed and rubbed his forehead.

"Oh wait, I forgot to tell you, I was burgled last night. They stole my laptop. I was hoping we could enlarge my iPhone photos on your computer."

"You've been through the mill."

"There's been a spate of burglaries locally. The police say it's junkies looking for quick cash."

"Do you believe them?"

"I don't know."

Colin connected her phone and dragged her Albanian album onto his desktop, double clicking on the gallery of images. "There, that's the one," Kate told him, touching the screen. Patrons sat beneath space heaters in the far-corner café. "Can you do anything to magnify the image?"

"This isn't CSI, you know. The more you zoom in, the

more pixelated the image becomes. The government or MI5 might have kit like that, but it's not commercially available."

"Just anything you can do to make it sharper."

"I can put it through some rendering software. Might help a bit."

They waited while the computer got to work, patiently filling in the dots. For the first time in years, Kate desperately wanted a cigarette. Instead, she sat down in the corner and flicked through Wired magazine, figuring out what she was going to say to the bank. Things can only get better wasn't much of an argument. If the bank turned them down, that was their last option. As Paul's executor, she would have no choice but to wind up the company.

"There, it's done. You're not going to get it any clearer."

There was Charles Lazenby, seated in the café with the waiter behind him. His bulky camera was on the small round table. Tourists braving the November cold were sitting all around him. It was exactly how she remembered, but the image was much sharper now.

"What about the other photographs? Can you do the same for them?"

"It'll take a few hours. I can leave the software running in the background if you want."

"I haven't got anything else on. Just lunch with Jackie and the bank at two."

People got up from their desks at lunchtime and drifted out of the office. Kate went to find Jackie, and together they walked to a sandwich bar in Bishopsgate. Kate occupied a table while Jackie queued for their order. Sitting there, she brooded about life and how things had turned out. "Cheer up, luv, it might never happen," said a jolly-looking builder at the next table. Oh, but it has happened, she thought, the very worst thing you can imagine has happened.

Jackie set their food down, a sandwich for her and tomato soup for Kate. Soup was the only thing she could stomach.

"So, how are you doing?" Jackie said.

"How do you think I'm doing?" Kate gave a brave little smile. "Paul killed himself four days ago because he was having an affair with a teenage prostitute who, by the way, was pregnant. Probably with his baby."

"Colin told me what'd happened. He didn't tell me that."

"Meanwhile, he left me in charge of a failing company. You know the books. Unless we get this bank loan, we might as well close the doors." She felt herself going again and made a face to stop herself from crying. "I'm sorry, it's not your fault," she said, recovering.

"You really had no idea?"

"You know that we'd been arguing, mostly about money.

What I don't understand is the cruelty. Who does that to another human being?"

"What you mustn't do is blame yourself. This had nothing to do with you."

"It would be nice to think that, wouldn't it? Anger, disappointment, resignation: I feel them all at the same time."

"The kaleidoscope will shift." The bookkeeper reached across and held Kate's hand. "You've got to hang on in there. Every moment, every hour, every day is a fresh start, you have to believe that."

Their local bank was further down Bishopsgate. She had an appointment with Umar Omar, Kate said when she got to the teller window. The teller said he would be with her shortly.

Umar Omar looked as if he'd just left school. His hair was almost shaved bald at the sides and that reminded Kate with a pang of the Balkans. He also had a surprisingly chunky paste-diamond stud in his ear.

They sat down in a bland side office and he put his hands together.

"So how can I help you?"

"I'm a director of my husband's business, the East London Hosting Company. We've banked with you since we started. My husband died last week when we were abroad."

"I am sorry for your loss."

"I've come here because I need a loan. We've never asked anything from you before. We've regularly made a profit since we opened our doors. Except for the past couple of years, that is. Here, I've brought the accounts." Kate dug into her bag and pulled out a profit-and-loss statement. "We made a loss two years running, and that loss is only going to get bigger this year. We need to cut costs."

Omar studied the paper. "Let's see what it says on the computer."

He frowned and tapped a few keys. "Everything's all right today, though. Look, see for yourself. Five hundred grand went in this morning."

He turned the screen towards Kate and there, right at the top, the cursor blinked beside "500,000".

"It must be a mistake. I've got no idea where that money came from. Can you see who sent it?"

"I can put a trace on a BACS transfer. You're sure nobody owes you money?"

"I'm certain of it. All our invoices have been paid."

Kate's mind was reeling as she trudged back to the office. It was raining and the water exploded on the pavement, splattering her tights. It really was pestilent. Half a million pounds paid into their business account. The bank must have made a mistake. She stepped into the road without looking first, and a taxi driver shouted at her. Kate glimpsed a face contorted with rage as the cab shot past.

Colin was still hunched over his computer when she knocked on his door.

"Somebody paid five hundred thousand into our bank account this morning. Does that make any sense to you?"

Colin looked askance. "None whatsoever."

"Do any clients still owe you money?"

He shook his head. "Does the bank know who sent it?"

"They'll phone when they've completed the trace. It could be the middle of next week though."

Leaning over his shoulder, she could see another photograph was up on his screen. It was the photo she'd taken of the roofs of buildings facing the hotel. There was the man she'd spotted in shadow standing on his balcony, watching the fireworks. Colin had cleaned up the image so you could see what he really looked like. Her scalp crawled. It seemed that Charles Lazenby was not the only person Kate knew who was in the square that night.

John Priest stared back at her.

CHAPTER NINETEEN

KITCHENER ROAD IN STREATHAM was a rundown parade consisting of a bookies', a nail parlour and an Afro-Caribbean hairdresser. The nail parlour where her dead husband's pregnant lover had worked – until she, too, had killed herself. Or had she?

The police suggested that Paul had at least witnessed her taking an overdose and had done nothing except watch her die. He hadn't phoned for help or an ambulance, and that touched on manslaughter, if not murder. Kate's thoughts flicked to the dead woman herself: had Tran An Na's parents even been told that she was dead? Did they know how their daughter made a living? Or that they were going to be grandparents? She blipped the car locked and walked towards the row of shops, taking care to sidestep a gnawed rubbish bag spilling out what looked like chicken bones.

Her heels clacked on the pavement and she thought about what a liar John Priest had been. If that was even his real name. Kate had been coming out of the Tube station earlier when she'd spotted the car dealership he supposedly worked for across the road. Something said to her, find out if this John Priest really is who he says he is.

The showroom had brand-new models on display. All cars look pretty much the same, Kate thought, gazing around. Earnest salesmen were going through finance arrangements with anxious-looking couples as a salesman zeroed in on her. "Can I help you?" he asked. The way he pronounced "you" as "yow" in a Birmingham accent was reassuring. Maybe Priest had been telling the truth about working for a Midlands car dealership.

"I'm looking for John Priest. I think he works here."

The salesman thought for a moment. "There's nobody of that name here."

"I know that he covers the south-east. Perhaps he works at a different office."

The salesman called out over his shoulder, and Kate noticed the tiny diagonal writing on his dealership tie for the first time. "Hey, Raj, do you know if a John Priest works in Romford?"

His Indian colleague looked blank and shrugged. "There's just us and Romford covering the London area," the first salesman said. He segued smoothly into his sales patter. "Perhaps I could help you instead. Now, when were you looking to change your car?"

So why had Priest made up this story about where he worked? What had he been doing watching their hotel room?

Kate waited until she was outside the showroom before rummaging in her bag for her mobile phone. Priest answered on the fifth ring. She tried to keep the anger out of her voice.

"John, it's Kate. Kate Julia. I wanted to apologise for last night."

"It were nothing. Forget about it."

"Grief's a strange thing. Your mind plays tricks…"

"Look, I understand. You're still in shock."

"I was wondering if you wanted to meet tonight. For dinner."

There was silence on the other end of the phone. Then, "We could do that. I've got some food at home, if you like. I enjoy cooking."

"Okay. I'll bring a bottle of wine. Would that be all right?"

They rang off, and she was amazed at her own temerity. Who did she think she was, Jane effing Bond? Did she really think that John Priest was going to give up his secrets that easily? The police were not going to be interested in yet another wild accusation: this time, Kate needed proof to back things up. She pictured her dress whispering to the floor as she stood before him, Priest watching from the bed. Then making an excuse while he waited, discovering his office, the laptop on his desk that would give up his secret.

The question was, just how far was she prepared to go?

Wind chimes jangled as she pushed her way in to the nail parlour. The first thing she noticed was the overpoweringly sharp smell of nail polish. It was a finger-marked, down-at-heel place with ugly pink walls and MTV playing on a wall-mounted TV. Even the fish nibbling a customer's feet seemed listless, having gorged themselves on so much dead flesh. A large black woman was having her nails done by a young Vietnamese girl wearing a face mask. Two other girls sat behind white plastic desks fiddling with their iPhones. An older woman, clearly the manager, asked Kate if she had an appointment. No, she said, looking round the mostly empty salon.

"What you want?" asked the manager.

"A manicure. I'd like a pedicure as well."

"One hour, okay? Sixty pound, okay? She do you now."

The manager said something in Vietnamese and one of the girls stood up. With her baseball cap on back to front, she looked barely more than a child.

"This is Phuong. She take good care of you. Any problem, you see me, okay?"

Kate sat down beneath the Anglepoise lamp while Phuong inspected her hands. She glanced at the woman next to her, whose nails were being buffed by what looked like an electric toothbrush. Kate breathed in the acrid smell of acetone. Phuong's touch was so tentative and featherlight, the thought of men raping this girl – and that's what it really was, rape – was too horrifying. As Phuong turned over her hands, Kate saw a crude homemade tattoo on the underside of her wrist. A single letter Z.

The same tattoo Paul told her he'd done as a teenage bet on a night out.

"You put hand here." Phuong pulled a plastic bowl of warm water towards Kate, who dunked her hand in it while the manicurist gently started filing her nails.

"How long have you worked here?" Kate asked.

There was a flutter of panic above the blue face mask. "One month. New."

"Where do you come from? Vietnam?"

The girl next to her twittered something and Phuong didn't reply. The tangle of wind chimes above the door sounded and a young, tough-looking man walked in. He walked straight into the back through a beaded curtain.

"What's through there?" Kate persisted.

"Sunbed."

Phuong snipped the nails on her left hand and dabbed her right hand dry. Kate reached into her bag with her free hand, pulling out her iPhone.

"I knew somebody who used to work here," Kate said. "She was a friend of my husband's."

Phuong pretended not to hear. Kate felt the woman tense as she concentrated even harder on doing her nails. "Perhaps you knew her," Kate continued, putting the iPhone on the table, sliding to the CCTV snapshot with her forefinger and pushing the phone across.

Phuong shook her head slightly. You could tell she was pleading with her to stop.

"Oh come on, you must have known her. Tran An Na. She worked here."

Phuong became so flustered that she knocked over a bottle of nail polish. The red liquid spattered the floor tiles, and the young woman stood up abruptly. Sensing a disturbance, the manageress walked over. "Everything okay?"

"Everything's fine," Kate said brightly. "We were just chatting."

The manageress said something and Phuong replied, keeping her eyes down. The older woman regarded Kate suspiciously and dismissed the girl.

"She no good. I get someone else."

"It's not a problem. Really."

The woman barked in Vietnamese and the tough-looking youth came out.

"He my son. He the best."

Her son, who looked like a surly lout, sat down on Phuong's

stool while she excused herself. He pulled up his face mask and gripped Kate's hand, inspecting it before picking up a fearsome-looking implement and jabbing at the fleshy ridge around the nail. This time Kate winced as the manageress's son dug harder.

CHAPTER TWENTY

THE REST OF THE DAY, Kate felt as if she was standing on a scaffold waiting for the drop.

She hooked her bra together and looked in the bedroom mirror. Paul had given her this Agent Provocateur underwear for her birthday. The trouble was that it never stayed on for very long, so she supposed it had the desired effect. The hangers jangled as she pulled out her black catsuit from the wardrobe. Once it was on, she pinched the material this way and that, adjusting in the mirror. If this didn't turn him on, nothing would. The catsuit zipper was crying out to be pulled down, while the bra pushed her boobs up, making them even more succulent. She slipped her feet into her stilettos before taking one last look in the mirror. Too tarty?

A bottle of wine was sitting on the kitchen table. She grabbed it and made final adjustments to her hair in the hall mirror. Kate had taken off her glasses and inserted her contact lenses, hoping for a sultry Vampira effect. It wasn't too late to back out and put everything in the hands of the police. Leave it to them to find out who John Priest really was. Yet an iPhone photo blown up to the point of incomprehensibility wasn't much by way of incriminating evidence. "Oh, and I believe that he had something to do with my husband's murder," wasn't going to play well with DI Sumner.

Kate felt stupid the moment Priest opened the door. He was dressed in jeans and a tee-shirt, and he wasn't even wearing socks. She felt ridiculously overdressed.

"Hi, come in. Wow. You look fantastic."

"Here. I brought you this."

He glanced at the label as she handed over the bottle. "Looks expensive. I haven't even started making dinner yet. I got back home late. A customer changed his mind after buying a car and tried to return it."

"Does that happen often?"

"Buyer's remorse, we call it. Happens all the time."

You had to admire how he stuck to his story, even though it was all a pack of lies. Priest said he'd go and open the bottle. His flat was the same layout as hers – a long corridor with rooms running off it and a sitting room at the end. Priest banged about in the kitchen while Kate looked around. "Mind if I use the loo?" she called out. Go ahead, he said, turning his back as she walked down the hall. The bathroom was on the right. Instead, she gripped what she guessed was the doorknob of the second bedroom, turning it as gently as she could. Her ears strained for any noise and her heart was beating madly. It was locked. This was not how she had imagined things going. What was inside the bedroom that he didn't want anybody to see? Part of her wanted to ask straight out what he'd been doing in Tirana; another voice urged caution. Softly softly catchee monkey, her nan used to say. Kate busied herself in the toilet, flushed the loo and washed her hands. The whirr of the extractor fan couldn't disguise the vague smell of damp.

Priest almost collided with Kate on her way out. He was holding two glasses of wine.

The main room was bare except for a squashy black DFS sofa, a coffee table that was too big for the room and an ugly plasma TV set. Nothing on the bookshelves apart from an iPod dock. Nowhere to hide a bedroom key. The background jazz playing was so smooth it was almost spreadable. Priest set both glasses down. The sitting room appeared primed for seduction, and Priest dimmed the lights even further. Kate's mouth was dry with apprehension. They clinked glasses, and suddenly she didn't think she could go through with it. She felt like a little girl who'd raided the dressing-up box and was clomping about in her mother's shoes.

"So how was your day?"

"Pretty awful. My husband's business is facing bankruptcy and I had to gather the staff together to tell them we were going out of business. Looking at all those faces, I just couldn't do it. There we were, about to pull the plug, and half a million pounds appears in our company account."

"From where?"

"The bank doesn't know. It's trying to trace the payee. Wherever it came from, it had something to do with my husband."

Priest ignored her lead to talk more about Paul's death. "Could you still get somebody to buy the company?"

"A couple of years ago, maybe. But we've been in the red since then. There's not much value left in the lease either. They're going to tear down the building and put up another office block."

Priest smiled sympathetically and placed his large brown hand over hers. Kate hated herself for doing this, but she had to find that bedroom key. She was convinced that the solution to Paul's death lay in that spare room.

Suddenly she leaned forward and kissed Priest. His lips tasted soft and pulpy.

"Wait," he said, pulling away. "This isn't a good idea."

"I want to," Kate said thickly.

This time he returned her kiss and their lips parted, the tip of his tongue searching for hers. Now they were kissing hungrily, and she felt him pull her zipper down. "You smell wonderful," he said, burying his face between her breasts.

She stroked the kinky frizz of his hair. You can do this, Kate, she told herself. It helped to picture what she was doing at a distance, as if she was watching somebody else. She saw them sitting on the sofa, as if she was high up in a corner looking down, as one hand dropped to his crotch, where she could feel his erection straining against his jeans. Then, Christ, what was she thinking? Her husband's ashes were strewn less than a ten-minute walk away.

A kettle started whistling in the kitchen, shrieking as it came to a boil. Priest pulled away and laughed. "That's how I feel," he said.

"Perhaps we should take this into the bedroom," Kate said. "Can you give me a minute?"

"Sure. I'll go and turn everything off."

Watching him pad down the hall, she panicked, wondering how she was going to get into that spare bedroom. A few more minutes and she would have to go through with it.

Priest's bedroom was next to the sitting room. She heard him coming back down the hall. "John, why don't you get the bottle of wine from the kitchen?" she called out. The room itself was spartan. Monkish. How fitting, Kate thought, except that John Priest probably wasn't his real name at all. He had invented an identity to inveigle his way into the lives of her and her husband. But why? A duvet was casually thrown over the double bed and there was a desk in the corner opposite a built-in wardrobe. Blood roared in her ears. Carefully she slid the desk drawer open and felt the splintery wood with her fingers. Nothing. All she was conscious of was the sound of her own breathing. He could walk in any second. Kate pulled the wardrobe open and saw a row of grey and blue suits. My God, his cover was deep. Beside his underwear and balled-up socks was a brown leather drum – just the place to keep a key. Her fingers scrabbled inside the box but felt only cuff links and plastic collar stiffeners. Desperate now, Kate reached into the pile of folded-up shirts and touched something hard and metallic – the burnished metal edge of a laptop. Kate pulled it out to get a better look at it. So she had been right, Priest was the one who'd burgled her flat.

"What are you doing?" he said behind her.

Her heart contracted with fear.

"Finding out more about you," she said, pulling out the first thought that came to mind. She dangled the tie from her fingers. Priest was holding their glasses of wine, and you could see the question on his face. She didn't think he believed her for one moment. He set the glasses down. "What did you find out?" he said. Playfully she touched his chest, pushing him down into the chair. Priest laughed as she walked round the back of it, pulling his hands through the support strut. "That you're a very bad boy," she breathed into his ear, touching his earlobe with her tongue. "I wouldn't have thought you would be into the kinky stuff," he said. "You don't know anything about me," she replied.

Roughly, she tied his hands together. He laughed again, a little nervously this time. His hands weren't tied together strongly enough. This time she yanked the knot hard. "Hey," he yelped. Slinking round to the front, Kate stood over him.

"So, who are you really?"

"I dunno what you're talking about."

"I went to the car showroom where you told me you worked. They said they'd never heard of you."

"Where did you go?"

"The one on Parsons Green."

"I told you, I don't work in that one. I cover the South East, Kent and Sussex. Could you untie me please? I'm not enjoying this."

"Why were you in Tirana on Friday night? You were watching our bedroom. Why? What did you have to do with my husband's death?"

"I dunno what you're talking about." He yanked at the tie. It wasn't going to hold him; a couple more tugs and he would be free.

"Just tell me the truth. Why was my husband murdered? Who pushed him off that balcony?"

"You need your head examined."

"You were the one who broke into my flat. You stole my laptop."

"I'm not listening to this anymore." This time he jerked his shoulders hard, struggling to free himself. The tie was coming apart.

"Here," she said, pulling the wardrobe door open. "I found my laptop you stole."

"That's not your laptop," he said flatly.

"No? Well it certainly looks like mine."

"Why don't you start it up, then?"

Priest looked almost amused as she set the MacBook down and turned it on. Together they watched the colour sundial spinning, and she felt deflated as the desktop appeared. Clearly this was Priest's own MacBook.

"Now," he said coldly. "Are you going to tell me what's going on?"

CHAPTER TWENTY ONE

"SO WHO DID YOU THINK I WAS?"

"When we were in Tirana, a man was watching our room from a balcony the night my husband died. I thought it was you."

"Why on earth would you think that?"

"I told you. I was taking photographs. A friend at Paul's work blew them up so I could see the man's face." Kate put her head between her knees and exhaled deeply, as if she was coming up from under water too quickly and had the bends. She looked up. "A line is stretched so tight in my head that it's about to snap."

"I don't even know where Albania is. Is it somewhere near Russia?"

"There's another thing. I think I'm being watched."

"Who's watching you?"

"It's a feeling I get. As if somebody had walked over my grave."

Priest paced the floor while Kate sat on the candlewick bedspread. She had never seen him angry before. "Look here, your husband died only a few days ago. You're in shock. When Kelly died, I didn't want to speak to anybody. You've gone straight out and tried to get help, and that's good. But you're putting two and two together and coming up with five. It's like I told you, sometimes things don't make sense."

"But there are so many things that don't add up." Kate banged her head with her fist in frustration. "My husband getting that text. My downstairs neighbour in the square. The man on the balcony … I swear, he's your double. It's all connected somehow."

Priest said sharply, "For God's sake, give it up."

"I went to visit that nail bar in Streatham, by the way, the one where my husband's lover worked." She practically spat out the word "lover". "The girl doing my nails flinched when I showed her Paul's picture. She knew who he was for certain."

"I told you before. These are not nice people. Even if it is a knocking shop, what would happen if they found out who you were? Leave this to the police."

"I suppose you're right."

The car salesman stopped pacing and placed both hands on her shoulders. "Kate, look at me. Forget about all this. What you need is a decent meal and an early night. Come on, I'm going to show you how to make a souffle."

"A souffle?" she repeated dumbly. A souffle represented the furthest shores of culinary ambition, beyond which lay only meringues and profiteroles.

Kate stood under the vaguely dehumanising kitchen light watching Priest deftly crack eggs into a bowl with one hand. The strip light overhead was strobing ever so slightly, just enough to bring on a headache. "There's a whisk in the drawer. Can you pass me it?" he asked. There, lying in a jumble of knives and spoons and kitchen oddments, was a silver key, a key that looked as if it might fit the spare bedroom. Her fist closed around it. Here you go, she said. The key's teeth bit into her palm flesh. There was a clop clop clop as Priest beat the eggs before saying he needed the toilet. "Here, you take over," he said, showing her the bowl.

She made sure he was safely locked in the toilet – she heard him switch the light on and lock the door – before she crept out along the corridor. The key slid into the spare bedroom lock. The tumbler mechanism was so loud, she feared he must be able to hear it. Inside was another cell-like room, empty apart from a couple of computer screens on a cheap pine desk. It was just how she had imagined. The screens showed Kate's flat from different angles: divided into quadrangles, there was the entrance hall, her empty bedroom, the sitting room and the study.

So Priest had her under surveillance.

Her legs turned to water. Priest was the one who had overturned her flat, as a distraction for installing spy cameras. He must have been watching her, seeing her get undressed. This was the man who'd been watching them from across the square, the man who'd sent Paul the text. The man who had condemned her husband to death. The thought of staying here for another minute disgusted Kate.

Priest's cooking was predictably excellent. He refilled Kate's wine glass while she pushed the gossamer-light souffle around her plate. It was ashes in her mouth.

"Tell me more about your parents," Kate said. The wine was making her reckless.

"There's not much to say, really. Me mum was a cleaner who worked in the local hospital. Me dad was a bit of a rude boy when he was younger. He played in ska bands around Brum. Then he fucked off with another woman. I was too young to understand what was going on. We never saw him again ... no wait, that's not true, I did see him again. He was living about one street away and I saw him staring out of a bedroom window. He looked straight at me and then he turned away. All through my childhood, he was only living in the next street. Makes you think, dunnit?"

"Makes you think what? That everybody has a secret?" Careful Kate, you're pushing this too far.

"Dunno about that. I think I'm a pretty boring person, to be honest. What you see is what you get. How about you? Do you have secrets?"

"Paul and I made a promise to each other on our wedding day not to keep any secrets, no matter how bad they were. If you can't trust each other, then the whole marriage collapses."

"But your husband was keeping a secret, wasn't he? Sorry. It's none of my business."

"You're right. It is none of your business."

Priest's fork tined the last of his souffle before he scraped his plate clean. "You're not eating much," he said.

"I'm not very hungry."

"Well, if you're not eating it..." He reached across, tipping what was left on her plate onto his. He said between mouthfuls, "Have you ever thought he was trying to help this woman?"

"Help her how?"

"Like he knew she were in trouble and he wanted to help her."

Kate thought about what he'd said for a moment. "Where would he have met her, though? My husband spent his whole time in the office. It was the only thing we ever rowed about."

"Hotel bars are full of them. Maybe he met a client in the West End and they got talking."

"Sounds a bit far-fetched."

"I'm trying to make you feel better."

"I know, and I thank you for it." Now was the moment she could get out of there. The idea of being alone with this voyeur made her skin crawl. She scraped her chair back on the wooden floor. "I'm really tired. Now that I know it's over, I feel exhausted. I was fine the first few days. Now I feel as if somebody's hit me over the head."

"I felt the same way. Here, I can walk you home if you like."

"There's no need. Really."

They stood in his hallway, and Kate flinched when he tried to kiss her cheek. The touch of his skin was almost unbearable, and she almost fell over herself in her hurry to get out. Priest stood in the doorway looking bemused. "Thank you again for today, I'll call you at the weekend," Kate said, pulling the garden gate behind her.

So, she had been right all along: Priest was the one who had been watching her. Her brain churned as her heels clicked on the pavement. She racked her brains trying to think of what Priest wanted, of what possible interest she could be to him.

That was when she realised she was being followed.

She could see a man's shadow just out of the corner of her eye. Suddenly the thought gripped her that this was her burglar, that he was about to grab her and push her onto the railings, a metal spike going through her eye.

She stopped to confront her attacker, and the footsteps stopped as well. Relief flooded through her. For God's sake, Kate, you've got to stop being so paranoid. You've become frightened of your own shadow.

Her car was parked up ahead, and her car keys were in her bag. It was still fairly early. Kate knew that another piece of the puzzle lay in that nail bar, and that she needed to see the manicurist again, the one who'd done her nails. Kate was certain that Phuong had recognised Paul in the photo. The car lights flashed as she blipped the car open. Kate reckoned it would take about forty minutes to drive to Streatham at this time of night. She thought about what Priest had said, about Paul wanting to help Tran An Na. It was true that Paul did have a social conscience: he'd run a marathon once to raise money for Middle Eastern refugees. She remembered cheering him on as he staggered past on a windswept East Sussex beach. But the idea of him trying to save fallen women sounded unlikely. It must be something else, it had to be.

Of course, the nail bar was shut by the time she arrived. Some lights were on upstairs.

Did Kate think she was just going to ring the doorbell and be let in? Inventing some cock-and-bull story about leaving her mobile phone behind wouldn't work. She imagined the suspicious flat-faced matron telling her to wait on the pavement while she searched inside. No, that wouldn't do. Kate was thinking about going home when another car slid into a parking space up ahead. The nail bar manageress struggled out holding LIDL shopping bags. She dumped the bags and pressed the doorbell before waddling back to her open boot. The lights came on and the tough who'd done her nails came out. The two of them hefted the bags into the shop and Kate saw them go through the beaded curtain. They must live upstairs.

The spare tyre and the nut jack lay beneath the grey felt in the boot. Kate wrestled the jack out, feeling the weight of it. Not quite believing what she was about to do, Kate walked up to the manageress's car and swung the jack against the driver's window. It bounced off. Next time she hit the window harder, smashing the glass instantly. When she opened her eyes, diamonds were strewn across the driver's seat and the window had spidered. A moment later the car alarm went off. Kate ran back and crouched down, breathing heavily. The shrieking car alarm covered the sound of the nut jack clanging to the pavement. Her breath steamed as she watched the nail parlour lights go on. Sure enough, mother and son came out to investigate. The mother shouted in Vietnamese and the son shouted back. Leaving the two of them arguing, Kate crept along the pavement and pushed the front door further open. The wind chimes made her nerves jangle. The beaded curtain that led upstairs lay straight ahead. All she was conscious of was the terrible danger she was in. The beads draped over her hair as she pushed her way upstairs.

Kate emerged onto a landing, wondering where to go next. Everything was dirty on this floor, like a squat, and she noticed a strong, acrid smell. Not acetone, something much sharper. She stood there, tensed, surveying her surroundings, when a man emerged from a bedroom, a dim red light behind him. He seemed just as surprised to see her. Kate smiled inanely before continuing upstairs. Just look as if you know where you're going, she thought.

She noticed there was damp on the walls as she took the steps two at a time. A floorboard creaked. If anything, the smell was even stronger here. "Hello," she called out. There was just one bedroom up in the eves and she made straight for it, unsure what to expect.

It was a child's bedroom, with faded rose wallpaper and a filthy, brown-stained mattress on the floor. It had been a nursery once. Except pornographic pictures had been Sellotaped to the wall: anonymous torsos violating women, yanking their heads back, making them bark. Phuong must be downstairs. And that's when she spotted a small wooden door beside the chimney breast. Vietnamese voices were coming upstairs, and Kate realised that her escape route was blocked off. Panicking, she knew her only choice was to go through the tiny door. The mother and son were getting nearer, talking as they came upstairs. Feeling like Alice about to go through the rabbit hole, Kate got down on her hands and knees; the space was just big enough for her to crawl through.

Kate emerged into a jungle.

Thick, lush plants filled the attic, stretching far into the distance. The owners had knocked through into next door's attic as well, so the place was one enormous forest. Kitchen foil covered the walls while newspapers blacked out the dormer windows. There was a timer on one wall controlling the twenty-four hour lighting, watering and heat, and infrared lamps glowed like false suns from rafters down onto a Christmas-tree-sized mother plant. She trailed her hand along the spiky fronds and only now did she recognise the sharp smell. This was a cannabis farm.

It was also as hot as a sauna. Sweat beaded her forehead as she spotted the beautician up ahead. Phuong was dressed in shorts and a vest, scissoring a bush. "Hey," Kate called out. Phuong stopped what she was doing. Kate called out again, and the Vietnamese teenager moved deeper into the plants. Kate pushed on through, fronds slapping her in the face. "I want to help you," Kate said. It was like a dream where you never quite reach the person you're after, she thought. Suddenly Kate caught her foot on a flex on the ground, pulling an old-fashioned bar heater with her.

Phuong was cowering against the back wall. Christ, it was hot. Kate had landed badly and twisted her ankle. She limped towards Phuong. "I'm your friend," Kate said.

Something in Phuong's eyes made her look back: smoke was rising from where she'd knocked over the heater. Firefly sparks drifted up and Kate realised that a fire was catching. "There must be another way out," she said, touching Phuong's shoulder. She shook her head, looking scared.

That was when they heard Vietnamese voices getting nearer. Kate glimpsed the brothel keeper and her son, if it was her son, moving through the plants. She pulled the petrified teenager down and they crouched beside the foliage. The smoke was stinging Kate's eyes. Don't give us away, she begged silently. Suddenly flames sheeted up as the fire really took hold. Thick black smoke roiled up to the ceiling. The madam shouted as fire ripped along the burning plants. The place was getting thicker with smoke. Kate didn't care if anybody spotted them, she had to get air into her lungs. She simply could not breathe. The attic was so full of smoke now that it was also difficult to see.

Flames leapt up, cutting them off from the only way out. The girl was becoming hysterical, shouting and crying. Kate spotted an old chair against the wall and ran over to it. She picked it up and jabbed its legs against the newspapered window above her head. It just wouldn't reach. Setting the chair down, Kate gestured for Phuong to help her. They were hemmed in by a wall of burning plants. Coughing from the smoke, Kate stood on the chair and reached for the window bar. Her fingers strained, but still she couldn't quite manage it. Nearly all of the plants were on fire now. She gestured with her interlocked fingers that she wanted to give Phuong a leg-up. At least one of them would get out of here.

They stood wobbling on the chair with Kate cupping her hands. Her muscles ached as she lifted the girl up and Phuong squeezed through the narrow gap in the Velux window. Now it was Kate's turn, but there was no way she could reach the opening. The entire room was ablaze, and she looked around for another way out. Please, God, let me get out. Suddenly a man's arm reached down through the ajar window. She grabbed it, and whoever it was lifted her up, grunting with the effort. Kate hauled herself up with everything she had, her muscles screaming. Strong arms also helped her out. She was dimly away of Phuong sitting off to one side of the roof as she lay on the slates, coughing and retching.

When she turned over, it was John Priest who smiled down at her.

CHAPTER TWENTY TWO

THE CORDONED-OFF STREET was full of fire engines and police cars, and the shop windows strobed with flashing blue light. People stood watching behind police tape, wondering how they were going to get home. Hoses snaked along the road and there was water everywhere, lots of it. Despite the hum of generators, there was a sense that whatever drama there had been was all over now, and that everything was coming to rest. Two green-suited paramedics were helping Phuong into an ambulance.

Kate shivered with cold. A no-nonsense blonde took hold of her arm, and she looked back to where Priest stood huddled with police. He was telling them something. Then he spotted her, excused himself and almost ambled over.

"Just give me a second," she said to the paramedic.

"We need to take you to hospital."

"I need to speak to this man. It's important," Kate said, wresting her arm free.

Priest grinned and stood with his hands in his bomber jacket. He looked insufferably pleased with himself. "I can't leave you alone for five minutes, can I?"

"Who the hell are you really?"

"I told you. My name's John Priest."

"You were the one watching us from the square. All that stuff you made up about your wife being murdered. It was all lies."

"I was trying to protect you."

"You were the one who sent my husband that text. Murderer."

He raised his hands. "We had no idea what he was going to do. You must believe me."

"Why would you do such a thing?"

"There's things you don't know."

"Such as?"

"That he was being blackmailed."

"Blackmailed? Who on earth would blackmail him?"

"I'll tell you on the way to hospital."

"Why should I believe you? Everything you've told me has been a pack of lies. I can't believe anything you say."

"You have to trust me."

Uncertain, the paramedic took her arm again. "Please. We need to take you to A&E." This time Kate allowed herself to be led away. The two of them climbed into the back of the ambulance, where Phuong was lying on a trolley. She really was barely more than a child. Priest got in after her and the paramedic pulled the doors closed. The ambulance juddered as the diesel engine started up. What did Priest mean when he said that Paul was being blackmailed? How could she trust anything he said? If he could lie about his wife being murdered, he could lie about anything. All men ever told her were lies.

"Who was blackmailing Paul?" she began.

Priest cut her off with a gesture of his hand. He leaned in to Phuong and asked her how long she had been in the country.

"Six day."

"How did you come to England? Were you in a lorry? Who brought you?"

"Boat. Man say to parents I get new job in England. They give money."

"But that's not what happened, was it?"

Phuong shook her head and turned to face the wall. She began to shake. Really, it was too heartbreaking, and Kate wanted Priest to stop.

"Who brought you here? I'm a policeman. I am not going to hurt you."

"They take me to apartment. There was another girl. They hurt me. They tell me I belong to him now."

"Belong to who?"

Phuong turned back and extended her arm, showing Priest the tattoo Kate had noticed before. Z. The same tattoo that Paul had on his arm. Priest sat back in his fold-down seat and threaded his fingers together, looking as if he'd just received bad news. The saline drip and equipment jangled as they lurched over a pothole.

"Did Zogaj bring you here? Is Zogaj in this country?"

Phuong traced a line from her eye to her cheek. "Crying man. He bring me."

"Who is Zogaj?" Kate interrupted.

Priest looked up. "He's the gang boss. They offer these girls jobs in Europe, and even get the parents to pay their fare. Then they beat them and rape them and use them as slave labour. That was the cannabis farm you saw. When these girls aren't being raped for money, and that's what it is, they look after these dope farms. The whole of England is being flooded with the stuff. And we're not talking about a few spliffs, the kind you had at uni. This stuff is laced with all sorts of shit."

Her mind flashed back to sitting on her boyfriend's single bed at art school, watching him crumble what looked like cake into a cigarette paper. She had lost her virginity that night. He'd draped a scarf over a bedside lamp, going for a louche, Keith Richards effect, and she'd sat back and exhaled as the room turned hazy and indistinct.

"What's this got to do with my husband?"

"Your husband was the British end of the operation. Or one of them anyway."

"Are you saying that my husband was a drug dealer?" It was so absurd that Kate wanted to laugh.

"I'm not saying that. He was the money side. I think they'd threatened his family back in Albania as well."

Priest was about to say more when the ambulance came to a halt. It was clear they'd arrived. The blonde paramedic got up and opened the doors onto a loading bay. Kate and Priest got out and stood watching as the paramedics lowered Phuong onto the ground, kicking down the wheels of her trolley. She looked in a bad way, and Kate thought about what these people had done to her. They crashed through heavy plastic flaps straight into A&E, where a doctor and a competent-looking nurse took over. Kate caught a last glimpse of Phuong as they wheeled her into a cubicle and whisked the curtain shut.

A man was groaning "Ohmygodohmygodohmygod" behind another cubicle. The A&E was operating a triage system, so the doctors could see Kate only when they'd got other, more urgent cases out of the way. She prepared for a long wait. A male nurse showed Kate and Priest into a waiting room. "I could murder a cup of tea," Kate sighed. Priest offered to get her one from the machine. A group of girls were sitting in the other plastic seats looking like a bunch of bedraggled fairies, with smeared mascara, wonky halos and crushed angel wings. Blood seeped through the head bandage of one of them who was sitting in a wheelchair. A hen night gone wrong. Priest walked back in gingerly carrying two Styrofoam cups. Kate took one and gratefully sipped the hot sweet tea – he'd put sugar in it, and it tasted silky and delicious. It was too hot to drink right now, and Kate placed hers on the ground.

"So you're a policeman."

"I work for an organisation called Europol. It's the European version of Interpol."

That made her smile. "You can't work for Interpol. You're from Wolverhampton."

Priest didn't rise to the joke. "We've been watching this Albanian gang for months. They smuggle these girls into Britain, promising them work. Then they turn them into slaves. They're completely controlled. Even when we do free them, they go back voluntarily. It's as if they can't see the bars of the cage. And it's not just drugs and prostitution, but increasingly cybercrime as well. Stealing people's credit card details and cash from their bank accounts. There are about thirty of these gangs operating in Eastern Europe who have tech as good as any government's. We're just a small office in Holland. These people aren't constrained by budget cuts. Every time they need more money, they just go and steal it."

The hen party were playing some sort of game. They were

behaving as if it was perfectly normal for a night out to end up in A&E.

"So you think Paul was being blackmailed."

"I don't think so, I know. He was the one they used to pay off British officials. They were using his company to pay them off through the internet. Have you heard of the Dark Web? It's the part of the internet you can't see with a browser. Criminals love it." Priest lowered his voice. "We don't know who they were paying off. Bitcoin payments are untraceable."

"You're saying that my husband was paying off the police?"

Priest sat upright. "Look, I'm not making this up. I can show you evidence if you like – photos, phone calls. That money you were telling me about, the five hundred grand that turned up in your account, came from beyond the grave."

"Why did you send him that picture?"

"Tran An Na was our informer. We were trying to help her. Your husband was doing the same thing. Both of them were trapped and wanted to get out."

"Instead he killed himself."

"Believe me, there isn't a day goes by that I don't regret what I did. She was our only way in. I wanted your husband to know that we knew who he was, that we could help him find a way out. I never thought he'd do what he did."

She felt a surge of anger and she slapped Priest across the

face. Hard.

The girls stopped what they were doing, and Priest rubbed his cheek with his large pink palm.

"I deserved that."

"Why were you watching me?"

"Because we didn't know how much you knew. My boss was convinced you were in on it. Paul must have told you what was going on. He had a valuable piece of information."

"What was that?"

Priest glanced at the girls before lowering his voice again. "The names of every British official on the take."

"You think I knew about that?"

Priest shrugged. "That's why you were under surveillance. Hey," he said sitting up straight, "if it wasn't for me you'd be dead."

"That's it, then, isn't it? Case closed. Paul's dead and now you know I had nothing to do with it. I can go home now."

Priest shook his head. "We need to get you and Phuong to safety. The Albanians don't know Paul kept you in the dark. They'll think that Paul told you everything and that you'll blow the whistle. They want you out of the way. I'm sorry, but that's how it is. I'll telephone my boss."

"What are you talking about?"

The hen party leaned in together, noisily posing for a selfie.

Priest turned around and snapped, "Jesus, could you shut up?"

"I don't understand. Why can't I just go home?"

"We need to get you away. You'll have to start again. Change your name."

Inside, a corner of her mind was laughing uncontrollably. Kate said coldly, "Don't be ridiculous. I have a life here, a business. I can't just start again in the ass end of nowhere. What if I say no?"

"You really don't get it, do you?" Priest lowered his voice to a whisper. "Anybody could be working for them. Any doctor, any nurse, any policeman. Trust no one. Believe me, you have no other choice."

Kate looked down at the grey-blue floor and noticed the sparkly mica in it. Albanian gangsters, politicians on the take, Bitcoin payments – really. The whole thing was absurd. "How long do you need me to disappear for?"

"A month, six months … I dunno. Your husband was going to be our way into the gang. The Albanian police want to get these people off the streets as much as we do."

"I suppose I'll need to get clothes from home," Kate said reluctantly.

"I'll get them for you. They'll probably be watching your place. First I need to phone my boss and get the safe house ready."

Priest stood up and got his mobile out of his pocket. To Kate's surprise, he spoke in French, and he nodded at her before stepping outside and pacing up and down the corridor. Somewhere a mournful alarm sounded. Safe houses, new identities – it was all like something out of a bad spy novel. Did he really expect her to give up her life and start again in some remote Australian town? It was all so silly. Five days ago Kate had been in a happy marriage with a husband she loved, and now–

Priest put his head round the door. "We're good. Come on, let's go."

"What about Phuong?"

"We're taking her with us."

They kept their heads down as they walked purposefully back along the A&E corridor. Kate felt as if she was doing something wrong, leaving before a doctor had seen her. Phuong's cubicle still had its curtain drawn and Priest sharply whisked it back.

The bed was empty.

CHAPTER TWENTY THREE

PRIEST AND KATE just stood there, not knowing what to do. Priest stopped a passing male nurse and asked what had happened to the girl in the cubicle. Two porters had taken the girl in a wheelchair, he said, presumably down to X-Ray to photograph her lungs. "Assumption is the mother of all fuck-ups," Priest muttered.

"What do we do now?" Kate asked.

"Come on, we've got to get going."

He was walking away so fast that Kate struggled to keep up with him. "Shouldn't we ask the police to take us home?"

"Trust nobody. My car's parked round the side of the nail bar."

Stepping out into the cold, they waited for a taxi, but all had their lights off. Priest said they would have to walk. There were few cars on the road at one o'clock in the morning, and Kate felt ghostly with tiredness as they trudged past betting shops and kebab takeaways. Every nerve ending felt exposed, as if she'd turned her skin inside out. If she could just close her eyes for a moment, to try and forget what was happening to her.

"Isn't there somebody you could call? Not everybody in the police is corrupt, you know."

"We don't know who is and who isn't. Best get you to the safe house. We can figure out what to do once you're there."

Her head ached with cold, which was making her slightly deaf. Her catsuit felt like tissue paper, and it was cold enough to split stones. You read about this kind of stuff happening to other people – that family shot to death in a forest, or Madeleine McCann going missing, big news stories that stayed on television for days – never thinking it could happen to you. Yet here she was caught in something ripped from the pages of the morning's tabloid. "Albanian gangsters silence grieving widow" would be the headline. She wasn't even meant to be here. I'm only thirty-three, she thought, my life has barely begun.

The plan was to drive round to her flat and Priest would pack for her while she stayed in the car. It was too dangerous otherwise, he said. Priest turned to Kate. "You're a threat to them," he said. "They don't know you're an innocent. Do you understand?"

Priest's car was a souped-up silver Mitsubishi Lancer with a spoiler on the back. The engine growled reassuringly as Kate buckled up in the rally-driver seat. The street almost became a blur as they accelerated, pushing her back a little. "A bit boy racer, isn't it?" she said as Priest swung a sharp right.

Forty minutes later and they were back inside Priest's flat.

She stood watching from the doorway as he threw down a nylon sausage bag and packed a pair of waterproof trousers and a jacket, a thick oiled-wool jumper and his toiletries. Priest packed in a hurry. They would be in a safe house for a week until they figured out what to do with her, he said, probably taking Kate back to The Hague for more questioning.

Next she followed him into the spare bedroom, where he checked his camera feeds of her flat. There were blurry black-and-white views of the rooms of her apartment. Had he seen her getting undressed, shimmying out of her panties, studying herself in the mirror? Suddenly she didn't like the idea of John Priest rummaging through her knicker drawer.

"I want to come with you," she said.

"I told you. Best wait in the car. They might be watching."

"There's things I need. You won't know where to find them." He hesitated. "For God's sake," Kate persisted. "You're telling me I've got to start a new life and you won't even let me pack? You won't know how to find my passport. It'll be quicker if I come in."

"Okay. But you've got to be fast. In and out."

Finally he pulled out what she guessed was her MacBook from a bottom drawer.

"So you had it after all," she said coolly.

"I was looking for the data, those names and addresses I told you about."

The MacBook was the last thing he threw into his holdall.

They ran across Fulham Palace Road to where his car was parked. A couple of minutes later they turned into her street and Priest pulled into a parking space. "Come on. Let's get going," he said, switching off the engine. Already he was out of the car, scanning left and right. Was there anybody lurking in the road? What about somebody waiting in a car? All clear.

Her fingers felt thick and clumsy as she fumbled with her own front-door keys. Priest stood with his back to her, watching for anybody coming into the entrance hall. Eventually the right key slid in and Kate pushed her front door open.

Priest said he would wait for her in the living room.

"I'll go and change," Kate said, closing the bedroom door. Finally she was alone. Getting her stilettos off was a relief, and she wriggled out of her catsuit before opening her wardrobe. What do you pack for a new life? She stood there, unable to decide, seconds tightening like a noose around her neck. They could be here at any moment. This wasn't the time to think. Finally she decided on black jeans and a tee-shirt – she threw on a leather jacket and pulled her hair into a ponytail through a baseball cap. Her carry-on suitcase was in the wardrobe. She dragged some blouses off their hangers and tossed the suitcase on the bed. Underwear next, and she nearly trapped her fingers in her hurry to slam closed the chest of drawers.

Her passport was in the sitting room, in the right-hand drawer of a table she'd inherited from her grandmother. There were photographs on the table and she paused to look at one of them: she and Paul standing beneath the tree in Bishop's Park on their wedding day. It had felt like the start of a great adventure; there had been no doubt in her mind that she and Paul were going to be married for a very long time. Till death us do part. Kate peered more closely at Paul's face. Whatever Priest had said about him being blackmailed, he'd allowed himself to be their pawn and had taken their dirty money. He could have gone to the police; there was always a choice. By now she was so close she could make out individual dots on the photograph. There was something not quite right about it; some of the pixels on Paul's face were differently coloured.

Taking the magnifying glass from a pencil pot on the desk, she looked even more closely. Yes, there was no doubt about it, some of the flesh tones were wrong. Kate tapped the magnifying glass ruminatively against her teeth.

"Could you get a move on?" said Priest. He was standing in the doorway.

"Here. Come and look at this."

"Jesus, Kate, we need to get out of here."

"Wait. This is important. There's something wrong with this photo."

Priest sighed and took the magnifying glass. "What am I meant to be looking at?"

"Look at the flesh tones on Paul's face. Some of them aren't the right colour. Like he's got acne."

Priest peered at the photo with her. "Where's the original? Do you still have it on your laptop?"

"I think so. Why, what are you thinking?"

"We'll need to get it from my car. Give me your keys. You draw the curtains."

She watched Priest cross the road before pulling the curtains closed. The odd car shushed past up the street. What had he spotted that was so important? A black van turned into their road and she had that feeling again, as if somebody had walked over her grave. The vehicle looked as alien and menacing as an insect. Hurry up, John, and get back here. She let the curtain fall and found her passport, slipping it into the leather jacket.

She was thinking about taking some food for wherever they were going when she heard keys in the door. Her heart thumped against her chest. "They're microdots. Or rather they act like microdots," Priest said, letting himself in. "Here. Show me your wedding photographs."

The buffering laptop seemed to take forever to start up. "I was looking for Bitcoin codes. I thought Paul might have kept them on the computer."

"What's a Bitcoin code?"

"It's a unique key that unlocks money. Criminals love it. That's what the Albanians were using to pay off the police. It's untraceable."

The folder where she kept their wedding photographs was spread out before them. Priest double-clicked on the one they'd had framed. They compared the two.

"Look, see how it's different. Do you have TOR on this machine?"

"I don't know. What's that?"

"It's a browser. We use it for pulling stuff off the Dark Web." He paused and turned to her. "You really have no idea what I'm talking about, do you?" He might as well have been explaining hang-gliding to a mole. Priest shook his head. "All this time I was searching for Bitcoin and here it was, right under my nose. I'll need to download some software. I can run a decryption program."

An arrow pulsed as Priest downloaded the software he needed. The sound of the front door shutting floated upstairs. When would she next see this flat? How would she explain to mum and all the others who knew her? You don't just disappear; you can't just walk out on your old life and start somewhere else. She pictured a hot Australian street in the middle of the Outback somewhere and shook her head. No, that was not going to happen. She wasn't going to let them bully her into being somebody else. Suddenly she was very tired. All her brain capacity was used up, and she felt drained. If only she could close her eyes, just for one second. She'd had enough of today.

She must have fallen asleep, just for a millisecond, because when she opened her eyes Priest was staring at a grey bar scrolling across the screen... 75 per cent ... 80 per cent ... nearly there. "Won't be long now," he said. The software was scanning the files agonisingly slowly, trying millions of different combinations to unlock the photo. "Come on, come on," he said quietly.

There was a knock on the door.

They both froze. It was two o'clock in the morning, so this wasn't just any casual passer-by. Kate thought about the black van and how it had been parked outside her flat for days. They both had the same unspoken thought.

"Don't answer it," said Kate.

Right at that moment, the decryption completed and Priest double-clicked on what was now an Excel spreadsheet: hundreds of names and addresses, columns of figures.

"Clever boy. Everybody's names are right here." He looked closer. "Not just here but all over Europe. He could always blow the whistle on them. This was your husband's insurance policy."

"An insurance policy he never got to cash in."

"Have you got a memory stick?"

The knocking started again. More insistent this time.

"No, I don't think so ... wait, there's a memory card in my camera."

"Here, you save it."

She heard Charles Lazenby's papery voice from the hall.

"Who the hell's that?"

"It's all right. He's my downstairs neighbour. The one in the square that night."

"What does he want? It's past two in the morning."

"It might be important," Kate said reluctantly.

"I'll go and check. You've got a spy hole."

Her old DSR was in the bottom drawer of the desk, and she popped the memory card out while Priest peered through the fish-eye lens. She heard him say "Who is it?" as she dragged the Excel file onto the memory card. Priest could give it to Europol or whoever he wanted; she never wanted to see that wedding photograph again. Maybe trying to protect her hadn't been the same as lying, but she still felt violated. Kate heard Charles Lazenby's voice from the hall once more.

Suddenly the front door crashed open and there was a commotion. Shouting. In her panic, Kate deleted the original from the MacBook as Lazenby was thrown into the room. The sitting room door shuddered. Kate's neighbour fell over the sofa looking old and frightened. A man she had never seen before stood in the doorway: he was tough looking, dressed in a nylon bomber jacket and camouflage trousers. What was odd about him was his face. There was a teardrop tattooed beneath one eye, as if he'd done something he was sorry about. She remembered Phuong drawing a line under her eye.

So this was them. The men who had killed her husband.

Kate stood defiantly in front of the man, shielding the laptop. "Please don't hurt me," Lazenby whimpered from the sofa. "Where is computer?" said the thug. Kate stood with her hands behind her back, rigid with fright. At the same time, her fingers searched for the memory card slot. This was what they wanted, she was sure of it. The tattooed thug stepped closer and she shrank back. The memory card popped out and she closed her fist around it.

The thug, who had a sensitive, almost melancholy face, pulled out a Stanley knife and dropped down onto the sofa, digging his knee into Lazenby. The thug held the knife against the old man; it pressed white against his cheek. "You want me to cut him? Please, I am not fucking you. Where is computer?" Lazenby let out a strangulated moan. Kate stood to one side, revealing the laptop, and Teardrop got up, pulling her away. She fell against Paul's favourite armchair. Teardrop grinned as he held the MacBook, revealing an ugly row of horse's teeth. Clearly, he had what he wanted.

A second man pushed Priest into the room. This accomplice was small and baby-faced, almost a dwarf. His close-cropped hair and bug-eyed sunglasses made him look even more sinister. He also had a gun pointed at Priest's head. Kate remembered somebody telling her once that the small bouncer was the one you had to watch out for on a nightclub door. He was the vicious one.

"Who are you, and what do you want?" said Kate.

"She say what do we want?" said Teardrop.

The dwarf snickered. "I dunno. What do we want?"

"Lady, why don't you tell us why we're here?"

"Look," Kate said. "We don't want any trouble. I think you'd better leave."

"I think you'd better lee-eave," mimicked the short one in a high, camp voice.

"Who the fuck are you?" said Teardrop. "I'm a neighbour," Priest replied. The little thug took a running kick at Priest, putting his boot in the back of his leg. Priest crashed down onto both knees. The dwarf then rested the gun against the back of Priest's head. Kate was so frightened she felt a drop of pee running down her inside leg. Teardrop pulled a mobile phone out of his pocket and stalked into the hall. Lazenby was still sprawled on the sofa.

Kate could hear Teardrop in the corridor speaking in what she guessed was Albanian. The skinhead smirked as he held the gun against Priest's head – he behaved as if this was one enormous joke. Priest looked shaken.

Teardrop didn't look too happy when he came back in. "You. Where is sheets?" He jerked his head for Kate to follow him. They walked down the hall to a wardrobe where she kept bed linen. Her fingers trembled as she turned the knob. "You have what you wanted. Why can't you leave us alone?" Teardrop pulled sheets down into a billowing heap and then picked up two pillowcases. All he said was "Move".

Priest was kneeling now, with his hands behind his head. "I've got some shirts to do while you're at it," he quipped. The runty one stepped forward and smashed Priest across the back of the head. What shocked Kate was how casual and unexpected the violence was. Priest toppled sideways onto the carpet. "My God, you've killed him," Kate said. Teardrop extracted what looked like a nylon cord from his pocket, the kind you use on an electric light-pull, knelt down and roughly tied Priest's hands together. He yanked hard and Priest groaned. "You next," he said. Kate held her hands out and Teardrop turned her around. Up close he smelled really bad, a strong goatish smell, and the way he looked at her made her fear she might be raped. The tight nylon dug into her wrists, and she circled her hands to keep the blood flowing.

"Can't you leave the old man alone?" she said. "He's done nothing to you." Teardrop told Lazenby to lie face down on the sofa while he hogtied his hands together as well. Next he pulled a roll of duct tape out of his pocket and sliced off a strip, slapping it crudely across the old man's mouth. "Zogaj say no witnesses," his accomplice said. Teardrop ignored him and did something curious: he adjusted the cushion beneath Lazenby's head, trying to make him more comfortable.

Teardrop hauled Priest up by the scruff of his neck and got him to stand. Priest was unsteady on his feet, as if he didn't know where he was. A trickle of blood ran down his temple. Teardrop pulled a pillowcase over Priest's head, shrouding him. For a moment it reminded Kate of a lynching in the Deep South, except the black man was the one wearing the hood. Priest stumbled again on his way out; the blow to the head must have really affected him.

Now it was Kate's turn.

Teardrop yanked the pillowcase over her head and everything went dark. Her breath felt hot inside the cotton as Teardrop pushed her towards the door. She was frightened she might trip over something. The thug steered her into the hall and she smelled his body odour again. Please, God, let a neighbour come out and see us. For once Kate wanted the nosy woman who lived across the hall to wonder what was going on. Teardrop steered her carefully but she stumbled over the threshold. The entrance door clicked open, and then they were out in the night air. This is it, she thought, the moment of no return.

CHAPTER TWENTY FOUR

A VAN DOOR SCRAPED OPEN and Teardrop told Kate to climb inside. She was shaking as he lifted her in, although she wasn't sure whether it was from cold or fear. The icy interior had a sharp, acrid smell that she couldn't put her finger on. Of course: this was the van that had so freaked her out a couple of days ago, the one with the dildo on the dashboard. All this time they must have been watching her, seeing where she went and who she met. Teardrop led Kate to the back of the van and pushed her down. She sensed Priest beside her. They were both sitting on what felt like a small wooden box. Teardrop leaned down and whispered in her ear: "You fuck with me, I kill you."

His boots rang out on the metal floor and then he jumped down. The van doors slammed shut. They were finally alone. That was when Kate became aware that another person was in the van. She heard the snuffling sound of somebody crying.

"Phuong, is that you?"

"They going to kill us," she said. Her voice trembled on the edge of hysteria.

"Listen to me. They are not going to kill you. You're worth too much to them." Phuong let out a surprisingly deep moan. "You must believe me."

"I'm sorry, I should never have got you into this," Priest said. His words were muffled through the pillowcase.

"It's okay. I think they'd been watching me for days. Why do they need us now they've got the laptop?"

"We can identify them. We know what they look like." There was an uncomfortable silence as he let the implications sink in. They both knew what that meant.

"I don't know anything. You know that."

"They don't care. These are hungry people. The worst. It used to be the Italians, then the Russians. Now it's the Albanians. Listen, I want you to promise me something. I want you to escape if you get the slightest chance. Promise me that. Okay?"

"What about you?"

"They don't know who I am. I'll take my chances."

The diesel engine started up, wobbling the van slightly. The vehicle lurched out of the parking space, throwing the two of them together.

"Where do you think they're taking us?"

"I guess to meet the big boss, Zogaj, the one I was telling you about. The Albanians control all the prostitution in Soho."

They swayed together, and she tried to imagine the route they were taking. They turned right onto Fulham Palace Road and left at the roundabout, so they must be heading east towards the West End. They turned right, then left, and then seemingly turned in on themselves, so she gave up trying after that.

They rode on. Metal dug into her back and she shifted position, trying to get comfortable. Strangely enough, she thought the opposite to Priest: she felt relieved that she'd been blindfolded. If they were blindfolding her, that meant they didn't want to be identified, and if they didn't want to be identified, it meant they didn't plan to kill them. At the same time, she knew she was grasping at straws.

"I wish I could put my arm around you," Priest said. "Tell you everything's going to be okay."

The van banged them about. "What you said about your wife being murdered. That was a lie as well."

"I'm divorced. I've got a three-year-old girl." The van bumped over something and Kate was thrown sideways.

"How did the divorce happen?"

"It was my fault. It's the usual story. I was spending more time at work and Kelly felt ignored. We moved to the country so she could be with her horse. One day I was on my way to catch the Eurostar when I realised I'd forgotten my passport. I had a sense something was wrong as I got to the house. Anyway, I let myself in and went upstairs, and that's when I heard them. She was having it off with a local taxi driver."

"I'm sorry. Are they still together?"

"No. He was married as well. He just fancied a bit on the side. She thought he was going to leave his wife, so now she's left with nothing. She's got our baby, Kristin, though."

"Couldn't you get back together? For the sake of your daughter?"

"You can't go backwards. I don't think even she understands why she did it."

They lapsed into silence, each of them alone with their thoughts. They must be in the West End by now, and Kate wondered what meeting Mr Big would be like. The van jostled them as it downshifted. She was desperate for sleep but her mind was churning – she kept asking herself, why me, why me? She saw the knife pressing down on Charles Lazenby's cheek, the flesh turning white as his skin was about to break; her fingers trailing along the spiky cannabis fronds; and Phuong's cold and filthy bedroom. Oh, Paul, you should have told me you were up to your neck in it. Together we could have found a way out.

Eventually Kate whispered, "What makes you think they're taking Phuong up north?"

"It's what they usually do if the police know who they are. Give her a new name. I told the hospital who she was, so she's in the system. That's one of our frustrations. There's not much cooperation between regions."

Kate quietened her voice even more. "They're going to be angry when they open up the computer. I deleted the wedding folder. There's nothing there."

"You did what?"

"Don't worry. I saved the photo we were looking at. The one with the names and addresses. It's on the phone memory card. I need you to get it out for me. In case they search us. We need to keep it somewhere safer."

"Where is it now?"

"In the back of my jeans pocket. I want you to put it down my knickers."

"If they find it, then we're both dead. They'll torture me to find out what I know and then they'll get rid of us. Without the data, at least we can pretend to know nothing. The data's incriminating. We need to keep it hidden."

"First you need to unbutton my jeans."

Kate shifted up and Priest's fingers struggled with her top metal button. He tugged the zipper down. Next she turned around and felt his fingers delicately lifting out the memory card. Careful, don't drop it. They were both dead if it fell on the floor. Kate tried turning around so Priest could slip it into her underwear, but it was too difficult.

"Here. It'll be easier if we both stand up."

They stood swaying as Priest tried to find her unbuttoned trousers. This was like a perverse game of pin the tail on the donkey, but there was nothing erotic about it. Kate guided him towards her knickers and felt his fingers brush her pubic hair. The memory card was now tucked safely inside her panties. The thought occurred to Kate that they might want to strip search her, and she pictured herself trembling, trying to cover herself in her modesty. After that...

Suddenly the van braked sharply and they were both thrown forward. Kate righted herself and she and Priest sat down quickly before the van doors opened. Flashback. Being caught with a boy in the hot, damp interior of a bike shed. Pressing her back against a dank, cobwebby wall as a teacher peered in. She bent over to cover her undone jeans. Would they notice? The Albanians were coming for them, climbing into the back of the van, and she wondered where they'd brought them to – an abattoir with hanging carcasses, or a strip club with cavorting dancers, where Mr Big waited in a camel coat? One of the men hauled her up and she stood uncertainly, wondering what was happening now. She felt Teardrop's knife hacking through the knotted cord binding her wrists.

Her pillowcase was pulled off and she breathed in the sharp night air. Beyond the open van doors was a dark cobbled side street that she recognised immediately. This was the street where Paul had his office.

One of the thugs led her out while the other climbed up. "I don't understand," Kate began. Please, God, somebody notice us. This was a London street that hundreds of people walked down every day. "Open the door," Teardrop said. Now she understood why he had untied her: he needed to get into the building. Her wrists felt sore from the cord, and she shook them to try to get the blood flowing. Furtively, she zipped her jeans back up, trying to dawdle. The longer they spent out on the street, the better their chance of being spotted. How many CCTV cameras were there in London? Her numb fingers tapped the door entry code, and the street entrance unlocked softly.

Paul's company was on the third floor. Teardrop unzipped the back pack he was wearing and handed Kate her lanyard with her keys on it. He nodded for her to unlock the office door.

The tell-tale warning beeps sounded, and Kate's heart lifted for a moment until Teardrop quickly unarmed the alarm. She didn't have time to question how he knew the disarming code because he roughly shoved her forward. Now she knew where they were going: the server farm: one petabyte of data, every Google search, financial record and credit card transaction of thousands of people. A digital brain that remembered everything you had ever said or done. A skein of other people's memories. Nothing was ever forgotten. Paul once told her that the data it contained was worth millions if it was sold on the market, to advertising companies, credit rating agencies, direct mail outfits.

The server farm had been her husband's pride and joy. He had even helped design it. Paul had specified that the servers be protected by the highest security and cooled by the latest green technology. "Really, it's just about moving air around," he had told her. Instead of rattly air-conditioning units bolted onto the side of the building, his data farm sucked in air and scrubbed it through a series of filters. "Just like a hospital operating theatre," he had said, beaming.

Whatever was on the other side of the bulletproof window lay in pitch black, except for tiny LEDs like dozens of cat's eyes. The lanyard also held Kate's swipe card, and she yanked it through the reader. Next, she placed her finger inside the fingerprint scanner. The light turned green once she had been positively identified, and the door clicked open.

The lights came on the moment they stepped into the room. It was so clean. Paul was right – it was like being in a hospital. The only sound was the shrieking hum of the servers. "So here we are," Kate said. "What are you going to do?"

Teardrop slung off his backpack and laid it on the ground. Unzipping it, he pulled out an ugly brown-paper brick slapped together with a crude metal box. There was a clock face embedded in the grey steel and a simple on/off switch. It looked so much like a bomb that he might as well have brought out a cannonball with a fuse sticking out of it. Kate wanted to laugh, the way you do at a funeral. Unfolding his clasp knife, Teardrop secured the bomb to the wall using duct tape. He flicked the switch. So he was planning to destroy the evidence – all that money laundering they'd forced Paul into, what and how much was paid to whom – incinerated the moment the timer counted down to zero.

"Come, we go now."

"I'm not going anywhere."

Kate sat down and crossed her legs. Her voice sounded close to normal, but when she looked down, her hands were shaking.

"Are you fucking crazy? We leave now."

"Why should I? You've taken my husband from me, the man I wanted to spend the rest of my life with. You've destroyed everything we worked for. What is there left for me?"

"Shut up. I fucking kill you." He was an electric wire of hate, always twitching, moving. He just couldn't keep still.

"Are you the one who killed my husband? Was it you who threw him off the balcony?"

"Unlock door or I swear I cut your finger off."

"It doesn't work that way. The finger has to have blood in

it. It's called vein recognition ID. My husband designed it that way."

Kate tried to look smug. She was enjoying this new, contrary role. Instead, Teardrop grabbed her wrists and pulled her up. She resisted, her Converse trainers slipping and sliding on the floor. They tussled as the thug edged her hand towards the fingerprint reader. He grabbed her little finger and started bending it backwards. The pain was excruciating. Any moment her little finger would snap. "Okay, okay," Kate whimpered, letting her index finger be guided into the Perspex hood.

Less than three minutes later they were back in the van, and the thugs left her pillowcase off this time. The four of them sat opposite each other. Priest and Phuong still had their hoods on, while the baby-faced thug kept an eye on Kate.

"They've planted a bomb in Paul's office. They're going to blow up the server room," she said.

"Destroying the evidence," Priest said.

"Whatever they were using looked professional. It wasn't a bag of flour in a rucksack."

"I told you, a lot of these gangs trade dope for weapons. They're easier to sell. Extremists either use them for bank jobs or they end up in the Middle East. It's a dirty business."

The little thug sat there with a faint smile on his lips; Kate wasn't sure how much he understood of what they were saying. The thought occurred to her that everything they had done had been caught on CCTV, and that Teardrop hadn't cared about being spotted. Wherever they were going, she realised, they weren't coming back.

They must have been in the van for another hour before they stopped again. The back doors opened and Teardrop climbed up. He snatched the pillowcase off Priest's head, pulled him to his feet and dragged him outside, down onto the asphalt. At least he could see where he was going now. The little one jerked his head, indicating that Kate should follow him.

Her legs felt stiff as she jumped down, looking all around her. They were in a reservoir car park. There were dinghies moored beside a clubhouse, and some of the bigger boats were covered up for winter. The tocking of rigging against their aluminium masts sounded like wind chimes.

Kate realised she knew the place. She and Paul had come cycling here one Saturday afternoon, renting bikes from the closed hut in the distance. It was somewhere off the M25 heading towards Kent, she knew that. The reservoir was on the other side of the hillock of stones they were facing – she remembered the uppermost spire of a church rising from the middle of the water. They'd had to flood a village to build the reservoir, and people said you could still hear the dreamy tolling of the church bell beneath the water. Teardrop dragged Priest up to the water's edge and forced him to kneel. He put the gun to Priest's head. Kate's mouth went dry with fear.

"Who fuck are you?" he said.

"I told you. I'm just a neighbour."

"You fucking lie to me."

He grabbed the back of Priest's head and pushed him down. Kate couldn't see properly, but she knew the Albanian was drowning him. "Who the fuck are you?" Teardrop must have pulled Priest up again because she could hear him coughing. She had a hollowing sense of what they were going to do to them: they would shoot Priest and haul his body into one of those boats before tipping him overboard. Nobody would find him in the reservoir. Teardrop shouted at Priest again and pushed his head back down. This time he held him under for longer.

"Stop. STOP," she heard herself shouting. "He's with the police."

Teardrop reacted as if he'd just been scolded. Priest was coughing and retching on his haunches as Teardrop slid back down the stones.

"What you say?"

"He's a policeman. He works for Europol. They know all about you."

"Fuck."

Teardrop ran his hand over the iron filings of his hair. Then he raced back up the stones and asked Priest if this was true. Whatever Priest said was lost in the wind. Teardrop was clearly agitated and he started pacing, making another call on his mobile phone. He gesticulated and spoke in Albanian. He reminded Kate of a caged animal, and in a funny way, this unexpected turn of events made him even more dangerous. Kate glanced at his accomplice with his wraparound sunglasses: in profile he looked like Mr Punch. No emotion there. A moony psychopath, the sort who when he was a child took a magnifying glass to insects to watch them burn.

Priest was hauled to his feet again and pushed down the hill. "Have you got a towel?" Priest coughed as Teardrop shoved him forward. The top half of his body was completely wet through and Kate thought she saw blood running down the side of his face.

The Albanians herded them back into the van, except this time both their pillowcases were left on the floor. Phuong was still sitting there with a pillowcase over her head. Both of them shuffled onto the wooden shelf, huddling for warmth, as Mr Punch sat down opposite with the gun resting on his thigh. The doors slammed. Mr Punch leaned across and touched Kate's cheek. "So soft," he said. Then he sat back and giggled.

Thursday

CHAPTER TWENTY FIVE

THE STINK OF PETROL in the back of the van was nauseating. "So where is Zogaj?" Priest asked. Mr Punch just shook his head. Kate couldn't decide whether he was simple or he just didn't understand English. "Ooh, Zogaj," Priest mimicked, pretending to shiver. Still no reaction.

"I don't think he speaks English," Kate said. "The man they're taking us to. What do you know about him?"

Priest lowered his voice. "Not much. He blipped on our radar when a nasty turf war broke out between gangsters in Tirana. They were fighting over who ran illegal file-sharing sites. They use them as a way to get credit card details. A few years ago, a rival gang was herded into a garage and shotgunned to death, an Albanian version of the St Valentine's Day Massacre.

"They say the Greeks were poets and the Albanians were pirates. Zogaj's family started out smuggling booze over the mountains, then graduated to selling arms to the Kosovans during the war. The Albanians and the Kosovans are really the same people. When the war ended, they began selling marijuana to the Italian Mafia in exchange for weapons. The weapons they sell on to Isis and other terrorist groups: Al-Qaeda, Al-Shabaab, they don't care.

"Albanian police are terrified of him. They sent an agent under cover to infiltrate his gang. Zogaj knew there was a mole, he just didn't know who. So he invited three of his men to his castle. According to an eyewitness, Zogaj moved down the line, hitting each of them in the back of the head with a baseball bat until one of them confessed. Our man was so terrified, he told the truth. Zogaj shot him, buried him, dug him back up again and then dissolved him in acid." He grimaced. "Sorry, you did ask."

Kate imagined the terrified policeman screwing his face tight to stop the sleet of bone and blood and watery stuff from seeping into his mouth, then opening his eyes, only to realise he was next.

"But two of them were innocent."

"They were just collateral damage."

"Jesus." Kate paused. "John, I'm really frightened."

"It's going to be all right. Look, he's not daft. He doesn't want a copper's blood on his hands. They only kill each other. And we've got a bargaining chip." He looked meaningfully down at her crotch, where she could feel the memory card. He glanced at Mr Punch, who was still smiling as they swayed along.

The cold made it difficult to think straight, and it was all too much to process. Despite herself, Kate could feel her eyelids growing heavy. By now it must have been three or four o'clock in the morning, and her brain was crying out for rest. She tried getting comfortable and leaned against Priest before closing her eyes.

The van doors banged open, and beyond them she could see the grey lunar dawn as the landscape revealed itself. She must have fallen asleep, just for a moment. Teardrop climbed up into the van, and through the open doors Kate could see a car transporter parked up alongside them. They were in a petrol station she recognised as being on the M25. The Albanian picked the dirty pillowcases up off the floor and turned to them. "Not again," said Priest. Teardrop pulled the case over Kate's head and the world went dark.

She could hear Priest shuffle towards the back of the van and then jump down. Hands got hold of Kate and lifted her up, guiding her towards what she figured were the van doors. "Step here," said Teardrop. Her trainer felt for the lip of the van and she jumped down. Hands released her and Teardrop said, "You. Come." Priest's words about escaping if she ever got the chance came back to her. Here she was, standing in a petrol station forecourt with a pillowcase over her head. If she ran, somebody would help her, somebody would see what was going on. There wouldn't be another chance.

Kate started running, not knowing where she was going, terrified that she was about to brain herself on something: a petrol pump or a parked car. She called it running, but really it was just a lurching stagger. The ground was rising now, and she guessed she was scaling an embankment. Her breath felt hot and ragged inside the pillowcase. There was shouting in Albanian behind her. She tried screaming for the first time, but it came out feebly. "Please help. Help. HELP." She sensed the men coming up fast. The ground was falling now, and she reckoned she was stumbling down onto the hard shoulder. A lorry buffeted past and the ground shook. Surely somebody would stop once they saw this handcuffed woman with a pillowcase over her head? Kate began screaming until she thought her lungs would bleed. A car horn blared and she felt an articulated lorry slam past, vibrating the air. "My God, I could have been killed," she thought. She was running blindfold across three lanes of motorway. Any moment another car would hit her. Why wasn't anybody stopping? Couldn't they see what was happening?

Suddenly she felt hands take hold of her. Thank God she was safe.

"You fucking crazy. I no hurt you," Teardrop hissed. He smelled rank, even through the pillowcase. Kate recoiled and began struggling, but the gangster's arms were around her chest, half-lifting, half-dragging her back the way they had come. He pulled the pillowcase off, and she really kicked this time. She couldn't believe nobody was stopping – a woman was being kidnapped, disappearing out of the world, and no-one was lifting a finger. Everything seemed to be happening in super slow motion. Kate was yelling and fighting as the Albanian dragged her up the embankment. Suddenly, though, she had nothing left to give. She felt drained. Her body dropped, and Teardrop dragged her back down the hill towards the car transporter. Mr Punch and another man, who she guessed was the driver, were waiting. He was a big, bald-headed guy who looked like a bodybuilder who had let himself go. The bottommost car boot was open, and Kate knew what they were going to do. "Wait," she said as Mr Punch grabbed her trouser legs and all three of them lifted her up. She glimpsed bare trees and the sky cartwheeling as they threw her into the boot. Priest was already lying there, and she landed heavily on top of him. Priest struggled and tried to tell her something but his mouth was taped up. "Please," she tried again as Teardrop reached down and slapped duct tape across her mouth. The last thing she saw was the car boot slamming down.

Darkness. The two of them were finally alone.

CHAPTER TWENTY SIX

KATE'S CHEEK WAS JAMMED against the felt of the car boot. She and Priest lay awkwardly against each other, panting as they got their breath back. Priest shifted his legs so Kate could get comfortable. The tape was suffocating, and Kate panicked as she tried to get air into her lungs. Muffled Albanian voices outside.

Kate felt uncontrollable fear: she wasn't ready for dying, there was still so much of life that she wanted to live. Pressure built on the bridge of her nose and she knew she was about to cry. They would kill her, and there was nothing she could do to stop them. She wished she could reach out and hold Priest's hand, anything for the reassuring touch of another human being. Instead, they were trussed like animals for slaughter. Paul, I miss you so much. She thought about all the people she would never get a chance to say goodbye to, imagining Estelle's happy snort of laughter as she recounted her latest adventure, Colin's wry smile as he came towards her in his electric wheelchair. She had a vision of her mother standing over her freshly dug grave before she finally turned away.

Kate wasn't ready to say goodbye. Was Priest thinking

the same thing? That he would never see his ex-wife or daughter again? You've got to stop thinking like this, Kate told herself, you can't just give in.

The engine started up and they lurched forward.

Teardrop said his Big Boss, this Zogaj, wanted to see them. If they were on the M25, she guessed they were on their way to Dover, and that could only mean they were heading back to Albania. "And what shall we do in Illyria?" A line of Shakespeare came back to her. She had played Viola in a wooden school production of Twelfth Night. Illyria was the old name for Albania. Now she dreaded the answer. The police would never find them. They would be tortured and killed, their bodies dumped somewhere and quickly forgotten. "Kate Julia," she told herself. "You have got to get a grip."

Her body was starting to cramp, too, as they tried to get comfortable. If only they could speak and comfort each other, that would be something. Kate thought she was starting to hallucinate as she lay there in the darkness. Mad, scary images piled on top of one another as she imagined being buried alive in an open coffin, while dirt took ages to reach her as it fell slowly from above. Finally it covered her face.

The engine roar kept her tethered to reality, though. Their only chance to escape would be when they stopped at border control: they could attract attention if they made enough noise. A customs officer or a policeman might ask the driver to open the boot. It was the only thing she could think of. After that they would quietly disappear into Eastern Europe.

After what felt like hours, the lorry downshifted and they began to slow. The transporter veered to the left, and Kate guessed they must be turning off for Dover. The urge to pee was also building. Oh, God, please not now. She couldn't bear the thought of humiliating herself like this. The gears kept shifting down and finally the air brakes shuddered as they came to a stop.

Her ears strained in the velvety blackness. Sure enough, she heard voices. Kate started banging on the floor with her feet. This must be passport control. She tried shouting, but the effort was useless. Instead, she redoubled her efforts with the one bit of body she could move. Priest, cottoning on to what she was up to, shifted around and he, too, started thumping. Kate stopped and listened. Her eyes were watering in her overwhelming desire to pee, but the voices seemed to be moving away. The lorry started up again, reverberating. So that was it, the idea of escape was useless. She moved away from Priest as much as she could and finally allowed self-pity to take hold. She started reciting the Lord's Prayer, sorry for all the things she'd got wrong in her life – "Our Father, who art in heaven" – only she couldn't remember what came next.

The transporter stopped again, and this time the engine

was switched off. Cramp was setting in, and Kate and Priest shifted around. It was both cold and claustrophobic. Kate thought she could hear the plangent bark of seagulls, which meant they must be at the ferry terminal. The gangsters would load them onto the ferry and they would roll off at the other end, disappearing into the continent, never to be heard of again. Goodbye, everyone.

A gnawing hunger was building, and she tried to remember the last time she'd eaten, pushing food around her plate in Priest's flat. It felt like a lifetime ago. Her voracious hunger took hold as she lay there with Priest's knees digging into her. Finally they were on the move again, up a ramp and into what she guessed was a ferry hold. She could hear other lorries. The engine switched off. The only way she could take her mind off food – the idea of gorging herself on salty peanuts, something she normally never ate – was by trying to go to sleep.

Psychedelic freak-show images of neon cathedrals and Teardrop's looming clown face crowded her mind. She wanted to let go and felt herself falling. Teardrop's spinning face was the last thing she remembered before she slept.

Her head banged against the metal boot, and she realised they were on the move again. Kate felt the transporter roll off the ferry. She wasn't ready to wake up yet. How long had she been asleep? A minute? An hour? Exhaustion saturated her bones like cancer. The rocking continued and she opened her eyes, dimly able to see in front of her. Light must be coming in from somewhere, because it wasn't totally dark. She shifted around. Priest, who was lying with his back to Kate, found her hands and gave them a squeeze. Hello to you, too. The transporter thumped over something, and she wondered how many hours of this there were to go. Her hunger pangs had returned with a vengeance; it felt as if they'd spent eons already in the boot.

Finally the transporter stopped again – she heard the shudder of air brakes – and she felt the engine idling before it died with a final shake. They must have arrived. Kate shrank at the prospect of what was going to happen. Voices. The boot popped open with a hydraulic suck, and it took a moment for her eyes to adjust to the view: Teardrop and Mr Punch silhouetted with a grey porridge sky behind them. When Teardrop pulled off the duct tape, she thought he was taking her lips with it. My God, that hurt. As the men pushed her onto the ground, she was too much in shock to speak. Her legs felt wobbly as Teardrop cut the ties, his clasp knife yanking upwards under the nylon cord.

It was early morning. They were parked in a forest and the air felt cold and wet, as if a heavy fog had just lifted. Every part of her body hurt. What are we doing here, she thought, as she watched a magpie fly up into the trees. One for sorrow. Priest, too, was hauled out of the boot, and the

Albanians cut his hands free as well. "You okay?" he said hoarsely. Kate nodded. They had both become unused to speaking.

Phuong, too, was being manhandled out of a boot further up the line. So they were taking her back to Albania as well, now she had become too hot for them in England. "Where are we?" Kate asked. Mr Punch said nothing but held out a cardboard sandwich box and a bottle of water. Kate tore into the sandwich, wolfing it down as her stomach groaned with pleasure. The processed cheese tasted like the finest fillet steak. Her tongue ran the pulpy mess around her gums, trying to extract as much goodness as possible. Priest was gobbling his sandwich as well. Only when she uncapped the bottle did she realise how thirsty she was – Kate drained the water in three or four long glugs.

"Why are we here?" she gasped, wiping her mouth. "Long way yet," said Teardrop. He really did have the saddest face, as if he was crying inside. Mr Punch grinned and jerked his head towards the boot. "No, you can't put me back in there," she said. Seeing that she wasn't going to go quietly, the men picked Kate up and bundled her back into the car. Her scream ripped the early morning air. But it was useless: there was nobody around to hear her. This time they were being separated. Priest was led off to another car stacked on the transporter. Phuong was also being herded onto the metal gangway. "Remember your promise," she heard him say as the boot slammed down.

The engine started up again and she lay there in the dark trembling and frightened, trying to imagine their route. She saw it as one of those animated lines working its way across a map of Europe: eight hours to Italy, and then another eight to Croatia, before dropping down the Adriatic coast to Albania.

They were definitely on the motorway now. The transporter rattled as they went over a rough piece of road. Claustrophobia started to build again. As she lay there in the dark, lurid images crowded her thoughts. She tried thinking about something else, but it was impossible. The moment she recalled a happy time with Paul, unnameable dread would seep into her heart. It was like she was looking over the edge hundreds of feet below.

Finally the van stopped. Kate's mind momentarily jumped with hope before another kind of panic set in – she was impatient to be out. She couldn't bear to be kept waiting.

It was dark outside, so they must have been travelling all day, although she had no idea if it was evening or morning. They were in a lorry park, and a motorway service station was lit up in the distance. How funny to think that all around her everyday life was still going on. Teardrop helped her out onto the ramp. "Please. I am sick," she began. There was no sensation in her arms and legs, and she felt feverish. The red tip of Teardrop's cigarette glowed in the dark. Mr Punch lifted his sweater to show off a handgun jammed into his waistband. "Period," she continued, miming rubbing her stomach and inserting a tampon. Teardrop said something in Albanian and Mr Punch stepped forward and gripped her wrist, pulling her towards the service station. She thought she saw his lip curl in distaste beneath the acid-orange street lamp. His body emitted a fishy odour. Teardrop just stood there smoking his cigarette. Kate tried memorising the transporter licence plate as Mr Punch pulled her away. Even at night he wore his bug sunglasses. It had begun to snow, and Kate thought about her mother and Christmas as they approached the motorway services entrance. Her mother was expecting her this weekend. Mummy would know something was wrong when she didn't answer her phone, and the alarm would be raised. Stop fooling yourself, Kate thought grimly. Nobody would come.

Inside, carols played: the cosy melancholy of Silent Night parped over the loudspeakers. People milled around her, going about their business, oblivious to the fact that she was being taken against her will. Kate thought about screaming and making a run for it but, as if he could read her mind, Mr Punch tightened his grip. They veered towards a shop selling newspapers, magazines and confectionery. Tampons and other loosely medical products were in a middle aisle. Kate glared at Mr Punch and shook her hand free, squatting down in front of the mouthwash and aspirin. She picked up a box of tampons while deftly slipping a marker pen into her leather jacket.

There was an ugly black bulb in the ceiling that she guessed was the CCTV camera, and she deliberately stood up slowly, letting herself be seen. Somebody would recognise her, she thought wildly. Mr Punch handed Kate a ten euro note and stood to one side as she approached the counter. There was a box on the counter selling loose balloons, and she picked up a couple of those as well. People were queuing behind her. "Please," she whispered, sliding the money across. "You must help me." "Non capisco," said the cashier flatly. "Call the police," Kate persevered. The queue was becoming restive and somebody said something. Mr Punch appeared between people's heads.

Back in the service station atrium she pulled Mr Punch towards the ladies toilet. Reluctantly he released her when she made it clear she needed to go inside.

Once through the turnstile, Kate saw a couple of women standing in front of mirrors adjusting their hair. There was the sharp, sour smell of urine. Her eyes scanned the room, looking for a way out. Just cubicles and tiled walls. Nothing. "Does anybody here speak English?" Kate called out. The women regarded her before continuing their conversation in Italian. Panicked, she knew she was running out of time. She locked the toilet cubicle and looked for a cistern to hide the memory card inside. More floor-to-ceiling tiled walls. She was afraid of the way Mr Punch looked at her and suspected he would enjoy hurting her. If the men found the memory card, their one bargaining chip would be gone. If she hid it here, she could promise to bring them to it, at least buying her and Priest some more time.

Except there was nowhere to hide the card.

Fine, she would do it this way. Unbuttoning her jeans and pulling down her knickers, she worked the balloon with her fingers. It was uncomfortable and hard going but finally she got there.

Uncapping the stolen pen, Kate wrote in large letters on the wall: "Kate Julia kidnapped. 4.12.15. Licence TR 1284 AA Call police." She was just looping the final "e" when the toilet stall door smashed open and Mr Punch grabbed hold of her, dragging Kate out. She let out an almighty scream, and she lashed out and kicked with everything she had. Mr Punch was dragging her towards the turnstile as she twisted and turned. He was not going to take her. She bit down on his forearm and tasted blood. Mr Punch grunted and backhanded Kate with his free arm, and she dimly recognised something spongy in her nose being thumped. First she was standing up and now she was sprawled on her back. She really was seeing stars. Mr Punch pulled Kate up again and this time she allowed herself to be manhandled, sniffing hard to keep blood out of her mouth.

Back outside they rejoined the shoppers and piped music. Kate was too dazed to do anything this time. It all felt so unreal. Why wasn't anybody doing anything – couldn't they see what was happening? Mr Punch dragged Kate through the sliding doors into the cold and towards the lorry park.

The car boot slammed with a definitive thunk.

The pungent fumes from the diesel made the atmosphere suffocating. Ohmygodpleaseletmeoutofhere. The darkness was pressing down. She could visualise herself far off, sitting in a corner with her arms over her head, and she felt she was slipping into madness.

She was buried alive again back inside the coffin. She could feel its silk walls as she pushed against the lid. She was going to get out of this, they were not going to kill her. The coffin became a boat dropped into the water as it headed downstream, gathering momentum as it approached the waterfall, before almost thoughtfully going over the edge, and there was a horrible weightless moment, except that she was now in deep space, far away from Earth, receding into darkness. Her body was floating further and further away. Silence. Just the sound of her panicked breathing. Hello, can you hear me? Please, somebody help me. Is anybody out there?

CHAPTER TWENTY SEVEN

THERE WAS A BLACK 4X4 parked up ahead. They were in a conifer forest somewhere. It was early morning and so foggy that it was as if they were sitting inside a cloud that had covered the mountainside. There was the sound of running water and, high up in the trees, the cawing of crows. Dank. A man she hadn't seen before got out of the 4x4 – this one was a big guy who looked as if he was all solidly built muscle – and walked towards Teardrop. He had a widow's peak and simian features. Some kind of handover was going on. Had they been ransomed and passed on to another group? Was this why they had stopped on this godforsaken road, so they could be sold on to another gang? Mr Punch grinned as if he alone was the recipient of a vastly amusing private joke. Priest looked shaken as they stood there in the lunar early dawn. This was the first time he'd been freed from the car boot, and, unused to the light, he kept blinking. Kate noticed he was unsteady on his feet again. They must have really worked him over. Teardrop and the big man stood talking, embraced and walked in opposite directions. The bald Albanian thug climbed up into the transporter cab and switched on the engine. So they were swapping vehicles. Mr Punch pushed

Kate's shoulder and she thought again about what Priest had said about trying to escape if she got the chance. The forest continued down the hill on their left. Her guts were twisting with anxiety, but she knew it was now or never. "RUN," she yelled, suddenly breaking free.

Kate plunged down the wet, mossy bank, almost losing control, and ran into the trees. Her legs were going so fast, she thought they would fall off. Priest had broken free, too. Out of the corner of her eye she could see Mr Punch scrambling down the bank while Teardrop got into the 4x4. "This way," Kate shouted. She could hit her head on a tree, or a branch might whip her in the face at any moment. Twigs and leaves crunched underfoot. If anything, the fog was getting thicker the deeper they ran. All she was conscious of was heart-clutching fear. Panic choked her as she expected the crack of Mr Punch's automatic handgun behind her, then everything turning white hot inside her head.

There was a clearing and, surreally, a banana-yellow boat stranded in the middle of it. What was a dinghy doing in a forest? Priest and Kate converged on it and hid round the back, landing heavily. The fibreglass hull was dirty and mouldy, but at least it offered protection. "You okay?" Priest panted. They crouched down, watching for Mr Punch to come through the trees. Kate nodded, too winded to speak. She wanted to vomit and shit herself at the same time. Cautiously she scanned the tree line for Mr Punch, aware that she could get her head blown off at any moment. Nobody there.

"We'll find something if we keep going downhill," Priest whispered, hauling himself up. Kate nodded. Dense fog obliterated the trees further down and they set off again, at a jog this time. The fog was clammy and she reached for Priest's hand. Their progress slowed as they sidestepped down the hill. The fog dissolved everything, and she could barely see in front of her. Weird tree shapes loomed out of the void, and Kate felt as if they had crossed into the underworld, the place where everything was dead. It was unearthly quiet.

A cable car station loomed out of the fog, as if somebody had breathed on glass.

It lay on the other side of a road, and a rumble told them it was still working. Thank God. They ran across the road and through an empty children's playground. The swings and roundabout looked forlorn with no one playing on them. This must be some kind of out-of-season tourist attraction, Kate thought. Running past a climbing frame, she looked over her shoulder and glimpsed Mr Punch scrambling down the hill they had just left. Priest grabbed her hand and they ran onto the platform, where a man sat in a glass booth. There was no turnstile, so presumably you paid at the other end. A cable car came barrelling towards them and abruptly slowed to a walking pace as the doors slid open. They both landed on its benches, terrified that Mr

Punch was about to appear. The doors took forever to slide shut. Sure enough, the second thug ran into the station as their cable car rattled over a grid and they were launched into space.

Kate was too winded to speak, and she just sat there with her head between her knees. Priest was looking back at the cable car following theirs. Their cabin shook as they went over a pylon. Kate's ears popped because they were so high up.

"What now?" Kate managed to say.

"We go to the police. Maybe we can flag a car down or something."

"What if the other one's waiting for us? The one with the tattoo"

"Somebody at the bottom will help us."

"I tried to escape in a motorway services. They let me use the toilet. I scrawled my name and the licence plate on a wall. Somebody must know we're alive."

"Do you still have the memory card?"

"Yes, I'm sitting on it." The memory card was always there, a not entirely uncomfortable presence. It made her feel full.

Priest did his best to smile, glancing over her shoulder at the next cable car following them inexorably down the mountain.

"He's following us, isn't he?" she said.

"We'll make a run for it at the bottom."

"There's a policeman in Tirana, the one I was telling you about. His name's Poda. He was investigating Paul's death."

"We'll go to him, then."

"Your friends at Europol, can't they help us?"

"All I need is a phone. There's a Europol field agent in Rome who could get us out."

Kate turned and saw the hazy sprawl of Tirana through the graffiti-ed Plexiglas. Their cabin rattled as they went over another pylon. Hundreds of feet below you could hear mooing from a toy-like farm. Kate waggled her jaw from side to side to get rid of the pressure.

Eventually she said, "John, I don't think I can do this."

"You just need to hold on. It's nearly over. Run like hell when we get to the bottom. We'll only have a few seconds."

"What if they're waiting for us?"

Priest had no answer for that. They went over another hill and the bottom cable car station hove into view for the first time. Priest stood up, prepared for a quick getaway. "Ready?" he asked. Kate nodded, slightly deaf with fear. Their cabin slowed abruptly and rocked as it came in to land. The cabin joined the stately procession and the doors slid open. Priest pulled Kate out and they ran towards the turnstile. Priest cleared it easily, while Kate managed as best she could with Priest helping her over. The attendant in the glass booth shouted. She glanced back at Mr Punch's cabin, whose doors were opening.

Outside there was no black 4x4, thank God. Instead, there was a sole taxi driver reading a newspaper. He looked alarmed as Priest tore the door open and they both jumped in. "Police," he said. "Pronto." The taxi driver folded his newspaper achingly slowly as Mr Punch skidded out of the swing doors. "Pronto," Priest repeated, banging the back of the driver's headrest. The driver reversed, the three-dimensional cross covered with Muslim names of God swinging wildly from his rear-view mirror. Kate caught sight of Mr Punch clutching his head as if he couldn't believe what had just happened.

Priest exhaled deeply, releasing a long sigh. Kate let out a happy bark of laughter. They had done it, they had finally got away. She wanted to laugh and cry; she had never felt so grateful to be alive. Priest put his arm round her and he, too, started laughing – the relief was just so overwhelming. It was all over. They were on their way to the police and to freedom.

"My God, I can't believe it. We're free," she said.

"Those bastards are gonna pay. We're going to put them away for years."

"We need to tell the police about Phuong as well."

"Don't you worry, love. Those bastards are going away for a long time."

"Will they know about Zogaj?"

"Oh, they know about him all right. It's a question of whether they can get to him. These people are protected. They make big donations to politicians' election campaigns."

There was so much construction going on, great tower blocks with the inevitable meringue wedding dresses in the shop windows. The road, though, was in a terrible state. It was a rutted brown track with gravel thrown in where the potholes were too deep to drive over. Kate and Priest lurched from side to side as their taxi slowed to a crawl, trying to negotiate its way through. They both had the same unspoken fear, and Priest leaned forward and shook the driver's seat. The driver turned round and glared.

They joined a proper street with a wider road this time as they headed into the capital. There were restaurants and cafés here, although most of them were still closed this early. On their left was what looked like a truly magnificent Roman mansion with stucco columns guarding its entrance and a trio of heroic-looking statues on the roof, which also sprouted an incongruous array of television aerials. Kate looked round for a sign of the 4x4, but they seemed to have given the men the slip.

At that moment, a bomb seemed to go off in their car.

There was a blur of black metal and a horrible grinding noise as the Land Cruiser bore down on them. The street waltzed around. Kate glimpsed Teardrop staring at her with furious hatred through the windscreen.

When she opened her eyes in the sudden stillness, she saw that the taxi driver's airbag had exploded. He was trapped behind the steering wheel. His windscreen had cracked, and there was a smell of smoke and battery acid.

The driver's side of the car had concertinaed, and Kate realised that Priest's leg was trapped in the buckled metal. Priest was pushing her with his free arm, and she dimly understood that he wanted her to get out. The problem was that she had gone deaf: all she could hear was a monotone, as if somebody had tapped a tuning fork inside her head.

The taxi's black innards had spewed onto the road, and petrol was snaking along the tarmac. Kate noticed how beautiful its rainbow colours were. Everything felt so unreal. The tuning fork in her head persisted, and she turned away in slow motion towards the Roman villa. Kate winced with pain as she loped along the road. She had done something to her leg, and putting weight on it was like hammering a nail through a bone.

Limping up the steps past the Roman columns, she pushed the swing doors open. An old woman in a housecoat was mopping a tessellated corridor with a greasy institutional smell. The cleaner leaned on her mop and looked at Kate suspiciously with bright currant eyes. "Please. You must help me," Kate said. Her leg was throbbing like a pump.

The woman said nothing. Kate limped over the newly washed floor and pulled open the first set of double doors. The cleaner barked at her this time, but Kate didn't care. What she needed to do was get to somewhere safe. It was like one of those old horror movies where the monster keeps coming after you no matter how fast you run; she pictured the corridor canted at a crazy angle with Teardrop bearing down. He was unstoppable.

Kate pushed down on a safety bar and walked into pitch black. She was in some kind of antechamber. She felt for another set of doors and pushed her way into what appeared to be a vast room with cables underfoot. Her hand felt icy scaffolding as she edged along in the darkness. It was colder on this side, wherever she was. What on earth was this place, she wondered, her eyes adjusting to the dark. Kate ducked to avoid clouting herself on an even blacker shape and realised that it was a heavy abandoned television camera. This was a soundstage with what looked like the hull of a spaceship taking up most of the floor surface. A vast cyclorama lay at the back. Now she could dimly make out lights hanging from the ceiling as she trailed her hand along the spacecraft hull, using it as a guide. Her ears strained in the darkness. At least the temporary ear-ringing deafness had gone. There had to be a way out of this place and, sure enough, she spotted another set of double doors up ahead.

Her hand groped for an old-fashioned metal light switch

and a series of government-issue overhead lights rippled into life. This corridor felt older and narrower, with rooms running off it and a sharp, musty linseed smell she associated with Albania. It reeked of Soviet-era bureaucracy. Kate hobbled down the thin strip of carpet trying every other door, almost weeping with anxiety. All locked. A door banged somewhere and she froze. Teardrop was definitely coming after her, she could feel it. Panic clamped down on her iron-hard, squeezing the air out of her lungs, and would not let go. A low moan escaped her lips.

She had reached a dead end.

The final door leading outside was locked. There was definitely the sound of doors banging and somebody coming. It was only now that she noticed the glass tank on her left – it was so dirty she hadn't realised what it was at first: a metal tank used for shooting underwater scenes. The glass was greenish-black with algae, and she knew what she had to do.

Steeling herself, Kate clambered up the metal steps and gazed down into the cold darkness. Oh, God, please don't make me do this. She sat down quickly and began lowering herself into the black water. Everything in her protested as the water came up to her waist and then to her chest. She took a deep breath, closed her eyes, and willed herself under.

The cold was unbelievable, yet somehow she swallowed a scream. The doors opened and she saw Mr Punch stalk into the room, still wearing his sunglasses. She knew she had to keep completely still. Her lungs were starting to burn, and she didn't know how much longer she could hold her breath. As if he had sensed her, Mr Punch's head swung round and he put a hand up to the tank, peering through the glass. Instinctively, she shrank into the gloom. The pressure was building, and she knew she had only seconds to get more air into her lungs or drown. The Albanian's gargoyle face nuzzled the scummy window like some monstrous aquarium fish. Inwardly she was frantic – her lungs were really on fire now – but Mr Punch finally turned and disappeared into the misty wall.

Kate's head broke the surface and she grabbed a great lungful of air, as if she was being reborn. My God, she thought, another few seconds and she would have drowned, imagining the propulsive kick as her lungs filled with water and she sank to the bottom.

Grasping the icy rungs of the ladder, she hauled herself up as water streamed off her body. She couldn't get enough air into her lungs because she was coughing so hard. Goddamn you, breathe. She inhaled as much air as she could before coughing overwhelmed her. Kate clambered back down, water pooling around her onto the floor. She had to get out of these heavy wet clothes before she froze to death.

Her body was shaking as she dragged herself along the corridor, clothes sticking to her like a wet shroud. Frantically she tested every door until, as if by magic, one opened smoothly. Why hadn't she found it before? The smell was even mustier in here, wherever she was, as she groped for the light switch. The light came on and Kate could have cried with joy.

The room was full of old costumes, racks and racks of them jammed on metal clothes rails. There were dusty wicker baskets on the floor. Pulling at the cracked leather straps, Kate threw one open to find old curtains. Thank you, Jesus. She tore off her wet clothes and stood there, pink and trembling, drying herself with the stiff, dirty cloth. It was so cold she couldn't think straight. She must find something warm to get into, she thought, her teeth chattering. One rail was full of old army costumes, and she pulled off a jacket and a pair of woollen trousers in roughly her size. The trousers felt scratchy and the jacket was too big. Another rail was full of military greatcoats, and she lifted one off its hanger. There was nothing she could do about her wet Converse trainers, though, she thought, as pressure built up in her nose and a sneeze exploded.

Kate squelched back down the corridor, pausing before she pulled open the doors to the soundstage. Nothing. Taking a chance, she slopped back along the main corridor, cursing the day she had ever set foot in Albania. She had no money, no passport and only one person she could turn to, the detective inspector investigating Paul's death. All she felt was a hand-wringing despair. Where was Priest, and what had they done to him? Would she ever see him again? The one thing she knew was that she had to get to safety.

The cold was biting when she stepped outside. At this rate, her wet hair would freeze into an icy headdress. Through the railings she could see that the taxi had been moved to the side of the road and the taxi driver was gesticulating to bystanders. There was a mess of plastic and glass shards all over the road. No sign of the 4x4, though. Where were the traffic police? She could throw herself on their mercy, she told herself, but then she remembered what Poda had said about most of his colleagues being corrupt. No, he was the one she needed to see.

Kate was so preoccupied with figuring out what to do next that she didn't register the sound of the engine quickly enough. She glanced up at a convex mirror above the road crossing.

Teardrop's black 4x4 was following at a walking pace down the street.

CHAPTER TWENTY EIGHT

THE FUG OF THE CAFÉ felt warm and inviting, and all she wanted to do was stay there. She took in the smell of wet wool and bodies, and of steam blasting as the café owner refilled the tea urn. For a moment, Kate allowed herself to be swayed by the idea of warmth and comfort before reality kicked back in and she barged past customers, looking for somewhere to hide. Anywhere. They would be here any second.

There was only one space available in the crowded café, and Kate sat down heavily at the free table. She hid her face in her hands. "Please don't let them find me," she prayed. There was a commotion at the door, and Kate glanced up to see Mr Punch struggling with a fat, overcoated man trying to get out. Neither of them would budge. In another life it might have been comic, but all she felt was heart-stopping dread.

Kate sensed that the man opposite was staring at her, and she glanced at him. She was appalled to realise who it was: the bearded dishwasher from the hotel, the one she'd wrongly accused of breaking into their bedroom, even of having murdered Paul.

The dishwasher was sitting over a cup of black tea in an old overcoat. In that split second he must have seen the fear in her eyes, because he looked over his shoulder and then rose to push Kate under the table.

Crouched beneath the Formica, Kate was certain she could hear Mr Punch's oddly high voice – it was girlish and asthmatic, the kind you might hear speaking feebly at a seance about the astral plain and messages from the other side. She certainly recognised his work boots: they were just inches away from her face. Her heart was hammering though her chest. Ba-dunk. Ba-dunk. Ba-dunk. The boots stopped and Kate knew then that it was all over. She had been discovered. Time stood still. She dared not breathe until the boots eventually swivelled and walked off. Kate could feel her heart turning over like a straining, reluctant engine. Baaaaa-dunk, ba-dunk, ba-dunk, ba-dunk.

The moment the dishwasher touched her she thought she would jump out of her skin.

Struggling back up opposite him, Kate saw that Mr Punch had gone. Why would he give up his search so easily? He knew Kate was in there. Of course, they would be waiting outside.

"He gone now. You safe."

"Why did you do that?" She could hear the hysteria in her voice, a panicked kind of gulp.

"That man. I know him. He is pimp." He looked as if he

wanted to spit on the floor.

"Those men want to kill me. We must go to the police."

The dishwasher harrumphed, "The police. They no good. Is better you stay with me."

"Surely the police will help me. I'm a British citizen," she cried, which she knew sounded pathetic even as she said it.

"The police, they all crooks. Corrupt. They all kopil. So why those men want you?"

Kate lowered her voice. "My husband, the man who died. They were blackmailing him. He was going to go to the police. So they killed him."

"Your husband at hotel?"

"They pushed him off our balcony, these men."

"Have you told police this?"

"Not yet, no."

"The police. They make life bad for me. You tell police I had nothing to do with husband?"

"Of course. I was wrong. I'm sorry for what I did."

"You have money?"

Kate shook her head. Marooned in a country a thousand miles away from home with no money and no passport. "I'll go to the British Embassy. I was there just a few days ago. They'll remember me."

The dishwasher looked thoughtful. "Come, we go."

He stood up, and Kate realised that he wanted her to follow. The air was thick with steam and grease. The dishwasher said something to the café owner, who jerked his head for them to go out the back way.

Outside they stood in a dismal courtyard where the rubbish was kept. Around them were piled-up sagging dustbin bags, one of them torn and spewing vegetable discards, leftovers and egg shells. Chunky dog turds were strewn on flagstones. The dishwasher tested a rotten-looking door, which shook a little on opening.

Now they were walking down an alley away from the café, parallel to the main road. Kate's wet trainers slapped the tarmac, and her greatcoat was dragging her down.

"I don't even know your name," she said, breathing smoke.

"My name is András–" he pronounced the "s" as "sh" – "and I am from Hungary. Why do I come here? I come here because of girl, you know. I work all over the place, I work in London at Ritz Hotel, Dorchester Hotel, Claridge's Hotel – you know Claridge's Hotel? Very good hotel. Everybody know András. I like London very much. Nice girls, football, Kings Road. We have party in Kings Road with Charlie George. You know Charlie George? Arsenal football."

"Your English is excellent. How long were you in London?"

"I live in Norwood." He almost crooned the name of the

south London suburb. "You know Norwood?"

It was hard to imagine this dishevelled man living it up on the Kings Road with Seventies dolly birds and Jaguar e-types. "So why did you come to Albania?"

"I meet Albanian girl, I come here. Big, sexy mountain girl. This was in bad days with Hoxha. Everybody here inform on each other. One day they come and take me to prison. They say I am foreign spy. They beat me, torture me, pull out my fingernails. I know those bastards, Sigurimi, police, they all the same. We go to my place, you be safe."

Kate wondered if he was drunk. He certainly smelled of booze, even this early in the morning. They trudged back along the potholed road, and again she wondered why this man was helping her. She'd cost him his job. She remembered Poda saying the hotel was going to charge him with theft, even though he had nothing to do with Paul's death.

She felt she had to apologise again.

This time the dishwasher shrugged. "I get another job easy. I have lots of friends."

Soon they were climbing the stairs in his apartment block. There were the same cooking smells as before and everything was painted shit brown. Halfway up she rested her hand on the banister – she felt grey with pain and all of her hurt. "You okay?" András asked. Kate nodded and girded herself for the rest of the climb. What would they do to John Priest once they realised the laptop didn't contain the information they wanted? What the dishwasher said about torture crossed her mind. Priest had told her to get to Poda, to get to safety, and that the police would contact Europol. They would know what to do. And then this nightmare would finally be over.

András's bedsit was just as she'd remembered it: the faded rose wallpaper and the window looking out onto a brick wall; the two-ring cooker and thin pink bedspread. All of a sudden she felt overwhelmingly tired; she had to close her eyes and let everything go. Her brain felt clogged, unable to absorb anything more.

"You want drink? Skanderbeg?" András asked.

"Do you have anything to eat?"

András cut a piece of black bread and handed it to her with a slice of thin cheese. "Your girlfriend, is she here?" Kate asked, wolfing down the sandwich. She had never tasted anything so delicious.

"She at work. Hotel let her keep job. Why she keep job? She hard worker, she good girl. Drita take care of András." He reached into the wardrobe and pulled out what looked like a bottle of brandy. "Skanderbeg. National hero of Albania."

András poured himself a tumbler and looked at Kate as if she was a puzzle to be solved. If only she could close her eyes for a moment.

"Tell me about your husband."

Kate went through the whole story, revealing how Paul had effectively been the bookkeeper for this criminal gang. "This other man, the policeman, he was trying to protect me," she said in conclusion. "They still have him. They were taking us to their boss, a man called Zogaj."

András took a sip and shivered, although she wasn't sure if it was from the brandy or fear. "Zogaj," he said softly.

"You know Zogaj?"

"Everybody know Zogaj. Newspapers know Zogaj, TV know Zogaj. Still they do nothing. Why they do nothing? Because he pay off politicians." András tapped the table with his index finger for emphasis. "Zogaj pay for their election campaigns. He has big cannabis fields in the north, plenty money, plenty guns. The police are afraid of him. They say, 'Zogaj not so bad, Zogaj gives us euros.' I tell you, this Zogaj is like cancer ... he–" András couldn't find the word and mimed spreading outward "–one day he kill whole country."

"Can you get me to the British Embassy?"

András waved his arm grandly. "Sure, British Embassy. No problem."

Her leg was throbbing as she limped past the bed. She knew she had done something bad to it in the accident but was afraid to look.

András noticed her limping. "Show me," he said.

Kate sat on the bedspread and hitched up her army fatigues. Her left leg was bruised and swollen, and just thinking about it made her sweat. András prodded and she winced. He tutted and rattled about in a desk drawer for what looked like a bottle of painkillers. "Here, you take this. You rest and then we go British, okay? No police." Kate nodded gratefully and swallowed two orange-jacketed pills without water.

She unlaced her wet trainers and stretched out on the bed, still wearing the military coat. András sat at the table smoking, and she noticed how cigarettes had turned his beard yellow. He coughed and turned the glass in his hand, contemplating it. Ah, the reward of Morpheus, she thought, and she imagined her shoulders and back spreading out as they oozed into the mattress, the bliss of oblivion. She simply had no more capacity for thought. Kate closed her eyes as the pills took hold and felt herself tipping backward, as if she was falling off a high-diving board.

There was a knock at the door.

Instantly she was awake. András put his finger to his lips and crept up from the table, motioning for her to join him.

"Kush eshtë?" he asked.

"Policia. Hapeni"

András mouthed the word "police" before turning back to

the door. "Jam sëmur. Cfare doni?"

"Gruan Angleze. Ne e dime qe ajo eshte me ju. Ne duam ta cojme tek zyra qendrore.

"Ketu nuk ka asnjeri. Largohuni."

András shook his head and gestured for her to help him. He was standing beside the wardrobe, and he nodded for Kate to give him a hand shifting it. Quietly, ever so quietly, they slid the wardrobe along the wall. Her eyelids felt so heavy – if only she could shake these damn pills off. The armoire was heavier than she expected, but now she could see what András was doing: there was a hole behind it you could just about squeeze through. It must have been where he kept stolen property from hotel guests.

Whoever it was on the outside lost patience. There was a hefty kick on the bedsit door, which bulged for a moment. Another couple of kicks and they would burst through.

Kate forced herself through the crack while András heaved the wardrobe back into place. Now she was standing in about a shoulder's width of dusty pitch black with rubbish bags against her legs. The dust made it difficult to breathe. She fought rising panic and the feeling of being suffocated. The one thing she knew was that she had to hold still.

There were raised voices through the plasterwork. Kate strained to listen and could imagine Teardrop and Mr Punch pushing their way in. Shouting. András must have been telling them she wasn't there. Then silence. András let out a terrible scream and she pressed her ear against the plaster, trying to figure out what was going on. The wardrobe scraped along the floor and light flooded her tiny crawlspace.

They had found her.

Her heart dropped through her ribcage and fear pooled in her stomach. "You come out," Teardrop said calmly in English.

András was sitting on the bedspread with a nasty burn on his forehead. His eyes said, "I'm sorry", and she noticed the cooker ring was deep red. A smell of burnt flesh hung in the air and a tuft of hair was stuck to the ring.

Teardrop and Mr Punch looked at her almost admiringly. Mr Punch was holding the automatic he'd revealed in the car park. They were laughing at her. "You come with us now," Teardrop said. "No more funny games." András looked in despair. "It's okay," Kate said, touching his shoulder as she went past. Reluctantly she took a step towards the bedroom door. The three of them were about to leave when András stood up and said something. Whatever he said must have antagonised Mr Punch, who stepped forward cocking the handgun. The men started arguing. The next thing she knew, András had gone for the pistol. The two men were wrestling for it when suddenly the gun went off.

The gunshot was so close it seemed to explode inside her head.

András appeared to sink like a ship turning on end, sliding down second by second. A kind of red mist hung in the air. The dishwasher settled on his knees, gazing directly at Kate as if he was about to ask her a question. Then he toppled sideways, bending at the knees with his legs doubling beneath him.

Nobody said anything, and she remembered the sound reverberating for the longest time. They were all in shock. Then, as if reading her mind, Teardrop made a grab for Kate, but she was too quick for him. She pulled the door open and threw herself outside, screaming her head off as she pelted down the corridor. Her banshee yell followed her as she crashed through the first set of double doors, throwing herself downstairs. She cleared the first flight in a single jump, clattering down the rest of the stone steps. She sensed people coming out of their rooms. What the hell was going on? Who was making all this noise?

The only thing Kate knew was that she had to get out of there. Get out. GET OUT.

CHAPTER TWENTY NINE

SHOUTS ECHOED AROUND the stone stairwell as she cleared another flight of steps. All she could hear was the sound of her ragged breath. One more flight to go, except this time she landed badly and pain shot up her left side. Dazzling pain. Grunting with the effort, she half-ran, half-dragged herself towards the outside door, which seemed to recede the nearer she got to it.

Pulling the entrance open, she felt tepid winter sun on her face and nearly toppled down the steps in her hurry to get away. There were cars at the other end of the alleyway – surely one of them would stop and help – and she set off, dragging her bad leg down the street.

She had seen a man murdered in front of her.

The side street was in shade, but rush hour must have started because the main road was gridlocked, cars and lorries bumper to bumper waiting for traffic lights. The air was thick with diesel smoke. She ran up to the first driver and banged on his window. "HELP ME," she screamed hysterically, thumping the glass. She didn't care what people thought. The driver shrank back in alarm, and she realised how she must seem: a deranged woman in an army uniform running between cars, looking as if she'd escaped from a mental hospital. Kate looked round frantically. The lights were changing and any moment her chance would be gone. Car horns blared for her to get out of the road. Traffic started moving, and if there was ever a moment that she just wanted to sit down and give in, this was it. Nobody was coming to rescue her.

The moving traffic revealed a queue of women at a bus stop. A couple of old men stood with them smoking cigarettes. A bus was coming down the street and Kate knew this was her chance. She could worry about where the bus was headed later. But then Kate realised that she had no money. She stood there impotently, waiting to cross the road. Then saw Mr Punch's head bobbing between the commuters going to work. He was weaving through, searching for her. Come on, come on, why weren't the lights changing?

The bus was pulling over just as she reached the stop. The pain in her leg was dizzying, and she felt as if her calves were bleeding. Her only chance would be to sidle past the driver as the other women boarded. Sure enough, the door wheezed open and the women pressed forward. She did her best to get caught up in the scrum. The driver shouted back at her. She ignored him, hanging on to a strap while pretending to look out of a dirty window. Just a stupid tourist who didn't speak English. The other women regarded her with suspicion. The driver shouted again, and still the bus would not move. Mr Punch had stopped and was looking straight at her. For God's sake, get the bus moving. An old man harangued the driver, who slapped the steering wheel in frustration before revving the engine. Finally they were off.

Only now could she start to digest what had happened. Teardrop and Mr Punch had murdered an innocent man right before her eyes. Priest was probably locked in the boot of the Land Cruiser, and now they were taking him to Zogaj. The words of the 23rd Psalm floated back to her: "Even though I walk through the valley of the shadow of death, I will fear no evil." She knew what she had to do. The police knew who Zogaj was and where his headquarters were, while she had the smoking gun that revealed which British officials were on the take. Who knew how far up this went? What Inspector Poda had said about the Albania State Police being corrupt came back to her; he was the only one to whom she could tell everything.

There were more billboards the closer they got to the city centre. Cute youngsters munching biscuits. Sexy women advertising shampoo, mobile phones and cleaning products. Now they were going past the jarringly camouflaged buildings, and she recognised the gulch running between the four lanes of traffic. Her clawing anxiety peaked the moment they passed the police headquarters – she dinged the bell, desperate to get off – yet she felt warm because she was finally in touching distance of safety.

Kate felt the effects of the pills coming on again the moment the bus doors slammed behind her. She had to get the damn things out of her system.

The solitary policeman on duty paid little attention to the woman hurrying through the gate. He slapped himself and breathed smoke while stamping his feet. Albania's police headquarters was a truly ugly building that could have been a modern hotel, apart from the red police shield on the wall. A smoked-glass atrium and central staircase divided the Seventies structure in two.

People sat on benches, waiting beside a couple of desk sergeants. "Please," Kate said, placing both hands on the counter. "I need to see Inspector Poda." Her voice was a panicky, breathless kind of gulp. The policeman turned to his colleague, who said carefully in English, "How can I help you?" She leaned in and repeated that Mrs Julia needed to see Inspector Poda. Urgently.

There were the usual posters on the wall for missing children, rabies and wanted criminals. Sitting there, she finally felt the enormity of what had happened. This time last week she and Paul had been an averagely happy couple, both struggling to pay the mortgage, he with a failing internet business and she as a freelance textile designer. Now she was on the run. She alone was the one who would bring down the whole house of cards.

Her mind was still running through what to say when she spotted Poda coming downstairs with his peculiar bandy-legged walk. He came through the turnstile, clearly puzzled as to what she was doing here. Kate stood up.

"Mrs Julia?" he asked.

"Thank God. You must help me."

"Sure. Are you okay? You don't look well."

"Please. Is there somewhere we can go?"

He walked her upstairs to his office, where there was the almost forgotten sound of telephones ringing along with the clack of typewriters. Police in Albania, she realised, still used old-fashioned electric machines.

Poda ushered out the two other detectives he shared his office with. Squeezed into suits with their Balkan meat-head haircuts, they resembled gorillas. She wondered if these two were on the take as well, and that was why Poda wanted them out of earshot. Her one piece of luck was the man sitting in front of her.

"I don't understand. What are you doing back in Tirana?"

"My husband didn't jump. He was murdered."

For a moment, Poda was about to roll his eyes. "Mrs Julia, I told you. The man we arrested–"

Kate interrupted, "No, you listen to me."

Once again, Kate launched into the story she had told

András, the chain of events that led to her sitting in this office. "Look, you don't have to take my word for it. There's another man with me, John Priest, he works for Europol."

Her words were tumbling out of her, falling over one another. Poda held up his hand. "Slow down. What you mean, Europol? Where is this man now?"

"They've still got him. The boss of this gang is called Zogaj."

Poda looked startled. "He knows Zogaj?"

Kate explained, "So, when Paul came to Albania last week for his uncle's funeral, my guess is that he told Zogaj he wanted out, that he'd blow the whistle unless they let him go." She was reaching here, but that did seem the most plausible explanation.

Something told her to hold back the ace in her hand – the names and contact details of everybody caught in this dark web. That she would give only to John's boss himself.

Poda looked as if she'd just slapped him across the face. She had forgotten quite how his glasses magnified his eyes so comically. "That's quite a story you're telling," he said.

"John said you knew where Zogaj has his headquarters. That's where they've taken him."

"Everybody knows where Zogaj is. That's not the point. Everyone is afraid of him. I told you, everybody here is on the take. This place is infested. It's all about..." He rubbed his thumb and forefingers together.

"But what are you going to do? You can't just leave him."

"Zogaj lives in Tirana's best hotel. Top floor. Private lift. He has men watching everybody who comes and goes."

"So why don't you go and rescue John?"

Poda looked at her as if she was mad. It was the first time she had ever seen him angry. "You think I can just walk in and say, 'Hey, Al Capone, give me this guy back?' You think it's easy? They have weapons, guns … better guns than we have. Listen. I need to speak to my boss, speak to the army, speak to Europol, do you understand? This will take time."

"But he might be dead before then."

"Before I speak to my boss, I need more information. Tell me more about who kidnapped you."

"There were two of them. One was small and bald and always wore sunglasses. The other had a teardrop tattoo right here." She dabbed the corner of one eye.

"Could you identify them if I show you pictures?"

Kate nodded.

"Okay, wait here. I'll go and get the file."

"Is there a toilet I could use? And a cup of coffee. I've been awake a long time."

"Sure, coffee. No problem."

It had been a struggle to keep her eyes open. Once she

was alone in the toilet cubicle, she knelt on the floor and lent over the bowel, sticking two fingers down her throat and gagged reflexively. After a couple of dry heaves, she vomited what was left in her stomach, wiping her mouth with the back of her hand. Stringy bile stuck to her fingers. There, that felt better.

Poda was back sitting at his desk when she returned, a large lever-arch file packed with mugshots open in front of him. The inspector looked concerned while she turned over the plastic sheets showing a toad-like man grinning in a pork pie hat, dead-eyed thugs, front and side shots of scarred farm boys. Finally she came across Mr Punch.

"He's the one I was telling you about," Kate said, tapping his photo.

Poda swivelled the lever-arch file back to himself and started reading out loud. "Saimir [Sammy] Rudaj, 35. Father unemployed and convicted of raping Rudaj's sister, aged 13. Worked as a dogcatcher ... then a plasterer before being convicted of theft and arson. Released in 1999 and conscripted to fight in the Kosovo War before he deserted. Sent to prison again in 2005 for attacking a woman with a hammer and raping her." Poda grimaced and set the file down. "Known associate of Zogaj crime family, for whom he works as an enforcer. Nicknamed 'The Butcher'. Suspected of murder of Gona Krasniqi, 26, after torturing her with an iron in her apartment. Her boyfriend, Zef Lika, had gone into witness protection after turning informer.

Suspected of planting a bomb in the car of Dardan Petrela after the Petrela crime family set up rival movie-piracy website."

"I've heard enough."

Poda put his hands together in prayer and rested his nose on his index fingers. "No hotel. Hotels are all watched. My parents live in the Highlands. You'll be safe there. My parents are poor people, but my mother will look after you. We'll wait few days, then we will take you across the border into Kosovo, okay?"

"Why can't I go to the British Embassy? Surely I'll be safe there."

"You think a portrait of the Queen on a wall makes any difference? I promise you, the moment you walk in there, they'll know about it."

"I find that hard to believe."

Poda leaned forward. "Mrs Julia, I wish everybody was as naive as you."

"What about my friend, the policeman?"

"We need backup, support. Not from here, they're all friends of Zogaj. There are other policemen I know, people like me. We can trust them. Do you like cowboy films?" Kate was nonplussed. Poda mimed lassoing something. "We'll get a posse together, just like in the movies."

This funny little man with his magnified eyes seemed more

like Mr Magoo than a tough, cynical cop, yet he made her feel safe. The detective punched in a number and waited a few moments before speaking. He'd said only a few words before the other person interrupted him. Poda shrugged helplessly as if to say, "Mothers". Finally, he was able to get in a word, and mother and son spoke rapidly in Albanian before Poda set the phone back down.

"It's all settled. We'll drive to my parents' village and you'll wait there."

"Why can't you just take me across the border now?"

"Do you have a passport?" Kate shook her head. "In any case, all borders are watched. We'll wait three days. Don't worry, I'll arrange everything. "

CHAPTER THIRTY

THE TRAMP PICKED the first of the collection of smoked cigarettes off the park bench and sprinkled what was left of the tobacco onto the paper. He flicked the butt away before taking the next one, all the while keeping an eye on police headquarters. Nobody ever paid any attention to him, he was just a fixture. An hour ago the Englishwoman had turned up, just as Zogaj said she would. Out of the corner of his eye, the tramp saw the gate sliding open and the woman clearly visible in the passenger seat of a Fiat car. He reached into one of his plastic shopping bags for his phone, pressed redial and whispered that the woman was heading north on the ring road.

Less than a mile away, a despatcher at the bus company replaced his handset and watched the Fiat on CCTV screens as it moved through Tirana, switching from one angle to the next as it queued in rush hour traffic. His fingers tapped out an email addressed to "all users" that plunged into the innards of the bus company server and out again to dozens of mobile phones that pinged with the same message. Like dogs barking across a city raising the alarm, the message read: "Registration #TR 467 28 AA … a man and a woman ... pass the word, tell Zogaj, tell Zogaj."

They were on the appallingly ugly highway out of Tirana when Poda pulled over for petrol. Kate sat in the passenger seat taking in the crazy Flash Gordon-on-Mongo architecture across the road as the detective inspector refilled the tank. "Here," he said, handing her a packet of crisps and a can of cola as he got back in. "Road food."

Car washes seemed to be on every third plot of land as Kate and Poda sped out of Tirana. They passed by ugly shops selling wipe-down plastic furniture, primitive farmhouses with satellite dishes. The mountain range, what Poda called the start of the Highlands, lay in the distance, and the air there was almost black. It had turned cold, indicating that a storm was coming. Sure enough, there was a tungsten flash, and somewhere far off the bronchial sky crackled. Seconds later, thunder rolled quickly across the empty fields. "You'll like my mother," Poda said, tapping the steering wheel. "She'll cook kackavall fure for you. You know kackavall fure? It's like a rich cheese fondue, set alight. You'll love it." The idea of going somewhere where there would be a bed turned down for her, where she would be looked after, seemed almost dangerous to contemplate. Kate felt raddled with exhaustion.

They were circling the main square of a small town when she saw what looked like an oddly bumbling statue of a man. "Is that George Bush?" she asked. "Oh yes," said Poda. "We love George Bush for what he did to help our brothers and sisters in Kosovo. We love Uncle Sam." He waved his hand as if he was holding a tiny American flag. "God bless America."

Outside the town they found themselves on a nasty, twisty road going upwards. In summer it might have been fun to drive fast round these blind corners with Primal Scream blasting on the car stereo, but today it felt like a long, hard crawl up the hairpin bends. Occasionally a lorry would appear out of nowhere and Poda would pull over sharply, cringing against the side of the mountain until the vehicle was safely past. There were fir trees on either side of the road. Thunder boomed and the first fat drops of rain started chasing each other down the windscreen.

"Tell me about your family," Kate said, glimpsing an upturned car resting at the bottom of a ravine hundreds of feet below. One wrong turn and they might join it. Rain drummed on the car roof.

"My father was a policeman, too. In those days, police were like Stasi – getting people to spy on each other, neighbours telling on each other, children betraying parents. Bad days. You have to remember that there was nothing here. Albania had no friends apart from China. Hoxha said that even Russia was too western. We were always at war. I remember marching like soldiers in my kindergarten. It was what we did instead of playing with toys."

"But things are better now."

Poda made a face. "Things are different now. Instead of Communism we have corruption, the Mafia. Everybody has a price."

"You don't think much of your colleagues."

"Some are good, some bad. The problem is that you don't know who to trust."

"You trust your boss, though?"

"Oh yes. He's a good man."

"What about my friend? What's happened to that posse you were talking about?"

"My boss says it's better if we do an exchange: two of Zogaj's gang for one British policeman. We have plenty of his gang in prison. Drug dealers. Pimps. Don't worry, your friend will be okay." He slapped her knee encouragingly. Don't do that, she thought.

"I still don't understand why I can't get a plane back to London. Or a ferry to Italy. Why do I have to cross the border on foot?"

"Zogaj controls the docks and the airport. He has eyes everywhere. In Albania, we call his gang Oktapod, the octopus."

They listened to the thock of the windscreen wipers as the rain eased off. Despite the ominous clouds, the thunderstorm had been brief. The Albanian countryside, though, reminded her of miserably wet family holidays hill-walking in north Wales.

Medieval castles dotted the landscape. "An Englishman's home is his castle, isn't that the saying?" Poda continued, as if reading her thoughts. "Same in Albania. Everybody wants to have their own castle. Lots of buildings are never finished. The recession hits, and developers go bust."

The fields here were all cultivated and, looking closer through the passenger window, Kate could see what they were growing. Cannabis. Fields and fields of it. "My God, is that marijuana?" she said. Poda kept on looking straight ahead. Perhaps he was embarrassed. "I told you. The gang bosses pay for politicians' election campaigns. The farmers make more money growing cannabis than regular crops. Nobody dares enter the cannabis fields because they are all mined. Leftover ordnance from the Kosovo War."

They passed a flatbed truck with a man sitting in it, as if guarding the marijuana fields. Kate turned back round and said, "I can't believe it's so open here."

"Better than growing olives," Poda said.

The village where Poda's parents lived was a delightful hodge-podge of a place, with what looked like a bazaar running down a side street. Its little white houses resembled nothing so much as a Cubist painting stuck on the side of a mountain. The Fiat protested as the detective inspector changed up a gear, and they turned into what Kate guessed was the main square. Suddenly an enormous unfinished tower block loomed over them. Floor after floor of empty concrete rooms and a staircase that abruptly ran out. It completely dominated the square. An old concrete mixer stood on a hillock of cement lumps and twisted metal. The site was fenced off, abandoned, as if the workers had just given up and gone home.

"Another Mafia building," Poda grimaced. "They build without planning permission, so the government stops them. Nobody knows what to do with it now. It was the same in Croatia. They destroyed the countryside. We don't want it here."

"You really care about this country, don't you?"

"Of course. The Mafia are rats, eating into everything. They steal copper wire, so there are no phones. They put crack in cannabis to get kids hooked. They win government contracts for roads that are never built, buildings that collapse. Somebody has to do something."

The Fiat bounced down a side street and, as it was now dusk, Poda switched on its old-fashioned yellow headlights. The road was really bad by now, and they lurched from side to side. Finally they drew up outside a high white wall with a doorway in it. They had arrived. A couple of boys were kicking a ball aimlessly against the wall, and Poda spoke sharply to them. They ran off down a plank of wood laid over the middle of the alley. Slamming her car door, Kate heard the ululating call to prayer floating down the mountain. Poda hurried over to an intercom and spoke quickly. A buzzer sounded and the detective inspector pushed the heavy door open.

They climbed up steps and emerged onto a patio with a swimming pool where somebody was doing laps. Steam rose from the water. Looking up at the house, Kate could see it was one of those vulgar castles that Poda had told her about, like something out of a creaky horror movie. Her scalp crawled. Something was very wrong. "I thought you said your parents were poor," Kate began. Poda wouldn't meet her eye, and she felt her kneecaps dissolve as Mr Punch stepped onto the patio. He was opening a clasp knife. Behind her she heard the person doing laps get out of the pool. She turned around and saw his strongly muscled back covered with tattoos as he heaved himself up onto the cement.

Of course. It could only be Teardrop.

He picked up a towel and dried his hair, moving with a kind of exaggerated ease, as if to show he was the one in charge. Poda, however, squirmed. All Kate could think to say was, "How could you?" Poda pulled down his shirt collar and revealed the letter "Z" tattooed beneath his collarbone. The same tattoo they had forced onto Paul. "All of us are caught in the web," he said, shrugging.

Mr Punch pushed her behind Teardrop and Poda, and they filed into the house, passing through a dining room with a suit of armour standing in the corner. A weapon, perhaps. Her fingers brushed a gauntlet. The entire thing was a stage prop made of cardboard. There was a hall with a staircase leading to the upper floors and a kitchen to the right. Kate stood trembling with fear. They would get rid of her just as they'd taken care of her husband. All loose ends tied up. "What have you done with my friend?" she asked. Nobody replied. She looked down and noticed her right hand was shaking uncontrollably.

Teardrop walked back into the kitchen, having changed into his usual black tee-shirt and jeans. He nodded for Mr Punch to pass him the clasp knife. The bad guys really do wear black, Kate thought, as Teardrop hoisted himself onto a work surface and began peeling an apple. He did so languidly, appearing to take great pleasure in curling the skin. Finally he speared a chunk and popped it into his mouth.

"I don't understand why you want me," Kate tried again. "You killed my husband and destroyed the servers. Anything he had on you is gone."

"You know too much." The implication hung there: there was only one way to solve the problem of somebody with too much information.

"Why not just let us go? Two people are already dead. You don't want more blood on your hands." She wanted to say that Europol was onto them, but she knew there was no cavalry riding over the hill to their rescue. A tinny bugle sounded at the back of her mind.

Sliding down, Teardrop said, "Zogaj say you make copy. With copy you betray us, tell police or ransom maybe. Zogaj tell me to search you. Turn around."

He stepped up behind Kate, sweeping his hands along her shoulders and arms and then down her torso and legs. This was the moment she had been dreading. If they found the memory card, she might as well have signed her own death warrant. Kate tried not to think about it as Teardrop dug his thumbs into her waistband and ran his hands around. Pulling Kate towards him, he patted down her front before stepping back. Nothing. There was only one other place the memory card might be, and they both knew it. Mr Punch arrived in the doorway. "Ai kërkon atë," he said.

There was a steep flight of steps down to the basement, and Kate had to duck as the men led her underground. Despite the dampness, she thought she could smell the fear down here. This would be where they tortured people, where those men Priest had told her about were battered to death. There was an anteroom in the cellar that was used as a tool shed. Hacksaws, pliers and handsaws hung from the walls, and a vice sat on a workbench. There were outlines where some of the tools were missing. Two men were sitting with their backs to the doorway on wooden chairs, their hands duct-taped to the crossbars and their ankles bound to the front legs. The man in the left-hand chair was John Priest: she recognised him immediately from his broad shoulders. He was slumped and looked in a bad way. The floor was discoloured with what could only be dried blood.

The man in the other chair was her husband.

CHAPTER THIRTY ONE

HER HUSBAND HAD COME BACK from the dead. She had crossed a line into another world, and nothing made sense anymore. Perhaps she had died back in that forest and had been ferried across the River Styx.

Kate slowly reached out to touch his beautiful face, making sure he wasn't a ghost. Paul looked haggard but still in one piece. All those questions she had crowding her mind – the dead prostitute he had betrayed her with in the hotel room, the agony he'd put her through when he had stepped off that balcony – disappeared. Her husband was alive and that was all that mattered.

Priest, however, had suffered a brutal going over. His face was bloody and swollen, and one eye had closed up. Paul smiled weakly, and with that Kate wanted to cry.

Lifting her face, she turned to Teardrop, "Haven't you done enough? How much more killing does there have to be?" Her voice had a righteous anger she'd never heard before.

"I told you I would never leave you," Paul said hoarsely.

"It's all right, my darling, we're together now," Kate said, stroking his face. "They're never going to keep us apart."

Paul shook his head. "You don't understand. I never wanted you to come here. I was trying to keep you safe."

"Darling, I love you so much. We're going to be together."

"Don't you understand, we're both finished. Being dead was the price I had to pay for keeping you safe. Kate, I never wanted to do this to you. I thought I had no choice. When they found me, I told them I would carry on hosting their payoffs as long as they left you alone."

"Don't listen to him, Kate," said Priest.

"This policeman is one of them. He was the one who told them you had to be watched. He said you knew where the data was."

"Kate, I'm telling you," said Priest.

"Where did you hide the data, Kate?"

"Don't listen to him. He's lying."

"Unless you give them what they want, they'll kill us both."

Priest raised his voice. "Don't do it, Kate."

"For God's sake, just give them what they want," said her husband. Paul started to cry. Part of her wanted to comfort him, another part was appalled by his weakness. "Priest said you'd copied the data. Please, Kate, just give it to them. I'm begging you."

Priest, however, just glowered at the floor. The thugs had already given him a real working over. Kate suspected the

dried blood on the floor was his. There was also the faintest
absurdity in all this, as if they were acting out an airport
thriller, the kind you'd find in a departure lounge.

Mr Punch, who had been standing by the workbench,
plugged an old-fashioned-looking power drill into a socket
and tested the trigger. Its sharp whine filled the basement
before snapping off suddenly. Paul began moaning and
Kate's heart dropped into her stomach. They all knew what
was about to happen. Nonononono her mind implored, and
Paul rocked his chair as Mr Punch trod softly towards him.
He was even smiling faintly. It was unbearable, and Kate
shut her eyes as the high-pitched whine changed to a dull
grinding sound as it bit into something hard – the bone of
her husband's kneecap.

Priest's scream was so loud that it penetrated the
brickwork.

The power drill snapped off, leaving a burnt smell in the air.
When Kate opened her eyes Priest was sobbing and he had
vomited over himself. Mr Punch, though, stepped back as
if admiring his own handiwork. You will pay for this. I don't
know how, but there is natural justice in the world, there has
to be, Kate thought. There was such a thing as karma, and
you did reap what you sowed. Teardrop barked one word and
Mr Punch revved the trigger again. This time he stood over
Paul. Priest's shoulders were still heaving. The smell of vomit
and fear in the room was nauseating.

Kate spoke quickly. "Even if you had the data, who's to say that another copy wasn't made? You'll never be satisfied. And you said yourself we know too much. You'll just get rid of us anyway."

"Please. Let them both go. I'll carry on working for you," Paul pleaded. "She's done nothing to harm you. She's an innocent." He turned to her. "I'm begging you. Just give them what they want."

Priest looked at her balefully. "Don't do it, Kate."

"She can go, but not him," Teardrop said.

"For God's sake, Kate, save yourself," Paul spat out.

May God forgive me for what I'm about to do, she thought, unbuttoning her trousers and pushing her fingers up as far as they would go. It was dry and uncomfortable to get at the memory card, but finally a relief to get it out; she had pushed it so deep inside. The others watched as she twisted around – Mr Punch looked disgusted – until she held up the balloon. She worked her fingers into the balloon's mouth and extracted the memory card.

Paul shook his head trying to get free, and Teardrop stepped smartly forward and cut through the duct tape with his clasp knife. Kate could hardly believe it: they really were keeping their side of the bargain. Paul muttered something in Albanian, and Teardrop crouched down to cut his legs loose. Finally Paul stood up, stretched and turned towards her while the thugs kept their distance.

Kate had the odd sensation that he was now the one in charge. She heard footsteps coming downstairs but she just stood there mesmerised, not understanding the change that had just happened. And then she got it.

Paul was the one in charge.

He had been the one in charge all along.

She had misunderstood everything. Paul had had never been taken prisoner. He had never jumped from that balcony, he had never even been pushed. He had faked his own death because he knew that Europol were onto him. Like a photograph emerging in a developing tray, he was finally exposed.

"You see?" said Priest.

Paul took the memory card from her and held it to his nose. "I'd forgotten what you smelled like," he said, inhaling deeply.

Kate couldn't think of what to say. The final veil had been ripped away.

Paul continued. "I thought our whole operation was blown – just burn down the servers, I told them – then I thought, no, Kate's cleverer than that, she'll figure out the one place where I kept a copy. And I was right. I know you better than you know yourself."

"Why not just steal our wedding photo back? You knew where it was."

"Because I wanted you to bring it. I wanted you here. I need you. With me."

With that, she spat in his face. Everything she had suffered, everything she had been through in her personal crucifixion, was all his fault. Paul flinched but did his best to behave as if nothing had happened.

"You disgust me," Kate said.

"Do you know what the new currency is, Kate, more valuable than dollars or gold? It's data. Personal details are the new oil, and you've just handed me a gusher. Of course, the English operation is over, but you've given me something even better, my darling. Really, I should be thanking you."

Kate said numbly, "The man who died, the one in the street, who was that?"

Paul looked meaningfully at Priest. "A rat. One of his informants. I gave him a choice – either he jumps or we take care of his family. He did the right thing."

"I don't understand. I saw you jump from that balcony."

"No, the man you saw was the informant. We pushed him off the balcony below. It was easy for me to cross over to the next patio."

"Exit, stage left," muttered Priest.

"So you killed another innocent." Kate looked at Mr Punch. "He murdered a man who was trying to save me."

Paul grasped her shoulders and she closed her eyes, like a suicide. "Do you think I wanted any of this?" her husband said. "I was happy in London. We were happy in London. When my uncle died, I had to come home and take over. This isn't something you can walk away from."

Priest started to laugh. "Jesus wept," he said.

"I still don't understand. Whose ashes did I bring back home?"

"Just some old fireplace ashes mixed with earth."

"What happens now? Are you going to get rid of us too?"

"That's your choice," Paul said quietly. "I don't want that to happen."

Suddenly Kate went for him, shoving him in the chest. Every molecule of him revolted her. The idea of being with Paul a moment longer made her want to vomit. "Get away from me. You're not my husband, you're not the man I married, I hate you." Paul just stood there taking it as she beat her hands on his chest. "You're not even Paul Julia are you? Your real name is Zogaj."

The final piece of jigsaw had clicked into place.

"Oh no, child," said a voice behind her. "I am Zogaj."

CHAPTER THIRTY TWO

Paul's aunt, the one whose husband had died, stood at the bottom of the stairs. She was leaning heavily on a stick and she surveyed the basement with a flinty, imperious look. The old woman regarded Kate with contempt.

Zogaj spoke.

"You despise us. You think you're better than we are because you never got your hands dirty. You've no idea how hard our life was here. People would pay good money for a little escape – alcohol, a woman – nothing has changed. Our family still offers the same thing. Our people have always been smugglers, his father and his father before him. We used to smuggle over the mountains. Today it's by car and boat."

"This isn't something innocent: you destroy people's lives," Kate said. "Those girls you take from Vietnam, you ruin them so they can't go home. What happens when they get pregnant? You just throw them away."

"Don't be so naive. Do you really think that the girls' families don't know why their daughters come here? The girls send money home. For many of these families, it's the only money they ever see. The fathers, the mothers … they know. Otherwise it's starvation."

"The girl I saved from the cannabis farm, she said you'd advertised a job in Tirana. Then you kidnapped her. She was locked up in a flat for days, handcuffed to a radiator, before you shipped her out. How do you sleep at night, knowing these girls are raped? And the cannabis you grow, you get people hooked."

"We're just providing a service. If we didn't do it, somebody else would."

"What's my husband got to do with this?"

"Child, Zogaj isn't a name, it's a title, like leader. It's passed on from generation to generation. Eventually Paul will inherit it."

"Like capo dei capi: the godfather," muttered Priest.

"Why not one of your own sons? I saw them at the funeral. What do you need my husband for?"

"What, him?" she said dismissively. Teardrop just stood there looking gormless. Of course. Teardrop was Paul's cousin, the one he'd told her so much about, the one he'd grown up with. "He was always a fool. No, Paul was the one with the brains. My husband said so. That's why we sent him to England. My husband was clear that he should inherit the family business when I die."

I hope that happens very soon, Kate thought bitterly.

Zogaj nodded, as if the exchange had exhausted her, and turned to go back upstairs. Mr Punch took her arm, guiding her up the stairwell. "I don't need your help," the old woman snapped, but her progress was painfully slow. Her breathing was bad, and for a moment Kate wondered if she was going to topple backwards. The four of them stood watching her arthritic progress upstairs. Only Priest did not bother to turn round.

"So what happens now?" Kate challenged Paul.

"We'll take you to a room where you can rest. Then we can talk some more."

"What's there to talk about? You've shown me who you really are. I hate you." Kate turned to Priest. "Can you walk? Here, let me help you."

Teardrop finished cutting Priest loose and stood back. Priest, however, just sat there. Sweat covered his face, as if he couldn't face the pain of standing up. He grunted with effort when Kate helped lift him, and he hobbled only a couple of steps with her support before shaking his head. "John, come on. Not far to go now. You can do this," she said, and together they limped towards the basement steps. "Where do you want us to go?" Kate asked. Teardrop jerked his head upwards.

Their attic bedroom was in the eaves of the house. Two metal single beds flanked a dressing table below a small window. The room was fearfully cold, and the window sill was black with rotted wood, as damp black as a coal seam. Kate touched the wood where it had rotted and brushed a weird butterfly growth with her fingers. Any thoughts of escape went out of her head when she looked out the window: it was a sheer, four-storey drop down the side of the building. Poda's car was still parked in the alley outside the main entrance, though. Suddenly the black 4x4 roared up and stopped outside the gate. Kate watched fascinated as a young woman she immediately recognised as Phuong got out. She'd had her hair cut differently, in a Japanese schoolgirl bob as sharply diagonal as a raven's wing. Dressed in a fake fur coat, she looked painfully young: a child who'd sat at her mother's dressing table and used her makeup. Paul escorted his aunt outside, helping her up into the passenger seat. God rot you both, Kate thought, as Paul stood in the alley watching the car leave.

"They've brought Phuong here," Kate said, turning from the window.

"She's a long way from home."

"What will they do to her?"

"Whatever it is, it won't be good," Priest said. "They think she betrayed them." He was stretched out on the bed and winced as he spoke.

"There's still a chance you could get away. I'm done for. Nobody knows we're here. Paul doesn't want to kill you, he wants to make you his queen."

"That policeman I told you about, he was the one who betrayed me. They're all in this together. Every last one of them."

"I did tell you."

"What's the expression, 'I was blind but now I can see'?" She patted his mattress. "What about you? Is there anything I can do to help? You should be in hospital, not here."

"I could use a drink, a double whiskey." He started laughing but grimaced as the pain got to be too much.

Kate banged on the door for attention and listened; the rest of the house seemed to be deserted. Had they left the two of them alone? She rattled the dressing-table drawers open, searching for anything they might use. And there, miracle of miracles, was a traveller's sewing kit, the kind given away in hotel bathrooms.

"What are you going to do? Stitch some sheets together?" Priest asked when she held up the sewing kit triumphantly.

"Try and fix your leg," she said, sitting down at the foot of the bed. "This is going to hurt, I'm afraid."

Kate helped Priest unbuckle his jeans, pulling them down to his calves. There was a nasty deep hole in the side of his knee about the width of a pencil. The blood, though, had dried, which was something. If only she had some water, she could at least clean the wound out.

"I'll tell Paul I will do whatever he wants, but he must let you go," Kate said, licking the thread and passing it through the eye of the needle.

"He won't go for it. I'm a policeman, not a civilian."

"You're going to need to bite on something. This is going to hurt."

Priest took hold of the filthy stiff curtain, stuffing the end into his mouth. His ridged skin turned white between her fingers. Blood popped on the needle as she passed it through. The cloth muffled his yell as she crudely stitched the hole together. "There. It'll hold," Kate said, surveying her rough handiwork. Priest tried to smile. What the man needed was painkillers, Kate thought indignantly. She got up and banged on the door again. Slowly, a plan began percolating in her mind.

Mr Punch answered her angry banging. "Tell my husband I need to see him," she said. Mr Punch turned and called down the stairwell. If Teardrop was driving Zogaj home, that meant there were only two of them in the house plus Poda, who she guessed wouldn't give them any trouble. She recognised her husband's heavy tread as he came upstairs.

"You wanted to see me," he said.

"We need painkillers and water," Kate said. "This man should be in hospital."

"If I do that for you, I want you to do something for me. I

want you to come downstairs and eat. There's things we need to talk about."

"All right," Kate said grudgingly. "Priest needs food as well."

It was absurd. Did he really think they were going to sit down together and pretend nothing had happened? Never underestimate how men are led around by their cocks, or what they will do for the comfort of a soft, warm pussy, a girlfriend had once told her. How right she was.

Paul nodded and went back downstairs.

It was Mr Punch who gave her the painkillers, watching Kate with cold, unfeeling eyes. He also held out a floaty chiffon dress for her to put on, the kind you might wear on a summer evening. Kate shut the door in his face. Did this dress belong to one of Paul's whores, she wondered, pulling it over her head. Priest watched her from the bed. "Thank you for doing that," he said. This time she went over to him and took hold of his large brown hand, turning it over to admire its pinkness. "We're going to get out of here, just you see," Kate said. Their eyes met, and this time she kissed him on the mouth. Mr Punch banged on the door again. "Hurry up," he called.

Going downstairs, Kate scoped out the house properly for the first time, scanning for any means of escape. The first-floor corridor, lit with electric candles in wall sconces, had bedrooms running off it, and there were more fake suits of armour. The whole place was decorated in mock Tudor, with wooden shields and fake paintings that were really just photographs of old masters.

Paul was downstairs in the kitchen making supper. She recognised what Paul was making as he dipped poultry into flour, then egg, and finally breadcrumbs. It was one of their favourites, breaded chicken escalopes. "Do you want a drink?" Paul said. Kate nodded, and her husband poured her a glass of red wine, which she greedily sipped, noticing the knife on the chopping board. "I don't think so," Paul said. He took the knife and speared the escalope before dropping it in sizzling oil.

"You think I'm a monster, don't you?" he said. "Do you think I wanted any of this? The family isn't something you walk away from. In Albanian, they call us the Octopus. Once they've got their tentacles around you, there's no escape."

"There's always a door," Kate said with a shrug. All the while she was looking for a weapon, anything she might use. The kitchen must be full of them. Careful, she thought, you mustn't let Paul know what you're thinking.

"I never thought I would become Zogaj. I assumed my cousin would take over. Of course, I knew what the family business was, but I always thought I could walk away."

"When did you first discover what your family did?"

"I must have been about five years old. It's one of my

earliest memories. I was in a car with my father. There was a woman in the passenger seat I'd never met before. My father was Zogaj then, you see. Not that I knew anything about it." Paul had stopped even glancing at her now, as if she was a coat left over the back of a chair. "I remember driving into the Block – back in those days it was the enclave of Party officials, ordinary people weren't allowed in – and then walking with this woman up to the front of an apartment building. We were walking back to the car and I was seeing food in shop windows I'd never seen before. One thing I remember in particular was the wind stirring rabbit fur outside a butcher's shop – it's funny the things you remember – when suddenly there was screaming behind us. The woman from the car was running down the street. She was completely naked. I had never seen a naked woman before. An army major with his tunic undone was chasing her, waving a gun. There was shouting, and my father tried to intervene. They scuffled and then there was a pop, more like a cap gun. Next thing I knew, dad was on the pavement making a ghastly wheezing sound. The major had shot him. Dad told me to take a notebook out of his pocket and give it to my uncle – he would know what to do with it. Only later did I understand that it was a list of Party officials who used his services. More names and addresses, you see."

If this was designed to elicit her sympathy, he wasn't going to get off that easily. "So your father was a pimp as well,"

Kate said coldly. "What about the girl who died, the one in the Savile Hotel? The police think you murdered her."

"I delivered a message from Zogaj, that's all. It was up to her what she did with it."

"Either she killed herself or her family would be harmed, you mean."

Paul turned over a browned escalope in the pan. It was nearly done. "Listen to me. Give me three years and we'll be out of this. Marijuana, girls... it's old school. The police know who we are. The politicians are on our side for now, but that could change. We're riddled with traitors who want to save their own skin. We're being attacked from outside and eaten away from within." He waved the knife dismissively. "I want to legitimise us. Government contracts, waste disposal, even data centres. That's the future. "

"So you can skim the government and build more shoddy houses that collapse."

"Zogaj was right, you really are naive. It's what all politicians do. Listen, there's a story about an Albanian politician who visits another politician in Italy. He goes to this guy's country villa and this ugly Italian's got a model girlfriend plus an apartment in Rome. 'Wow. How do you afford all this on a politician's salary?' the Albanian asks, goggle-eyed. 'Look out this window. What do you see?' says the Italian. All the Albanian can see is a track. 'That's the motorway the government gave me money to build,' says the Italian. Anyway, a year goes by and the Italian goes to visit his Albanian friend. Except this time, it's the Albanian who's got a castle and a supermodel girlfriend. 'My God,' says the Italian, 'being a politician in Albania must really pay.' The Albanian shows him the view. 'See that motorway?' he says. All the Italian sees is an empty field. 'Exactly,' says the Albanian. That tells you all you need to know about politics here."

Despite herself, Kate managed a smile. All the time she was thinking furiously. She would let him seduce her, anything to buy them more time. "So you're going to be the reforming Tony Blair of the Albanian Mafia," she said. It was too funny, almost priceless.

"You may laugh, but Blair and his wife are well known here. They're best mates with the prime minister. They can see this country's potential."

Kate hadn't realised how hungry she was. This was the first proper meal she'd had since Priest had cooked her supper, what, two days ago? She ploughed into what was on her plate, devouring the sauteed potatoes and crisp green salad. They ate quickly and mostly in silence.

"I don't understand why you couldn't have told me the truth."

"I guessed the authorities would be keeping a close eye on you. What I hadn't realised was how close."

"What are you going to do with him?" Kate let the implication hang that somehow they were in this together.

"It's out of my hands. I told the family there's been enough killing. What I said to you, I mean it," he said, changing the subject. "You wouldn't have to know anything. You could live in one of the big Venice hotels, the Cipriani or the Gritti ... you'd have unlimited spending money, everything would be taken care of... I would come and visit you at weekends. Think of it, living in one of the most beautiful cities in the world. Anything you want, you can have."

For a moment she glimpsed herself as Audrey Hepburn in a scarf and sunglasses, riding out to that beautiful lagoon in a speedboat or sipping a delicious Bellini in the chic warmth of Harry's Bar. No, instead this was like that scene in the Bible where the Devil tempts Jesus, showing him all the wealth and power he could have.

Kate pushed her empty plate away, tipped her chair back and put her feet on the table, spreading her legs in a most unladylike way. It was an unmistakable message. From the way Paul reacted, Kate might as well have rung a bell, and what her girlfriend had said about men and their cocks came back to her.

Paul said thickly, "You know I love you, Kate. I need you. I want us to be together."

Sitting forward, she lifted her face to be kissed. Paul took her hand and, without saying a word, led her out of the kitchen. So this was how it was going to be. She blocked her mind to the man her husband had become, the private crucifixion he had put her through. Kate numbed herself, preparing to be raped, because that's what it was, just like all the other women these people abused.

Paul always undressed in the same way. First his socks and then his shirt, and finally his jeans. It was a male way of undressing he'd seen on television, she thought.

And when he came, it was with an agonised, puppyish whimper.

Lying there in the dark, Kate thought this was the blackest black she had ever experienced. This hilltop village must be miles from anywhere. Paul had fallen asleep on top of her, and the weight of him was becoming claustrophobic. She had to wait until she could be sure he was asleep. Only when he started snoring did she gently roll him on to his side, slipping out of bed as quietly as possible. The door was on her right. She crept across the floorboards, gathering her clothes, preparing to dress on the landing.

The pain when she stubbed her toe was dazzling. She did her best not to cry out, and Paul moved uneasily in his sleep. Quickly she pulled on her knickers and reclipped her bra, cursing the silly chiffon dress she slipped on top of them.

As she crept up the stairs to where Priest was being held prisoner, a step creaked beneath her. She waited, heart palpitating, but nobody stirred. It would all be over if Teardrop or Mr Punch investigated any strange noises.

The door bolt slid back easily and she entered the tiny attic room. Priest was asleep, and Kate was pleased to make out an empty tray on the other bed. At least they had given him something to eat. Sudden lightning left an after-image like the pop of a camera flashgun, and moments later thunder lazily rolled over the mountains. A storm was brewing. "Come on, we're getting out of here," she whispered, shaking him roughly. Priest woke instantly. She wanted to give him confidence that she didn't really feel. In fact, all she felt was nauseating, gripping fear.

CHAPTER THIRTY THREE

IT WAS ONLY WHEN THEY WERE STANDING in the corridor that Kate realised how absurd her plan was. Teardrop or Mr Punch might be behind either of these doors. Her idea had been so simple when she had thought of it: she and Priest would come downstairs and steal Poda's car keys from his bedroom. Poda was just an employee, somebody else who had got infected after being bitten – she remembered what he had told her about *la mordida,* the bite. They stood for a moment, uncertain what to do. Electric candles flickered in their sconces. Apparently thinking the same thing, Priest shrugged and tested the door handle. If it was locked, then their whole plan disintegrated. Could they really just walk out of this hideous castle and disappear?

The door opened smoothly and Kate sensed somebody sitting up in bed. Poda snored loudly. "Shhh," she motioned, putting a finger to her lips. Thank God it was Phuong who sat up in bed. Please don't scream, Kate's mind implored, as Phuong pulled the sheet up higher around her chest and Kate tiptoed across the room to where she sensed a chair. Perhaps because she already knew Kate, Phuong wouldn't raise the alarm. "I will come back for you," Kate whispered to the frightened girl. She meant it. A pair of trousers was slung over the chair and there, oh blessed Mary mother of God, were the policeman's car keys. Poda emitted a particularly sharp snore. For good measure, Kate had the presence of mind to steal his glasses off the bedside table. Remembering his magnified eyes, she knew he would be blind without them.

Now they were creeping downstairs to the ground floor. The kitchen was at the foot of the steps on their left. Priest suddenly gripped Kate's wrist. They stood there poised, all senses stretched to breaking point. Men's voices murmured in the kitchen. It was well after midnight, but Teardrop and Mr Punch were still sitting up talking. Priest stood listening. If one of them came out unexpectedly or spotted them tiptoeing out, it was all over. Kate couldn't understand what Priest was waiting for. Finally he relaxed his grip, and they tiptoed silently past the kitchen doorway.

They slipped across the patio. What if the door to the street was double locked? If that was the case, they'd have to go over the swimming pool wall, and it was a good thirty-foot drop to the ground. There was an especially deep crack of lighting. Suddenly the heavens opened and pulverising rain came down like diagonal pencil leads. Kate was drenched. Her clothes stuck to her as the nasty, cold rain penetrated her bones. Here goes, she thought, depressing the electric lock, which gave way with a click once open.

Rain hammered on Poda's car roof as Kate fumbled with the keys. Her teeth were chattering, and she didn't think she had ever been this cold. Water sluiced down the gutters, churning the alley into mud. "You drive. My knee's too bad," called Priest through the freezing downpour. Mud oozed between her toes as she searched for the right key, cursing her bare feet and the stupid dress. Finally she found it, and Kate slid across and opened the passenger door. Priest slammed it shut, running his fingers through his curls. The car started first time and they lurched backwards into the alley. "Lights," said Priest. They swung round, the yellow headlights dimly lighting up a graffitied wall, as they barrelled down the alley.

It was like a nightmare switchback ride. They would accelerate towards a brick wall, only to suddenly veer left or right, searching for a way out. Fear choked Kate's throat.

Finally they came out into what she recognised as the village square with the unfinished block of flats, the ones the Octopus had built. The road out of the village was on the left. The engine protested as they careened down the hill. But Kate felt the stirrings of hope for the first time.

"Turn up the heating, for God's sake," she said. "I'm going to freeze to death." Her chiffon dress was wet through and her hair was plastered to her skull. She was also trembling violently. Trying to operate the pedals in bare feet was not helping either.

Priest started laughing. "What's so funny?" she asked him.

"That place reminds me of a restaurant me mum and dad used to take me to as a kid. A Berni Inn."

"With a medieval torture chamber in the basement."

"Yeah, when he got out that power drill, I thought I was done for."

"What do we do now?"

"I told you. There's a Europol office in Rome. All we need to do is sit tight. If we can find a phone, they'll come and get us."

"What were those men talking about?"

"I couldn't get all of it. My Albanian's not very good. I got snatches, though. They're meeting somebody in Venice next Thursday. It's not drugs this time, it's arms."

"Weapons? I thought they were in the dope business."

Priest gave her a look. "You don't run an operation like this selling a bit of wacky baccy. The whole of the Balkans is a weapons stockpile. Leftovers from the Kosovo War. They sell them to Muslim terror groups. Anybody, really."

They were out of the village now, and Kate had to contend with nasty blind corners going downhill. Rubber bit into her soles and the pedals were clunky to kick down. The rain fell interminably on. Glancing in the rear-view mirror, she saw the road brightening behind them, and she knew that could mean only one thing.

They were being followed.

Sure enough, another car was coming down the mountain, its headlights groping like an insect's feelers for whatever lay ahead.

Kate put her foot down, trying to get another few miles an hour out of the tiny Fiat. She urged it on. "Are you sure it's them?" Priest turned around, lit up by the other car's headlights. They were dazzling. There was no doubt in Kate's mind who it was bearing down on them. And this time there would be no more Mr Nice Guy. Paul would have to show the others how tough he was. For a moment, Kate thought about appealing for mercy, and then dismissed the idea: she had shown where her allegiance lay. She reached out and squeezed Priest's hand.

The road was flattening out now to the long stretch where Poda had pointed out the cannabis fields. The rain was pestilent, and Kate wondered how much longer they could go on. Wind rocked the car. The yellow headlights barely lit up anything, and it was as if they were plunging head first into a spuming, swirling vortex of water.

A thunkety-thunkety-thunk sound came from the engine, which lurched violently as if it was coming loose. Oh Christ, not now. The couple turned to each other. What could it be? Kate glanced at the dashboard and saw what the problem was.

The petrol gauge read empty.

CHAPTER THIRTY FOUR

THE CAR GROUND TO A HALT and they sat there for a moment, not believing what had just happened. The only thing Kate could think of was that the boys playing football had stolen the petrol. Rain drummed on the roof. "Get out of here," she said, pushing the door open. In this wind, even getting the door open was a struggle. And if anything, the storm was getting worse. There was another blue-white flash and moments later a catastrophic boom. Kate skittered and slopped round the back of the car, helping Priest out. The 4x4 was bouncing down the road towards them, lurching from one pothole to another. She couldn't see who was behind the wheel.

"Come on," Kate urged Priest, helping him off the road and down the verge. He hobbled as best he could. They were like awkward contestants in a three-legged race.

They slithered down the bank and staggered into the cannabis fields. Kate wanted to be anywhere apart from this godforsaken place, a desolate field in the middle of nowhere. They loped along the row of cannabis plants, barely able to see in front of their faces. Mud squelched over Kate's feet and the going got heavier and heavier.

Hopelessness had her by the throat. Suddenly Priest put his hand on her back and pushed her forward. The message was clear. Get down.

They lay face down in the churning, unforgiving mud, and only now did she understand.

Peering through the bushy fronds, she saw the 4x4 parked beside Poda's car on the embankment. Three men got out; one of them was holding a rifle. The 4x4's headlights were facing them, piercing the dark of the cannabis field. They would be spotted any moment. Worse, one of the men was clambering down the bank, and she knew it was Mr Punch. They always sent him to do the dirty work. It was Teardrop who held the rifle.

Mr Punch had a torch he was swinging left and right. A childhood memory: a hook-nosed man in a top hat searching for children in a storybook. Come out, come out, wherever you are. No matter how well they were hidden, the child-catcher would sniff them out. Mr Punch was walking towards them through the next row of plants, scanning this way and that. At least the rain covered their footprints. He was nearly on top of them. Kate whimpered and she closed her eyes. Ohmygodpleasejustgivemeonemorechance. Cannabis plants cracked underfoot as Mr Punch came nearer. Kate couldn't help making a strangulated noise like an animal caught in a trap. "Hold still," Priest whispered in her ear.

Given how hard it was raining, Kate had no idea if Mr Punch was standing right over them. Priest covered Kate with his body, pressing her further down, and they sank deeper into the mud, very slowly. If she prostrated herself any more she would suffocate. Mr Punch would be waiting for something to give them away; a movement, a rustle, anything. Oh, God, she thought, I'm going to drown in this mud.

That's when she sensed the torchlight on her face. "Mbi këtu," Mr Punch shouted. That was the moment she held her breath. Her brain stopped thinking, while her heart stopped beating.

CHAPTER THIRTY FIVE

MR PUNCH STOOD ROOTED to the spot as if they were playing a game of musical statues. Now Kate understood what had happened: she remembered Poda telling her that the fields had been mined. All that Kosovan War ordnance. Mr Punch must have stood on a mine and knew he would be dead the moment he lifted his foot. Priest, too, must have realised something had changed, because he let go of Kate. She felt him getting up. Slowly she stood up as well. What was left of her dress was a muddy rag; her legs, face and arms were covered in the stuff. Illuminated by lightning, Mr Punch smiled, as if he was sorry their little game was over.

At that moment, Kate's world turned silent. The blast rattled her teeth as the earth shook beneath her feet. She felt heat like a blast-furnace door being opened, a roar that started white and went red and on and on in a rushing wind. Then the sound came back, so loud it seemed to detonate inside her head. A sleet of blood, tissue and bone fragments flying at 22,000 feet per second knocked Kate to the ground. It was as if a sledgehammer had struck her in the chest. One moment she was standing up, and the next she was lying on her back. She felt a tremendous shock – no pain, only a tremendous shock – and, at the same time, a sense of utter weakness, of shrivelling up to nothing, as the rain-sodden field receded into immense distance.

Mr Punch had detonated the land mine.

A thick cloud of particulate matter roiled up into the night. The smell was wretched, a mixture of bad eggs and human blood. Kate didn't remember exactly what happened next, although she felt her body returning to her. All she knew was that she had to get away from this place. There was ringing in her ears. She must have staggered only a couple of paces before she felt Priest's arms round her, pulling her back. He sounded as if he was underwater. "Kate, stop. There are mines everwhere."

Kate allowed him to take hold of her, turning her back the way they had come. She felt like a somnambulist, unable to wake up. The tuning fork in her head was dreadful: a wincing monotone filled her brain as she stumbled through the cannabis bushes, not caring where she was going. All she knew was that she had to get out of there. Priest pulled her back to the cars, dragging his bad leg behind him. All the fight had gone out of her. She had nothing left to give.

The downpour eased up, replaced by a blustery, drifting rain. Paul and Teardrop were waiting, silhouetted by car headlights. "Leave me alone," she managed to say as they climbed up onto the road. Paul slapped her across the face.

Kate recognised that she had been punished for something, and she sniffed hard to stop blood running down her nose. The cold was biting. She didn't really care anymore whether she lived or died – she just wanted this all to end. Just kill me now, she thought.

Teardrop shoved Priest into the front passenger side, then pushed her in the back. Paul sat in the driving seat. "I'm glad that fucker has gone. He was trouble," he said. There was a ping ping ping as Paul started up the engine, and Kate recognised that at least her hearing was coming back.

The Toyota went back up the twisty road towards the village.

The dashboard lit up Paul's face like a cruel mask. She didn't recognise him as the man she had once loved.

"Let her go," Priest said. "She's got nothing to do with this."

Paul gave a sarcastic laugh. "You know I can't do that."

"She's done nothing to you."

"This is all her own fault. It doesn't have to be this way."

Nervous tension thickened the silence. The car entered the village and they passed the first houses in the empty, rain-slicked street. No lights were on.

Kate caught sight of herself in the black passenger window. "I'm dead already," she thought. Her mind flicked back to what Paul had said in the taxi on the way to the funeral. "I feel like a ghost." She had a vision of her and Priest shot in the head and dumped in an oil drum or dissolved in lye until they were sludgy mush. Whatever way they decided to kill them, she hoped at least their deaths would be quick.

Suddenly Paul shouted, and the car turned crazily left. Kate caught a blurry glimpse of the unfinished apartment block, and the headlights threw up a brick wall. Priest had grabbed the wheel. Paul must have hit the wrong pedal because they were accelerating towards the brickwork. Teardrop had his hands round Priest's throat as the building loomed straight up. Kate shut her eyes, braced for impact.

They jolted as they broke through the diamond metal fence, and there was a terrific thump when they stopped. Kate's head bounced off the driver's headrest, snapping back. The car was tilted at an angle. There was a moment of stillness before the sound returned. Teardrop still had his hand's round Priest's throat and was attempting to strangle the life out of him. Paul, though, was slumped forward over the inflated airbag.

Now, before they do anything.

Move.

Kate's fingers scrabbled for the door lock, and she practically fell out of the car. The Land Cruiser had smashed through the security fence and had run aground on the dirt pile, hazard lights blinking. Lightning flashed, and there was a shattering boom of thunder as Kate stumbled downhill, not caring where she was going. Something told her not to run into the square, though: the block of flats would protect her. Stones and builder's rubbish bit into her feet as she hobbled towards the building. Her progress was painful. She glanced back at where the Toyota was haphazardly perched.

The passenger door swung open and Paul began struggling after her.

CHAPTER THIRTY SIX

THE BLOCK OF FLATS WAS PITCH BLACK and smelled of cold as Kate groped her way in. A tungsten-blue lightning flash lit up the ground floor. A few plastic sheets had been stapled to a partition wall frame beside a central cement staircase. Apart from that, the ground floor was empty. That was her only glimpse of the building before everything went black again.

Kate reached out with her hands, feeling for the staircase. This was like an insane game of blind man's buff, her hands groping for something she could hold on to. The wind was really howling now. This was madness. Suddenly Kate barked her shin on sharp cement and realised that she'd reached the steps. Slowly, now. She edged upstairs, feeling for support. Her fingertips touched a solid wall on her right; she could feel nothing on her left, and she realised the steps rose up through the heart of the building, a winding stairwell. The banister hadn't been put in yet to stop people from falling.

She brought her foot down on nothing, and for a moment panicked, fearing she'd walked off the staircase. No, it was a landing. Kate trailed her hands along the wall, feeling her way around. Outside her name was being called. Paul. The wind swallowed his words. If only she could get up the stairs faster – there must be some builders' tools she could use as a weapon. She willed herself to pick up the pace, aware that one wrong step could mean death. Each footfall was a leap of faith.

"Kate. Where are you?" Paul's voice came up the stairs.

He was inside the building.

Fighting rising panic, she knew she had to keep going. She hugged the wall for support.

"Kate, come back. It's useless trying to run away. There's nowhere to run to. Kate, please. If you just let me explain, we could be happy again."

For a moment, she wavered. Then suddenly–

"Goddammit, you little bitch, come here. I'm going to stab up your cunt when I get hold of you. Liked his black cock, did you?"

Paul was incoherent with snarling, spitting rage, as if something had possessed him.

Fear made it difficult to breathe. She told herself not to cry, but nevertheless a tear formed. He was so close now. Worse, Paul had switched on a torch and its needle light was like a stiletto blade as he kept on coming. The moment his torch found her she might as well be dead. For God's sake, Kate, keep moving. The torch was slashing and scything its way up the staircase. Come out, come out, wherever you are. A game of hide and seek. A childhood memory: holding her breath inside a wardrobe as other children hunted her down. She was about to take another step when something told her to stop.

There was nothing in front of her.

She could feel the void where the staircase ended. One more step and she would have fallen to her death. Frozen, she stood there as Paul's stabbing torchlight got nearer. Think, for God's sake, think. There was a terrific lightning flash and almost instant answering thunder. The storm was right overhead.

In that instant, she saw that the staircase hadn't run out but that there was a gap between this flight and the next landing up. About half a body's length. Paul's builders had left the staircase unfinished, and she would have to jump up and across in utter darkness. Kate couldn't do it. Her legs refused to move. Hesitantly, she reached out, feeling for the lip of the cement landing, sensing the chasm beneath. Frightened to let go, she had no choice but to lie across the void and somehow haul herself up. As she willed herself forward, everything was telling her to stop. Her muscles trembled as she let go and dangled, her legs hanging in space.

With one supreme effort, she hauled herself up and lay gasping on the cement. She got onto her hands and knees as Paul emerged onto the landing below. The only thing she could do was to show herself. If he kept his torch on her, there was just a chance he might not see the void. "Up here," she called. What was he doing? The torch was roving around the floor below: Paul was looking for something. Then, to her horror, a strip light propped against a wall flickered into life.

Now he could see everything.

Paul called up the stairs, "Come down, Kate, it's over."

"What are you going to do with me?"

"Do with you? I'm offering you a new life. You'll live in the finest hotels, have anything you want. All you have to do is go along with it."

Paul kept on climbing the stairs.

"Or what? You'll get rid of me, like you did that informer. Have me killed like that man from the hotel."

"It doesn't have to be this way."

"Do you really think we're going to have a life together?"

"There's no place to go now, Kate. Nowhere to hide. I never wanted to hurt you."

Another voice shouted down below. Teardrop. He must have struggled in from the car. That meant that Priest was probably dead. Her shoulders slumped: she'd had the faintest hope that at least one of them would get away. It really was all over now.

"She's up here," Paul called out in English.

They both stood there breathing heavily, each caught on the Escher staircase. Teardrop emerged at the foot of the steps. "Bring her to the car," Paul said. Teardrop started walking upstairs, looking as if he meant business.

Suddenly he shoved Paul hard. There was a horrible crack as Paul hit his head on the cement. Kate's brain pulsed with a dizzying shock, but she could not move. Paul had grabbed onto the overhang and was clinging on for dear life, as the livid redness where he'd hit his head widened. He looked up at her beseechingly. "Kate," he said. All she could do was look on in appalled horror; her limbs wouldn't obey her. Casually, almost nonchalantly, Teardrop took a step back and swung a massive kick at Paul's head.

What happened next she would remember forever.

Teardrop trotted down the steps to retrieve the pencil torch that Paul had dropped. As he shone the light down into the chasm, she saw Paul lying at the bottom like an abandoned doll, his arms and legs at funny angles. Just like the first time. She thought about that moment, a week ago – when she thought he'd killed himself, except this time Paul really was dead. When Teardrop looked up, he was smiling strangely. "I was the one who loved him, not you," he said.

One week later

CHAPTER THIRTY SEVEN

SURELY VENICE HAD TO BE the most beautiful city
in the world. A feast for the eyes. Kate walked along the
quay wrapped up against the cold, taking in the delightful
mosaic of terracotta, biscuit and weeping pistachio up
ahead. It was a bright, sharp day in mid-December, one
of the last good mornings before winter set in. She had
been living in a small hotel for the past three days, seeing
nobody and having her meals sent up. It was good to be
outside.

She turned into St Mark's Square and walked along the
colonnade, past bored-looking tourists inside Florian's,
who seemed more interested in their mobile phones than
in the city around them.

Teardrop had turned himself in to the police. What he
wanted was a new life in exchange for betraying the
Octopus, and to her surprise the authorities had gone
along with it, agreeing to hide him in a witness protection
programme. When Kate protested, Priest said grimly,
"We've got bigger fish to fry."

Teardrop had pleaded for his life when Priest was fighting
with him in the car. Paul had murdered his father, he said,

while his mother watched. Teardrop had then made a run for it, and they'd got into a fight on the building site before the gangster left Priest for dead. The rest of the story Kate knew.

Zogaj, meanwhile. had gone to ground. The police came up empty-handed when they raided her farm. Paul's aunt, realising that her organisation had been destroyed, had simply fled.

Over the next few days, Teardrop laid bare how the gang operated. The air became blue with cigarette smoke as Teardrop stubbed butts out, occasionally daring Priest to believe him, as he explained the whole operation. Zogaj was meeting an Italian customs official in Venice on Sunday, he said, to discuss smuggling rocket launchers across Europe. These RPGs were being used in bank robberies: Dutch banks were being robbed to fund Islamic extremism. A bank teller had been clubbed to death only last week. That was why Kate and Priest had come to Venice: police would swoop in and arrest Zogaj as the deal went down.

"He gets a new life, just like that?" Kate asked incredulously. She thought with a pang of the dishwasher. Maybe none of this would have happened if she hadn't thought he'd been on their balcony. She had wanted to say something when she passed the dishwasher's girlfriend in police headquarters, but the woman had snubbed her. Anyway, what could she say? She had been wrong about her own husband as well. She'd been wrong about everything.

"He's sick of thug life. You get older, you start thinking about things."

"He's not even going to prison."

"There are still plenty of people who want him dead for betraying the syndicate. Think about it. Every morning he wakes up, he'll wonder if today's the day somebody recognises him. Imagine checking your car each morning to see if somebody has put a bomb under it. He's in prison for the rest of his life."

She had pleaded with Priest to be allowed to see the arrest: she wanted that poisonous old woman to go away for a very long time. She had never really thought of people being evil before, but now she knew it was a fact. All right, he said eventually, but you do exactly what I tell you.

They had flown to Venice after briefing the Europol office in Rome. Priest had told her to lie low, although they spoke every day on the phone. It would only be over once they arrested Zogaj.

Kate sidled past gawping Japanese tourists in an alleyway flanked with jewellers and sweet shops, their windows stuffed with bonbons and carnival masks. She could smell the salty, briny Adriatic as she crossed over the deep moss green of a canal.

Kate emerged into the square and spotted Priest sitting outside a café. She realised that she wanted Priest to be waiting for her for a very long time.

He was idly stirring a cappuccino. There was bubbling conversation around them in French, German and Italian as she drew up a chair.

"This coffee's amazing. It's not like that rubbish back in England with half a litre of milk in it."

"The Italians did invent it. The sandwiches are good, too. They serve them up at the counter."

"Do you want one?"

She shook her head. "I'm too nervous to eat. What if she doesn't show?"

"Don't talk like that. All she knows is that her nephew's dead and that her son is under arrest. The Albanians kept it out of the papers."

"Surely she'll pull out."

"Her buyers are people you don't want to disappoint. The customs official has been under surveillance and she hasn't made contact, so we can only assume it's still on. There'll be lots of arrests after this one. You'll hear about it on the news. We're lucky that your husband still had the memory card in his pocket."

Kate turned and looked at the statue of a bearded nineteenth-century figure on a pedestal. The black streaks from his sightless eyes reminded her of the dishwasher looming through the net curtains.

"You have to understand how difficult this is … somebody you loved, somebody you thought you knew, capable of such-" she searched for the word. "-cruelty."

A bird landed on the back of a chair, unafraid of humans. Priest placed a reassuring hand over hers. Once again, the touch of another person felt so good.

"Kate, listen to me. You did nothing wrong. Paul always had choices. He could have walked away, but he never did. You have nothing to feel ashamed of. There are only two things that matter in life: how much did you love, and how well did you let go? And you did love your husband…"

He was right, of course. It was time to let go of the past, but there were too many false memories, moments when she still believed she and Paul had been truly happy.

The competitive tolling of church bells echoed across the square, signalling that it was noon. "It's time," he said.

Priest stood up from the table, and she noticed that he was using a stick. "How does your leg feel?" she asked.

"It only hurts when I laugh," he replied.

Priest and Kate walked into the hotel behind the café, where the receptionist was running the front desk like a practised traffic warden. Priest limped up the art nouveau staircase to the second floor, where they turned right. The

Europol agent knocked once, paused and then rapped twice on the door at the corridor end. A man looked at them suspiciously through the door chain.

The room stank of body odour, greasy food and the unpleasant tang of cigarettes. There were two other men, Europol agents, in the Venetian-style bedroom, both standing beside the curtains. Both were bent over cameras on tripods, their fat telephoto lens peering through gaps in the curtains. One stood up and spoke into a walkie-talkie, "Repeat. Target one is in place. Target one is in place. Over."

"You're just in time," the other agent said. "He's only just sat down."

"Still no sign of the woman, though."

The motor shutter whirred as the agent kept his finger down.

Priest gestured for Kate to make a space among the rubbish on the bedspread. Instead, she said: "I would like to see."

"Kate, we can't do that. We're bending the rules even allowing you in here."

"None of this would have happened if it wasn't for me. I just want to see what he looks like."

"Three minutes to go," said the agent bent over the other camera.

Priest touched one of the agents on the shoulder. "Just let her look. This is my operation, I'll take responsibility."

The Europol agent went and lay on the bed beside an empty pizza carton. Kate wondered how long he had been up.

She took her turn at the viewfinder. The back of the hotel overlooked another square with a café. How ironic, she thought, how it ends is how it began. A pudgy middle-aged man with a moustache was studying a menu. She zoomed out to see what else was going on. The buildings above the café were either apartments or offices, she guessed, as she scanned the rows of balconies. Some windows were open, others shut. Kate panned back to the customs official sitting at the café table, enjoying the winter sunshine.

"One minute to go," said the agent, pushing her gently aside.

"All units get ready to intercept. We want a hard stop on the suspect."

God damn you for all the misery you've caused in people's lives, Kate thought. She and Priest had visited Phuong in a detention centre, where she was being kept before being deported. Sitting there in the interview room, the Vietnamese teenager was barely more than a frightened child.

A burst of static from a walkie-talkie interrupted Kate's thoughts.

One minute went past, and then another. You could feel tension like fog in the bedroom as Priest started pacing, his stick tapping the floorboards. The Europol agents poised over the cameras kept snapping away, but it was clear Zogaj wasn't coming. "Goddamn it," said Priest. "Something must have spooked her."

"He's signalling for the waiter to pay the bill," said the agent with the telephoto lens.

"What do you want to do, sir?"

"I don't know. All units stay in position."

"The waiter has come over and he's paying the bill. Target is standing up to leave."

"Sir, you need to make a decision."

The moment gathered like a drop of water about to fall. Priest nodded and the agent beside the curtains spoke urgently into his walkie-talkie: "All units move in. Repeat. Arrest suspect."

Kate put her eye to the viewfinder without being asked as the man behind her carried on talking. Black-uniformed riot police were converging on the café, forcing the government official onto the ground. She zoomed out and whipped the image back up to the balconies overlooking the square and *there*, just for a moment, she glimpsed Zogaj. The old woman had dyed her hair blonde and was wearing a headscarf and sunglasses, but there was no doubt in Kate's mind. Her apartment curtains fell back into place.

"She's on the third floor above the café. One of the flats up there. She was watching."

"Are you sure?" said Priest, coming up behind Kate.

"Positive. She must have been there all the time."

Priest spoke rapidly into the walkie-talkie, and a line of policemen ran towards the apartment block entrance. All the while, Kate kept her finger on the motor shutter and she thought of the last photo she had taken, of Paul standing in front of the hotel balcony.

She had never really known who her husband was, yet there had been moments when they'd been happy, she knew that. Feeling the afterglow as they lay in the hotel bedroom moments before Paul walked out onto the balcony; one lazy Sunday when they hadn't really done anything in particular, yet she had never felt so content; Paul diving cleanly into the sea from a boat on their honeymoon. And the way Paul had looked at her as they stood gazing out over the city at night on that bridge and she thought, "This is the man I want to spend the rest of my life with."

All of that was gone now.

They had loved each other once, but that was another time, and the moment of letting go was the most poignant of all. Kate raised her head from the camera and realised something. She had done it. She had finally let go of the past.

| | |

ACKNOWLEDGEMENTS

First, I would like to thank Matthew Smith of Urbane Publications for taking a risk putting me into print. Seeing your first novel on bookshelves is a thrill never to be recaptured.

Once again thanks to Catharine Browne for her assiduous copy editing, taking a hairbrush to my copy and brushing the tangles out. My Daily Telegraph colleague Susanna Hickling designed a striking cover, while Tim Cumming, another of my co-workers on the Telegraph, offered to proof the manuscript.

I also want to thank Simone Glover for helping me develop the plot. With all the mountebanks out there offering development services, finding somebody with true story sense is as rare as hen's teeth.

I would also like to thank Paddy Magrane, Henrietta Fudakowski, Philippa Juul and Rhian Davies for all reading an early version of the manuscript and giving me their comments.

Tom Williams of The Williams Agency has always been such an enthusiastic supporter, as has my nonfiction agent Laura Morris.

Finally, I want to thank my darling wife Kate Evans and my children Jack and Theo for being such a help. *Hold Still* was inspired by a moment of photographing my son jumping from high rocks into the sea while on holiday. Through the viewfinder it looked as if he was going to dash his head on the rocks. "What would happen if you did photograph the moment when the person you loved most died?" I wondered, setting my camera down. Such a thing happening in real life to the three people I love most is, of course, unimaginable, despite everything I've written.

Tim Adler London 2016

About the author

TIM ADLER is an author and commissioning editor on *The Telegraph*, who has also written for the *Financial Times* and *The Times*.

His debut self-published thriller *Slow Bleed* went to number one in the US Amazon Kindle psychological thriller chart. Its follow-up *Surrogate* stayed in the Top 40 psychological thrillers for more than a year.

The Sunday Times called Tim's most recent nonfiction book *The House of Redgrave* "compulsively readable" while *The Mail On Sunday* called it "dazzling". Adler's previous book *Hollywood and the Mob* – an exposé of how the Mafia has corrupted the movie industry – was Book of the Week in *The Mail On Sunday* and Critic's Choice in the *Daily Mail*.

Tim is former London Editor of *Deadline Hollywood*, the US entertainment news website.

Follow Tim on Twitter @timadlerauthor or contact him directly via his author website **www.timadlerauthor.com**

BOOKS BY THE AUTHOR

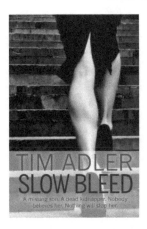

A missing son
A kidnapper who's dead
Nobody believes her
Nothing will stop her

When Doctor Jemma Sands' five-year-old son goes missing, only she believes that a vengeful patient has stolen her child. How do you convince police to search for a dead woman? As her world falls apart, Jemma realises she is the only one who can save her son. If somebody took your only child, how far would you go to get him back?

What the critics say about *Slow Bleed*:

"A tense and gripping crime read ... Slow Bleed grabs you by the throat." Raven Crime Reads

"One of those books you can't put down ... a great medical thriller." Book of the Month, Crime Book Club

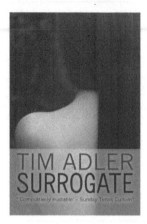

How much is your child worth? That's the question Hugo and Emily Cox must answer when they get a ransom demand for their child – from Alice, the surrogate mother they paid to carry their baby. The police are helpless. No law has been broken – the baby belongs to their surrogate. And Hugo has a secret he's keeping from his wife that makes their search even more desperate.

Now Hugo and Emily must find their missing daughter ... even if it costs them everything they own. Fans of Elizabeth Haynes, Sophie Hannah and Mark Edwards will love this gripping and fast-moving thriller.

What the critics say about Surrogate:

"A fantastic read ... wonderful plot twists." Thriller of the Month – E-thriller.com

"A great read ... if you loved Gone Girl, try this." Crime Reader

Urbane Publications is dedicated to developing new author voices, and publishing fiction and non-fiction that challenges, thrills and fascinates.

From page-turning novels to innovative reference books, our goal is to publish what YOU want to read.

Find out more at **urbanepublications.com**